START A WAR

ELLE THORPE

ELLE THORPE PTY LTD

For all the women who like their fictional men dark, sexy, and stabby. This one is for you.

V3.

Editing by Emmy and Studio ENP

Proofreading by Karen Hrdlicka.

Photography by Michelle Lancaster

Model: Tyler James

Cover Design: Elle Thorpe

I was always hungry.

Some days it wasn't so bad, and the gnawing feeling in the depths of my stomach could be ignored while I watched cartoons on the tiny TV in our trailer. Some days the bugs that bit at my skinny legs and crawled through my matted hair were more annoying than the ache of an empty tummy.

But some days, normally the ones where Axel hadn't come by for a while, the hunger was all I could focus on. It took over everything else and couldn't be held off with water or cartoons or staring out the trailer window at other kids walking to and from school.

Those were the days I searched the trailer cupboards silently, even though I knew they were all bare.

Those were the days I crawled around the floor, trying to hold in my whimpers because what good would crying do? Better to just search the cracked linoleum for any scrap that might have been dropped from a previous meal when Mom or Jerry had been feeling generous.

Those were good times. When Jerry came home, his eyes clear instead of their usual red. When Mom wasn't passed out in her bedroom, and Axel wasn't at school or working. When the smell of fried chicken with mashed potato and gravy permeated the air, covering up the rotting stench of mold and dirt and body odor.

I lived for those days, when the four of us gathered at the table, and for a moment, I could pretend we were a real family.

Even at five, I knew not all families were like ours. Some were happy. Some had food all the time. Some had parents who loved them and took care of them. The moms brushed their daughter's hair and kissed their chubby cheeks and told them they loved them.

Across the trailer, my mother lay spread-eagled across her unmade bed, her hair a knotted, matted mess around her head. I knew better than to interrupt her when she was sleeping.

I knew better than to hope she'd care that I was starving.

I tried to sleep, even though darkness had only just fallen and I wasn't tired. At least when I was asleep, the pain all went away.

I might have drifted off but it didn't last long. Jerry's boots pounded on the metal steps, waking me instantly. He jerked open the trailer door, letting it swing back with a crack that was loud enough to wake the entire park.

"Kim! You fucking ho. Where the hell are you?"

I curled slowly, tucking my knees to my chest, trying to make myself small.

Even though he wasn't looking for me, I knew that

tone in his voice. It was only a matter of time before his rage would extend to me too.

I slipped beneath the pile of dirty blankets on my bed and hoped if I stayed still enough, he wouldn't notice my breathing. I left only the tiniest of gaps so I could peer out, because it would not be smart to take my eyes off Jerry when he was like this.

He stormed into my mother's bedroom, his chest heaving with rage, spit collecting at the corner of his mouth. "Kim! Is this where you've been all day, you lousy bitch?"

She didn't move from the bed.

The urge to be helpful came over me, ready to offer up information on Mom's whereabouts. Not that there was really much to tell. Because she had been there on her bed, ever since she'd stumbled in early this morning.

"Tired, Jerry," she mumbled. "Leave me alone."

For a big man, Jerry could move fast when he wanted to. His fingers speared into her dirty dark hair and yanked her head back.

The scream she let out cut right through me, locking up all my muscles.

"You're tired?" he yelled. "*You're* tired? You've done nothing but sleep all day, you lazy cow. While I worked to pay your goddamn bills."

"I worked last night!"

He let out a harsh laugh. "Bullshit. Where's your money then?"

She struggled to her feet, but her eyes were more focused than I'd seen them in days. She glared at him with sparks of anger dancing in her gaze. "It's my money, and I ain't giving it to you."

He let out a roar of anger as he slammed her up against a wall. "I own you, bitch! Anything you earn is my money. Did you forget that? Did you forget that your dirty, used-up cunt always belongs to me, no matter how many men pound it? Do I need to remind you?"

The crack of his hand across her face and her responding cry had me closing up the gap in the blankets so I didn't have to watch anymore. I plugged my fingers in my ears, but there was no keeping out the sounds from my mother's bedroom.

When the blanket ripped off me, it wasn't a surprise.

I didn't even scream. I just squeezed my eyes shut tighter.

He pulled my hand away from my ears, and I knew better than to fight.

"Hey, Bliss. Do you want some Goldfish crackers?"

My eyes flew open.

Axel's gentle face loomed over me, a lighthouse in a stormy sea.

Those words...they meant one thing every time. He thought I didn't know but I did. Whenever Axel asked me if I wanted Goldfish crackers, it meant, *You're in danger, you need to go hide.*

I threw myself at him, my little arms hugging his neck and holding on tightly.

He squeezed me back, scooping me up and clutching me to his chest. "Come on," he whispered. "Let's get you out of here."

We slipped past Jerry and Mom in the bedroom, and I tried not to see what he was doing to her. It was nothing I hadn't seen before, but I shuddered at the dead look in her eyes as she watched us over Jerry's shoulder.

It was like she didn't see us.

Like we didn't exist.

Or like she just didn't care.

I turned away. I'd be back here tomorrow, and nothing would have changed. But for tonight, I'd been granted a reprieve in the form of my big brother and my favorite snack.

Axel carried me down the stairs and into the cool night air. Darkness wrapped around us, but a circle of glowing orange-red light pierced through the dim. I eyed it until we got closer and then realized it was the end of a cigarette.

"Jesus, fuck," Nash gritted out, dropping the smoke to the ground and stepping on it. "They're really going at it tonight. I could hear every word from all the way out here."

Axel kept walking, jerking his head for his best friend to follow. "Fucking prick. One day, I'm going to take a baseball bat to his ugly head."

Nash shook his head as we moved through the darkness. "The guy has a hundred pounds and six inches on you. He'd snap you before you even got to swing."

Axel didn't say anything. We all knew Nash was right.

A gangly teenager had no hope against a fully grown man. Especially not one as drunk and mean as Jerry.

Nash peered over at me, wrapped around Axel like a koala. "You okay, Bliss?"

"Hungry." That seemed the easiest emotion to pin down when so many worse ones coursed through my body.

Nash reached over and patted my back. "She's skin

and bones. Fucking hell. We need to get her out of here. Not just for a night. Permanently."

"I know," Axel ground out. "I'm trying to talk to her dad."

"He still got that big place in Providence?"

"Last I heard."

Nash took a hard drag on his smoke, keeping it in his lungs for a moment before blowing it out with a sigh. "Jerry won't let her go without a fight. You know he's looking at her like she'll be a paycheck in a few years. We gotta get her dad to take her."

Axel pinned him with a glare. "I fucking know, okay? I know!"

Nash's mouth pulled into a grim line as he watched over me. But when he took in my big eyes, his expression softened. "Sorry it took us so long to come back this time. But we gotcha two boxes of Goldfish, Blissy girl. And candy too."

I picked my head up off Axel's shoulder. "Twizzlers?"

Axel chuckled. "Of course. They're your favorite."

Nash nodded in agreement.

I grinned at him, letting the promise of a belly full of my two favorite things wipe out the memories of my mother's face and Jerry's anger.

Everything was better when Axel and Nash were around.

We trudged through the woods around the trailer park, going deep enough that the lights no longer touched the darkness, and both boys turned on the flashlights on their cell phones.

Eventually, their lights bounced over a small green tent, mostly hidden in the thick woods. Some leaves had accumulated on the tough green canvas since we'd last been here, but neither boy brushed them off. Axel dropped me to my feet and told me to wait while the two of them checked the ropes and pegs.

"It's held up okay." Axel stomped a boot down on one of the pegs, pressing it back into the dirt.

Nash tugged on a rope, tightening it. "She's a good secret fort. The guy did say it was ex-army. Built to last."

"He wasn't wrong. It ain't pretty, but it's strong."

"It is pretty," I disagreed, finally speaking up. I tugged at the zipper and let myself inside. "It's the best home I have."

Axel swore low under his breath. "That's so fucking tragic I could cry."

I didn't understand what he meant, but I squealed with excitement over the pink Barbie sleeping bag, nestled between two much larger blue bags. I turned to Nash, eyeing the backpack he carried, as he crawled inside the tent with Axel close behind him.

I held my hands out expectantly for my treats, saliva filling my mouth at the thought of the deliciousness he held in that bag.

Axel laughed at my impatience. "Where's your manners, kid? You need to say the magic password to get those candies."

I frowned, racking my brain for a password. "Sandwiches?"

Nash and Axel burst into laughter while they settled on their sleeping bags.

Axel ruffled my hair. "Okay, I was going for please, but sandwiches is a good password too. We'll work on your manners when you've got a full belly."

Then the two of them pulled out more junk food than I'd ever seen. I was so hungry I would have eaten anything, but they had all my favorite things, and I wolfed down the Goldfish crackers so fast Nash had to thump me on the back when I choked on them.

I didn't care. I grinned at him and went straight back to shoving more in my mouth, desperate to get as much in as I could.

The two of them let me eat, never asking me to share. And when I was finally done, the food washed down with root beer, Axel held up one corner of the little pink sleeping bag he'd found for me.

I snuggled in.

The tent was really too small for two tall boys, but neither complained. We lay there in the darkness, the boys talking quietly over my head while I watched them.

And when Jerry's deep, angry voice called my name from somewhere in the distance, I only snuggled in farther, safe and hidden between the only two people in my life who actually cared about me.

1

BLISS

I smoothed my hands over the silky sapphire-blue ball gown, doing a little twirl in the women's bathroom. The fabric flared in a circle around me, swishing softly around my calves when I came to a stop.

"Bethany-Melissa!" Sandra's eyes were wide, her head bobbing up and down in approval. "That dress was made for you. It's stunning."

I smiled happily at the other woman. "Isn't it beautiful? Caleb bought it for me especially for tonight."

Sandra leaned against the little sofa to the side of the room, her extravagant dress spread out around her. It stood out beautifully, its bright-red vibrant against the black-and-gold luxury bathroom. "He must have dropped a pretty penny on that one. At least you know he has good taste for when he buys you an engagement ring."

I studied my reflection in the mirror. She was right. The dress fit me perfectly, dipping between my full breasts, hiding the rolls on my tummy, and flaring out around my wide hips. It accentuated all my curves and hid the wobble in my thighs. I loved it. I'd gone to the hairdresser's that morning and spent hours letting them freshen up my color and then curl the lengths. A makeup artist had been my next stop, and she'd worked her magic until I felt like I was Cinderella, ready for a ball.

Which wasn't exactly where we were, but the charity auction did have the same sort of feel. A sleek black car had picked me up from my house, and when we'd arrived at the entrance to the fanciest hotel in Providence, Caleb had been waiting by the door for me like my very own Prince Charming.

I watched Sandra in the reflection of the mirror. "You don't really think he's going to propose, do you? It's only been a year. It feels too soon…"

Sandra tutted, coming to stand beside me so we both stared into the mirror. "Does it matter? He's handsome. Successful. Rich. And you're downright fabulous in every way—"

I laughed. "Not sure about that."

She waved around a manicured hand in dismissal. "Of course the man wants to marry you. Did you see there's a ring up for auction tonight? It's got an absolute boulder for a diamond too. Maybe that's what Caleb will bid for." Her gaze met mine in the mirror. "It's the smart move, you know? The two of you, I mean. It would be such a great union for your families. Your father must be so thrilled the two of you are dating."

I nodded. "He adores Caleb. They're playing golf every other weekend lately. I barely get to see my own boyfriend."

"Perfect! Leaves you plenty of time for shopping and lunch with me."

That was true. It did leave me with plenty of time to myself. I'd never exactly seen that as a good thing, though I liked that my boyfriend and my father got along. It was just that perhaps they got along too well. Their work talk tended to monopolize most conversations, to the point where anything I wanted to say was lost in business politics.

I tucked my lipstick away in my purse. "Anyway, we should get back to the table before my potential future husband forgets what I look like."

Sandra picked up my hand and swung it as we made our way to the bathroom exit. "There's no forgetting you in that dress, Bethany-Melissa. Every eye in the room is on you tonight."

I blushed at the compliment. "Thank you."

It was a little over the top though, when the entire ballroom was filled with beautiful people, all dressed to the nines. I found my date at our table and was once again blown away with how handsome he was. His blond hair was slicked back neatly, just like it always was. But tonight, his regular business suit had been replaced by an expensive tuxedo. He glanced up when I approached, and he excused himself from his conversation to pull my chair out for me.

I smiled at him. "Thank you, sir."

He smiled back. "The pleasure is all mine, mademoiselle."

I giggled, enjoying his attention.

It was short-lived.

Caleb took his seat beside me and fell straight back

into conversation with the man to his left. I tried to pay attention, but as usual, Caleb's business talk was an in-depth labyrinth of confusing numbers and terms, none of which I understood. He didn't try to explain them to me, nor did he introduce me to his acquaintance, and the other man didn't even spare me a glance.

I sighed quietly, telling myself to suck it up. If Caleb really was close to proposing like Sandra thought, I'd get all the attention I wanted from him. In the meantime, I needed to get used to these types of events and my role within them.

Which seemed to be, 'look pretty and be quiet.'

The role would evolve once I was his wife. Maybe I could get more involved with the charity and help run events like these. That might be fun. I'd need something to fill my time once I quit my job. None of his friends' wives worked in childcare centers for a miniscule wage like I did. It wasn't a good look when their husbands earned millions. They all filled their days with long lunches and Pilates and charity work.

The same would be expected of me once Caleb was my husband.

The master of ceremonies for the night cleared his throat from behind a podium on the stage. "Ladies and gentlemen. Would everybody please take their seats? We're about to start the main fundraising event of the evening—the charity auction."

Sandra squealed from across the table, her plastic surgeon husband at her side. "This is always such fun."

At the announcement, Caleb ended his conversation with the man on his other side, so I took the opportunity to lean into him.

"Are you going to bid on anything?" I asked in a whisper.

He sat back on his chair with a smug smile. "I might have my eye on a little something."

My heart lit up in a flutter. Maybe Sandra was onto something. If Caleb bid on that ring tonight, I could be an engaged woman by the end of the weekend.

The MC clapped his hands. "Okay, I think that's about enough time for everyone to get their credit cards out…"

There was a titter of laughter around the room, though I didn't think it was really supposed to be a joke. That was the whole reason we were here after all.

"Let's begin with the Titleist golf clubs."

"These are mine," Caleb muttered beneath his breath, his fingers curling around an auction paddle with his assigned number. He held it up in the air. "Twenty thousand dollars."

I widened my eyes. Twenty thousand dollars…for golf clubs? He already had three sets.

The master of ceremonies peered into the audience and pointed in our direction. "Okay then! Mr. Caleb Black, opening things up with a very strong bid before I could even suggest one. Thank you, Caleb. Do I hear twenty-five thousand?"

The man next to Caleb raised his paddle. "Twenty-five thousand."

Caleb laughed and elbowed his colleague before raising his paddle in the air once more. "Let's just skip to the good stuff, shall we? Fifty thousand dollars."

I tried to stifle the choking feeling that swelled my throat, but it just came out an uncomfortable cough.

Caleb glanced over at me, his forehead furrowed. "Are you okay?"

I nodded, taking a sip of water from my glass. "Of course. I'm sorry. My throat was a little dry." I forced a smile across my face. "Congratulations on your golf clubs."

He grinned, slinging an arm around the back of my chair as he leaned in close to me, his mouth hovering over my ear. "Truthfully? The clubs probably aren't worth a hundred bucks. I'll give them to Goodwill. But I couldn't let Norman one-up me. I'd never hear the end of it."

I snapped my mouth shut when I realized it was hanging open. The thought of spending that much money on something and then discarding it just as easily was crazy. I shifted uncomfortably in my dress. "It's all for a good cause, I suppose. Right?"

Caleb shrugged.

An assistant came around and handed him some paperwork for his golf clubs and swiped his card through a reader. Some part of me waited for the big red cross and the declined 'buzz.' Of course, it didn't come. The woman handed Caleb his receipt, and he thanked her with his charming grin.

The ring Sandra had thought Caleb might be considering for me was the next item up, and I held my breath while the master of ceremonies went into detail on the piece of jewelry. It really was beautiful. Close-up images of the ring sitting in a bed of black silk shone up on the screen behind the announcer's podium, and there was more than one gasp from the women around the room.

The bids came in thick and fast from a roomful of

men who seemed intent on buying their ladies some-thing special.

Caleb didn't raise his paddle once.

In fact, he seemed entirely uninterested now he had the item he'd come for.

Sandra shot me a pouty, sympathetic look when the auctioneer slapped his palm against the wooden lectur-er's podium and the gorgeous ring became the property of Mr. and Mrs. Kemp, an older couple at the back, for forty-seven thousand dollars.

Less than Caleb had paid for the golf clubs he didn't even want.

Oh well, so much for that.

The ringing of a phone cut through the next round of bidding, and frowny faces all turned in our direction. I gaze around, adding my frown to the ones around me.

"Is that your phone?" Caleb whispered.

My face heated when I realized it was, and that I'd forgotten to put it on silent as we'd arrived. Red-cheeked, I took my cell from my purse, frantically trying to silence it.

But the name flashing on the screen froze me to the spot.

Axel.

Caleb glanced at me like I'd lost my mind. "Bethany-Melissa!" he hissed. "Can you shut that thing up?"

I still couldn't move.

Caleb leaned over and peered at the phone. "Who's Axel?"

Hearing his name out loud was enough to finally shock me out of my stupor. "No one. Never mind. Sorry."

I silenced the ringer, pulling it away from Caleb and

pushing back in my chair so fast he had to grab the back of it to keep it from falling over.

"I'm going to the bathroom."

Without waiting to hear if Caleb said anything in reply, I spun on my heel and hurried for the safety of the ladies' room, my phone still vibrating in my hand.

I never made it to the bathroom. The moment I was out of the ballroom and into the hall, I hit the green answer button. "Axel?"

The sound of labored breathing came down the line. "Bliss?"

"It's me. What's wrong? Why are you calling?" I swallowed hard. "Is it money? If you need help, I can't ask Dad but I—"

"Do you want some Goldfish crackers?"

I stopped breathing.

Memories I'd fought hard to forget flooded back, swirling around my head in a tumbling dark mass, sinister and terrifying.

"Why would you ask me that?" The words came out as barely more than a croak, the tremble in my voice matching the one that had taken control of my fingers.

There was nothing but his breathing.

"Axel! Talk to me! Why would you say that after all these years—"

The crack of a gunshot, even down the phone line, ripped a scream from my chest. On instinct, I threw my phone across the hallway and covered my ears, shrinking down and cowering like I was five years old again, in my mother's vermin-ridden trailer, my big brother the only protection I knew.

I stared at the phone with terror clawing at my throat.

"No," I whispered, the word coming out as a sob. "No. No." I crawled across the floor, my dress tugging and twisting and dragging along until I had the phone to my ear again. "Axel? Axel!"

There was nothing but a deathly silence on the other end.

My heart pounded against my rib cage, and my whispers turned to screams. "Axel!"

There was no reply.

But I heard his voice in my head anyway.

Do you want some Goldfish crackers?

It had always meant one thing.

You're in danger. Hide.

2

BLISS

"*I* need your keys."

Caleb glanced up, irritation etched into his handsome features. "I was in the middle of a conversation."

Any other time I probably would have dipped my head and meekly apologized. Who was I kidding? I wouldn't have interrupted him in the first place.

But after pulling myself together in the hallway, there was only one thought pounding through my head.

Get to Axel. Because something was horribly, horribly wrong.

"Your keys, Caleb! Hurry!"

He chuckled uncomfortably and apologized to the man he'd been speaking to, who frowned like I was an annoying child, interrupting the adults' conversation.

It was all I could do not to scream in his face.

But Caleb was on his feet and tugging me away by the elbow before I could completely lose it.

"What's gotten into you?" he hissed, short fingernails

digging into the soft skin of my arm. "Is this something to do with that guy calling you? Who was he?"

I couldn't tell him the truth. He'd never look at me the same, and my father and I hadn't spent all these years covering up my past just for me to ruin it now. "There's an emergency," I explained. "Please. I don't have time to tell you everything. Right now, I just need your car keys."

He shook his head, his annoyance written all over his face. "Fine. Whatever. Don't ride the clutch, you'll burn it out..."

His warnings fell on deaf ears. As soon as his keys were out of his pocket, I snatched them from his hand and raced for the door, yanking off my high heels as I went. The plush carpet beneath my feet quickly turned into the rough asphalt of the parking lot, but it didn't slow me down. I ran through the night, searching in the dark for Caleb's black BMW.

I hit the button on the key fob, and the lights on the car flashed twice, giving away its location. Doubling down on speed, I yanked open the door and slid behind the steering wheel to hit the start button. The engine roared to life, mixing with the roaring of my blood circling my body too fast.

It was only then, sitting behind the wheel of Caleb's expensive car, that I realized I had no idea where I was going. I didn't know where Axel lived anymore. Did he have a wife? A family? It had been years since we'd shared anything personal about our lives.

That hadn't been my choice. He was the one part of my past I'd never wanted to deny. But it had been him who'd pushed me away.

"His bar," I muttered. "Shit, what was it called?" I got

my phone out, racking my brain. "Hey, Siri? Give me the names of dive bars in Saint View."

"Finding bars in Saint View."

I guessed Siri was insulted by the use of the term dive bar. But it didn't really matter, because every bar in Saint View was a dive bar. Saint View was the ghetto. The wrong side of the tracks. The cautionary tale parents of Providence told children when they let their grades slip from an A+ to a regular old A. *"Do you want to end up living in Saint View? That's what will happen if you don't apply yourself."*

My father had said the same things to me once. It was only after he'd said the words and we'd both stared at each other, that he'd realized how close to home that threat was for me. Neither of us had said a word and had avoided each other for days until it had blown over.

I scrolled the list of bars in Saint View, pausing toward the bottom of the list.

Saint View Psychos.

Something clicked in the back of my mind, and I gunned the engine, putting my foot down on the accelerator. My chest ached, and I tried to calm my breathing while I replayed Axel's phone call in my head.

It couldn't be what it seemed. I was blowing the entire thing out of proportion, and if I drove the streets like a madman, I'd end up writing off Caleb's car.

The ritzy upper-class neighborhoods outside quickly turned into the suburban houses on the border, but from there, it was all downhill into the depths of Saint View. The houses and businesses outside became more ramshackle with every passing street, broken windows the norm, and overgrown yards, long abandoned by their occupants. The main street boasted little more than a strip club with a neon-pink sign and a large crowd of men hanging around out in front.

I leaned on the door locks, popping the central locking, and drove faster.

Deep in the heart of the Saint View seediness, Siri directed me down a lane barely wide enough for Caleb's car and into a parking lot at the back. I blinked in surprise at the number of cars hidden back here, but I wasn't going to waste time driving around, looking for a free spot. I parked right up at the door before I could think about it and got out.

The building was huge, a big enough space for several businesses, and yet the only sign on the wall was one of a deranged clown, the letters, PSYCHOS, painted between his pointed, blood-dipped teeth.

I shuddered at the image, my brother's old warnings flooding back in from the one time I'd asked to go to his bar.

"This isn't a place for you, Bliss. I mean it. I don't care if you're twenty-one. I'll have the bouncer throw you out on your ass before you even step a foot inside the door."

I'd believed him, because he'd never lied to me before. If Axel thought his new business wasn't somewhere I needed to be, I trusted he'd said it for a reason.

So I'd put his bar out of my mind for years. I wasn't much of a bar-goer anyway. I didn't drink alcohol often, and if my friends and I did go out, there was no way their Louboutin soles would be touching the grimy floor of a bar in the hood.

Maybe once upon a time I'd been a hood rat kid from a trailer park just around the corner. But after my dad took me in, things changed. Day by day, I grew soft, fueled by a loving, safe home, and constant food on the table.

I'd put this life behind me.

And now I was about to reopen the door.

So I slammed my fist against the locked door. I pounded against the clown's terrifying face and wondered why Axel had gone for such horrible branding. It was hardly welcoming.

But maybe that was the point.

To keep out people like me.

The door opened, and two burly bouncers eyed me.

"I need to see Axel," I demanded.

The two of them glanced at each other, then the bigger one folded his arms across his chest. "Think you got the wrong place, sweetheart."

"I don't," I insisted, standing my ground, even though my knees trembled ever so slightly. I hoped the tulle of my dress hid it. "Axel Fuller owns this bar, right?"

The man shrugged, stepping aside. "This should be interesting."

I didn't stay long enough to ponder what he meant by that. I pushed my way past and into the darkness of the bar.

Deep, thumping music poured from hidden speakers. The bass vibrated up into the soles of my feet and through my entire body. It somehow managed to be both sexy and dark all at once. Nobody danced though. I weaved my way between bodies, all standing in groups with drinks in hand. I didn't say a word or make a noise, but every single person stopped their conversations to stare at me anyway.

I couldn't even blame them. I'd worn a ball gown to a dive bar. I didn't exactly blend in with their denim, leather, and bare skin.

I struggled by one woman in a tiny leather miniskirt, her top barely more than a strap that covered her nipples, and tugged my dress up over my breasts. She hissed at me, and I turned away quickly.

I wanted to turn around. With every step, my skin prickled with awareness I didn't like. One that screamed, *"Run. You don't belong here."* I knew it as well as every person I passed who stopped and stared. I felt their presences closing in until I was sure this was what claustrophobia felt like.

But that gunshot echoing through my ears couldn't be forgotten, and so I pressed on, searching the crowd of faces for my brother. One glimpse of his face, and then I'd be out of here and back to Caleb's side like nothing had happened. Maybe by then he'd be drunk enough to not even remember I'd made a scene and commandeered his car.

I yelped as somebody grabbed a handful of my behind, and spun around, trying to work out who it was. The men surrounding me all laughed, and heat burned in my cheeks. I scurried away from their jeers and taunts and wandering hands.

"Excuse me. Do you know Axel?" I asked a woman carrying a tray of glasses with a deep-brown liquid inside them. I wasn't sure if she worked there or if she was just carrying drinks back to her friends. It's not like anyone there had a uniform and a name tag with a cheerful, 'How can I help you?' greeting below it.

Her gaze raked over me before coming to land on my face. "Jesus Christ, what the hell are you wearing, lady?"

I smoothed my hands over my dress self-consciously. I didn't have much of a temper, but all the stares and the unwanted groping, mixed with a healthy dose of fear, pushed it right up to the surface. "A paper sack," I snapped at her. "Do you like it?"

Sarcasm and disdain barbed each word, and she raised one eyebrow.

I bit my lip, realizing how incredibly rude I'd been. "I'm sorry. I didn't mean that." I turned away, face burning and tears pricking at my eyes.

"Hold up, wait a minute." The woman placed her tray of drinks down in the middle of a nearby table of men, who were all more interested in me than drinking anyway.

I shuddered at their stares.

The woman followed my gaze and turned back to her table. "Hey! What do we say when someone gives you a drink?"

The guys all looked suitably chastised by the fairy-sized woman, and there were mutters of "Thanks, Rebel," as they reached for their glasses.

With her hands on her hips, she nodded. "Now, drink up and mind your own business. You ain't ever seen a lost Disney princess before?"

I stared at her wide-eyed. "I'm not a—"

Rebel sidled up beside me, taking my arm. "Sure you are, Disney. And they might be behaving right now because they just got new drinks, but if I don't get you out of here in about five minutes, you're gonna get eaten alive. And not in the good way."

I blinked at her, letting her drag me along. "There's a good way to be eaten alive?"

She raised one eyebrow. "What the hell are they teaching you people over in Providence? Your husband never eats your pussy?"

Shock and embarrassment punched through me. I opened my mouth to answer, then closed it, then tried again. But each time, I couldn't find words.

Rebel rolled her eyes. "Jesus, all that money but no pussy-licking? All the money in the world ain't worth it if he's a dud in bed, Dis."

We moved quickly through the crowd, now with her leading, and I shook my head, finally finding my voice. "He's not a dud in bed. And he does...do that."

Once. He'd done it once and never again, leaving me with a complete and utter complex that there had been something wrong with me. Rebel didn't need to know that, though. I hadn't told anyone. Not even Sandra.

"Well, good for you and your cunt. What do you want with Axel if it's not for his oral sex skills?"

I scrunched my nose up at the thought of my brother doing that. I didn't need that mental image. "He's my brother. I'm worried about him."

Rebel stopped and stared up at me. I wasn't tall, but she was really short. "You're Axel's sister?"

I nodded.

Her black makeup-ringed eyes widened. "Fuck, Dis! Why didn't you lead with that?"

"Sorry?"

She tugged me through the last of the crowd, muttering something about getting fired while elbowing aside patrons who stood waiting to be served. At the bar, she rested her elbows on the countertop and let out a piercing whistle that somehow managed to cut through both the thumping of the music and the buzz of shouted conversation around us. "Hey, boss man number two. Get your sweet ass over here. We got a problem."

The man behind the bar turned around, frown creasing the space between his eyebrows. He wiped his hands on a small towel and tucked it into the back pocket of his jeans. "Fucking hell, Rebel. What now? I'm sick of the shit toni—"

His gaze collided with mine, and his eyes widened. "Bliss?"

I was suddenly thrown back twenty years. "Nash?"

With shock etched into his expression, he moved past the other bartenders to where Rebel and I stood, his gaze wandering over me, sweeping all the way to my toes and back up to the gold chain hanging around my neck.

I did the same thing to him.

I hadn't seen my brother's best friend since he'd been a gangly teenager who'd come to save me in the night.

He was a gangly teenager no longer.

Nash was all man, with broad shoulders and a filled-out, solid-looking chest beneath a tight white T-shirt and a flannel shirt left undone. I took in every inch of his familiar face, reconciling all the changes there. There was scruff on his jawline now, and smile lines at the corners of his eyes, reminding me he was almost fifteen years older.

"Okay, you two clearly already know each other, so I'm just gonna..." Rebel jerked her thumb over her shoulder and disappeared into the crowd once more before I could thank her for her help.

"Holy shit, Nash. Where you find a hooker in a ball gown? And will you share?"

Nash dragged his gaze to the drunk sitting two stools down. The man leered toward me, his unsteady gaze flittering all over my body.

My skin crawled. Coming here had been a mistake. A huge one.

Nash seemed to realize it at the same moment and swore low under his breath. He reached out and took my hand, wrapping his fingers around my own. The noise of the crowd around me swallowed my gasp of surprise at his touch.

"Come on." He tugged me behind the bar and then through a door on the back wall.

I followed him inside and grimaced at another Psychos wall mural, complete with scary, crazy-eyed clown. I shuddered.

Nash noticed and shook his head as he closed the door behind him. "Fuck, Bliss. If a mural gives you the creeps, you're *really* in the wrong place. What the hell are you doing here?"

It was quieter inside the little office, and I babbled out the whole story as quickly as I could. "Axel called me. He said our code phrase. You remember? About the Goldfish crackers? It worried me. And then there was a noise that sounded like a gunshot, but it couldn't have been, right? It was probably a car backfiring or something completely unrelated. I don't know. I didn't want to come here. I know he said not to. But I just needed to check he was okay."

Nash frowned.

I finally sucked in a deep breath and tried to calm my racing brain. "Is he here? I didn't know where else to go."

Nash ran a hand through his hair. "He's not." His mouth pulled into a grim line. "He should be, but he's not. I was just cussing him out to the other bartenders because he's left us short-staffed."

The swirling vortex of worry that had been momentarily distracted by the club, Rebel, and now seeing Nash again, opened up once more, ravaging through me and centering on my chest, making it difficult to breathe. "Nash, the noise I thought I heard...what if it really was a gunshot?"

The swirling inside me threatened to drag me straight back into panic mode.

Nash's expression darkened by the second.

I grabbed his open shirt, trying to get his attention again. "He's at home, right? Can you give me his address? I'll go check on him."

Nash already had his phone out of his pocket and pressed to his ear. He moved around the windowless office while he waited for Axel to pick up, muttering beneath his breath.

I didn't dare move, my body rigid with a mounting worry for my brother.

"Pick up, you asshole. Pick up."

When Nash slammed the phone down on the desk, it was very clear that Axel had not picked up.

"What's going on?" I asked, watching him pull out the top drawer of the desk in the center of the room and pluck a set of keys from it.

Nash shook his head. "Your idiot brother isn't answering his phone, so now I'm gonna have to go find his dumb ass. Which is going to leave us another staff member down. Fucking jackass. If I find him dick-deep in some woman at his place, I'm gonna kill him."

"Has that happened before?"

"More than once."

I didn't particularly want to hear about my brother's sex life. But on this occasion, I prayed Nash was right. Because the alternatives playing out in my head were too terrifying to think about.

"You gotta go." Nash towered over my five feet, five inches, even with some extra height, thanks to my heels. He brushed past me, reaching for the office door, then strode by, leaving me behind.

There was no way I was staying here in this bar now that I knew Axel wasn't here. I ran to catch up to Nash. "Wait. I'm coming with you."

He stopped before we hit the main bar area and turned back to me. "Uh, no you're not. Go home, Bliss."

"He's my brother. I'm coming."

"Not a chance. You don't know this town. Or the people your brother hangs out with."

I ground my teeth together. I didn't remember him being this bossy when I was a kid. "I grew up in this town, if you've forgotten. And I know you."

Nash laughed. "Sweetheart, you don't know me from a bar of soap."

He was right. I knew his name, and his face, and that I'd always felt safe with him, but that was all. How well could a five-year-old truly know a nineteen-year-old? Neither of us had been those people in a very long time.

"Fine, I don't know you. But you don't know me either. I'm not that naïve little kid anymore."

He stopped and stared at me and then laughed. "No offense, but you have no idea what you're doing here. Do you even have a clue how close you probably just came to losing that fancy necklace hanging above your tits? Any one of those guys could have ripped it off your neck in a heartbeat, and you wouldn't have had a chance in hell of stopping him."

I was sure all the color drained from my face. "That wouldn't happen."

He leaned down, getting in my face. "It would. And a whole lot worse. Those guys out there aren't gentlemen. I toss 'em out if I see it happen, but I'm one person."

"Rebel's a woman, and she seems fine."

"Rebel keeps a set of brass knuckles in her back pocket and has never hesitated to use them. You got a set tucked into your panties?"

I scowled at him.

"Didn't think so." He grabbed my arm again and towed me through the crowd, shooting death stares at any male who looked in my direction. He clearly had their respect because they all stepped out of the way.

The two bouncers nodded at Nash, and then we were outside once more. Nash stopped in front of my car and stared at it like it was an alien spacecraft.

"Oh, fuck me. This is yours, I suppose?"

"What?" I snapped, pulling my hand away from his sharply. "You don't like BMWs?"

He didn't answer my question. "Go home, Bliss. Just… go home. Don't worry about your brother. I've had his back all these years. Today ain't no different."

With that, he left me at my car and strode to a beat-up black Jeep.

Anger coursed through me at the insinuation I hadn't had Axel's back. Like it was my fault we hadn't seen each other in years.

Nash's engine roared to life, and his headlights came on, shining directly into my eyes. "I go by Bethany-Melissa now, asshole!" I yelled as he drove past.

He didn't answer.

"I like Bliss better," one of the security guards spoke up.

I whirled around and glared at him.

The two of them burst into laughter.

I slid inside the car, well reminded why Saint View, and everyone in it, was the worst.

3

NASH

"Goddammit, Axel. Pick up your motherfucking phone."

The phone rang through the speakers of my car, each time hitting Axel's goofy voicemail greeting, until I was ready to throw my phone out of the open roof and watch it disintegrate on the road beneath my tires.

His place was ten minutes from the bar, on the other side of an annoying number of red lights. I tapped my finger on the steering wheel while I waited for one to turn green.

Headlights flashed in my rearview mirror as a car pulled up, idling behind me. I turned left when the light went green and then took a right at the next intersection.

The car stayed with me through each turn.

"Shit," I uttered, glancing in my mirrors. But the headlights were too bright and blinded the details of the car. "Axel, if you've got yourself into something bad, and now that something bad is following me, I swear to God,

I'm going to destroy your limited-edition baseball card collection."

Any other best friends probably would have thrown punches, but I wasn't a fighter. I mean, I would if it was a life-or-death situation, but Axel and I were brothers. I wasn't about to take up brawling with him over just anything.

His stupid baseball card collection was totally on the table though.

I took a wrong turn, not wanting to lead whoever was behind me straight to Axel's place, but I eyed the mirror as I did it. The side angle eliminated the blinding glare so I could make out the car's details.

"Oh, for fuck's sake, Bliss." While I was relieved it wasn't someone Axel had gotten himself messed up with, I didn't want it to be her either. What the hell was she thinking, driving that expensive car all over Saint View while wearing a goddamn ball gown? She was just asking for trouble.

That old protective instinct I'd had when she was a little girl reared its head once more, as fast and hard as it had slammed into me in the bar. She'd been such a tiny, skinny, runty kid. Always underfed. Always itching with bugs. But sweet. So stupidly sweet with her big eyes and complete and utter gratitude for everything Axel and I did. I'd always wanted to protect her from the world, and that feeling had come crashing right back tonight when she'd walked into my bar, a fully grown-ass woman.

Fuck.

I'd taken one look at her, and my dick had gotten hard.

There was nothing little girl about the swell of her tits

spilling out of that dress. Or the curve of her hips, shown off perfectly by the fitted satin covering. Her face had rounded, and her long hair was glossy.

Like she had enough food.

Like she had somewhere safe to sleep.

Like she'd had a good life.

That was all I'd ever wanted for her. Me and Axel both. The one good thing we'd ever done, besides Axel buying Psychos, was getting Bliss away from her deadbeat mom, her rapey stepdad, and getting her biological father to take her in before she ended up on the streets.

She didn't belong in this world. She never had. Axel and I were different.

There'd been no saving us.

But Bliss had needed sheltering back then, and she clearly needed sheltering now. Which was what I'd tried to do back at the club by sending her home.

There was no going back now though. We were only a street away from Axel's place, and something about the whole thing felt off. I'd played it cool with Bliss, acting like his disappearance was a mere annoyance, but there was worry gnawing at my stomach.

Things had been weird with Axel for weeks. I'd pressed him on it multiple times, but he'd refused to admit anything was wrong.

We didn't keep secrets from each other, so I'd let it go, knowing he'd tell me when he was ready.

But now, my stomach lurched as I pulled into his driveway with Bliss right behind me.

I should have killed the headlights.

I should have reversed, even if it meant running into her car. Whatever it took so she didn't have to see.

The scene lit up on Axel's front porch was ripped straight from my nightmares.

Bliss's blood-curdling scream turned me to ice. And then on instinct, I was pushing out of my car and running.

Not toward my best friend who lay slumped on his porch with a bullet through his brain.

But to his little sister, screaming hysterically beside her car, her eyes trained on her brother's still form and the slick pool of blood surrounding him.

I slammed into her, harder than I intended, cradling her to my chest and burying her face in my shirt.

"No! Let me go! We have to help him!" Her legs trembled, giving way now that I was there to catch her. But still, she fought me, slapping and shoving, trying to get around me to her brother, but she wasn't strong enough to put up any sort of real fight. Her sobs echoed through the quiet night air, piercing straight through my soul.

I'd always hated when she cried. I couldn't handle it at nineteen, and I found that now, even at thirty-nine, it was still my undoing.

Nothing had ever hurt me the way her tears did.

Except for the sight of my best friend, lying dead on his front step. The pain wrapped its way around every muscle, every organ, squeezing so tight. It was bloodied nails piercing every inch of me until I wanted to beg for mercy. Beg for it to stop.

Except I couldn't. Because Bliss was there, and her needs had always come before mine.

"Don't look," I murmured into her hair, inhaling the honeysuckle scent of her shampoo. "Fuck, Bliss. Don't look."

I was speaking to myself as much as I was to her.

She didn't respond, but she stopped trying to fight me. Her tears wet my shirt while I stared at an inky-black sky full of stars and cursed whatever fucking god was up there.

Axel was one of the good ones.

Dealt a shit hand in life that he had never deserved, and it had finally caught up with him.

I swallowed hard. I would be next. I was probably lucky to have lasted this long. This fucking shithole of a town and the people in it always won. There was no place for the good guys.

They just got chewed up, spat out, and left dead on their porches like it was any other Sunday.

4

BLISS

I stood protected in Nash's arms while the police asked questions for hours. He never let me go, not for one moment, and when I shivered uncontrollably, he took his checkered flannel shirt off and draped it over my bare arms.

It was lightweight but warm and soft. His scent engulfed me, and just like when I'd been a little girl, huddled in the middle of two teenage boys more than twice my size, his smell meant safety. Comfort.

I knew I should have stepped away. If Caleb had suddenly arrived on the scene, he would have turned purple over me standing so close to another man, no less wearing his clothes.

But I couldn't bring myself to do it. I was cold all over, from the inside out, and Nash was the only thing keeping me functioning at all.

I couldn't look toward the porch where my brother's body was now hidden by a swarm of officers and crime scene tape. Every now and then, there was a flash of light as their camera caught the sickening sight of my brother's brains blown out on the front wall of his house.

The questions droned on and on.

Did Axel have gang affiliation?

No.

Did he have any enemies?

No.

Any suicidal tendencies?

Nash had steeled the officer with a glare at that suggestion. "You think he shot himself in the head, execution style? Are you a fucking moron?"

"Hey!" the policeman snapped without an ounce of empathy for our situation. "If you want us to find the person who killed your friend, then shut up with your attitude and answer the questions."

I could see the moment the rage ignited inside Nash's heart. His eyes frosted over, the blue depths turning icy cold. It was like all his humanity had suddenly up and left the building, and he was considering tossing common sense out of the window and launching a fist at the arrogant cop's face.

I put my hand on top of his and squeezed.

He looked over at me and dropped his gaze to the ground, a little of the fight going out of him.

Relief rushed in, and I answered for Nash. "No, Officer. Axel didn't have any suicidal thoughts that we knew of."

Even without knowing Axel for the past few years, since he'd taken ownership of Psychos, I knew he would never commit suicide. If he'd been inclined to end his life, he would have done it well before now. God knew he'd had more than enough reason to with the way we'd grown up.

But that wasn't him. I knew it in my heart.

There'd been someone else standing in this yard tonight. While Axel had been warning me of danger, someone had turned a gun on him and pulled the trigger.

I'd heard my brother die.

Another sob built up in my throat, and I tried to swallow it down, but it was a losing battle.

Nash's gaze turned tortured, and he glared at the police officer. "Are we under arrest or what? Because if we are, you better tell me now so I can call a lawyer. If we aren't, I'm done answering questions and I'm taking her home."

The officer grumbled something about them contacting us with further questions, but Nash was already guiding me toward the passenger seat of the BMW.

I stared up at him through watery eyes. "Is this really happening?"

He brushed a stray lock of hair off my face, tucking it behind my ear. "Yeah, Blissy girl. It is. Get in. I'm taking you home." He reached around me and opened the door.

I didn't argue like I had earlier that night, outside the club. This time, I let him put me in the car.

We were halfway back to Providence before I even considered the fact he'd left his Jeep at the crime scene. "Wait, Nash. Stop. Go back. I live all the way in Providence. How are you going to get home? You'll be hard-pressed getting a cab or an Uber at this time of night. Not one that will take you into Saint View anyway." Nothing good happened in Saint View after dark.

He shook his head, keeping his gaze on the road. "Just tell me where you're going. You still live with your old man in that fancy-pants house up on the hill?"

I nodded. "Sort of. Technically that's my address, but I don't stay there much these days. As big as that house is, it's a little cramped there with Nichelle, Verity, and Everett." I glanced over at him. "That's my stepmom and my younger brother and sister."

"Shit, you've got other siblings? How old are they?"

"Six and eight."

"Shit, yeah. Handful."

"I like kids. And they're good ones."

Nash slowed the car at an intersection and waited for me to direct.

I pointed to his left, and he made the turn.

His eyes flickered in my direction. "So, you're staying with the fiancé then? Husband?"

"Boyfriend."

"How come he's not your fiancé?"

"He hasn't asked."

"How come you haven't asked him?"

I twisted to watch him drive, grateful for the conversation, because right now, anything was a good distraction from everything I'd seen tonight. "I don't know. I mean, I do. We've only been together a year. It's too soon."

"Or you don't love him."

I frowned at the certainty in his voice. "What?"

He shrugged. "When you know, you know. Time doesn't make a difference."

I sat back in my seat, my cheeks heating. "That's not true. People need time to get to know each other before they leap into a commitment."

"If you say so."

That felt decidedly like a brush-off, and any other time I might have argued some more. But we were already on Caleb's street, and I didn't have it in me. "You can just park in the driveway. It's that one over there on the left."

Nash let out a low whistle. "Does he rob banks for a living?"

"More like runs them."

"Fuck me."

I bit my lip. "Thanks for driving me home."

"Wasn't gonna let you drive yourself. You were trembling like a leaf."

I held a hand up. The tremor was still visible, so I tucked it beneath my thighs. "Do you have any idea who did this?"

Nash let out a long sigh. "Nothing concrete. But, Bliss, there's probably a lot of things you don't know about your brother. Hell, there's a lot of things I don't know about him. Clearly. If he knew he was in this sort of trouble, he didn't tell me." He looked at the clock. "It's really late. Or early, I guess. Your man in there is probably frantic with worry over you."

I doubted that. I stared up at the big house and the window to Caleb's bedroom. It was dark, like the rest of them.

Caleb wasn't waiting up for me. My phone hadn't rung once in the hours I'd been gone. He'd either gone to bed or was still out partying with his work colleagues.

I didn't want to tell Nash that. He'd already hit the mark a little too closely with his accusation that Caleb and I weren't in love. "I should go," I agreed. "I don't want him worrying."

We both got out of the car, and Nash tossed me the keys. I caught them easily, tucking them into my purse.

He raised a hand in farewell from the other side of the car. "Good to see you, Bliss. I know that's a fucked-up thing to say, considering..."

I didn't insist he use my legal name. Nobody had used that nickname in a long time, and I liked the way it sounded on his lips. At least I did now that I wasn't angry with him. He was right about the timing though. "There'll need to be a funeral. My mother..."

Nash shook his head. "It'll take time for the police to release his body. But I'll take care of it. You don't need to see her."

I nodded, knowing he would. Nash had never gone back on his word. And instinctively, I knew that some things didn't change. He walked backward down the street for a few steps, watching me, until the darkness closed in around him and his footsteps drifted away.

It was only as I was halfway up the stairs to Caleb's bedroom that I realized I was still wearing Nash's shirt. Without thinking about it, I pulled it across my nose, inhaling his scent one last time.

The overhead light flickered on, and a rumpled Caleb stood at the top of the stairs, rubbing sleep out of his eyes.

I dropped the shirt, but not quick enough.

Caleb's gaze narrowed in on the movement, his shrewd eyes taking in the unfamiliar piece of clothing. "What are you wearing? And where the hell have you been all night?'

He needed to know. "My brother..."

Caleb squinted. "Everett?"

"I have another brother. An older one."

Caleb bit out a harsh laugh. "Do you seriously expect me to believe that? You come tramping in here in the middle of the night, reeking of another man, wearing his clothes, and you expect me to believe he's your brother?"

He moved slowly down the stairs, but I almost wished he'd run. There was a sinister air to his movements. They were almost snake-like, stalking me, ready to strike.

I didn't dare back away from him.

He stopped in front of me and gripped the shirt, yanking it from my shoulder. "Get it off."

His closeness forced me back. "I am. I'm on my way to the bathroom to take a shower right now. You can go back to bed. I'll be in soon."

He moved in again. "Take it off now. You fucking reek of him."

I opened my mouth to explain again, but the back of his hand cracked across my face.

My head whipped to the side as the stinging pain speared through my cheek, and tears filled my eyes. I cupped my hand over the place he'd hit me and stared up at him, too shocked to speak.

There was no remorse in his eyes. He grabbed Nash's shirt again, yanking it so hard the seams protested with a ripping sound. "Take it off."

This time I listened. I peeled off the shirt with trembling fingers.

"And the rest."

I blinked, and a tear spilled over and down my aching

cheek. "We're standing on the stairs. Just let me go to the bathroom."

He twisted the front of my strapless dress, pulling down the front, exposing my breasts. "Take that dirty slut dress off. I'm not having anything in this house that's touched another man."

"I didn't!"

The tears rolled across my skin in a stream while he continued to rip at my clothes. I cried out when he stripped my beautiful dress away, leaving it a sad, crumpled mess at our feet. Alcohol tainted his breath. He was still drunk.

Fear coursed through my veins, but at the same time, I knew he was right.

I'd known I shouldn't have been wearing Nash's clothes. I'd let him put his arms around me and comfort me, when it wasn't his place to do so.

Caleb was right. I had acted like a slut. There was no excuse for it when I was supposed to be his.

It was in my genes, after all. How many times had I heard Jerry call my mother slut and whore? How many times had I seen him throw his fist into her face?

This was what happened when you acted inappropriately.

Caleb ripped at my panties, the only article of clothing I had left. He tore them off me until I stood naked and trembling in front of him.

His gaze rolled over my body, his dick hard beneath his pajama pants. He dropped down onto the same step and crowded in on me until I was pressed against the banister. It was cold across my lower back, and I curled my fingers around the railing.

Up close, his bloodshot eyes stared me down, and his breath came in hot, ragged pants. A mixture of desire and disgust played out all over his face. But the aggression in his stance frightened me, forcing me back until I knew that with one tiny push, he could send me over the edge and onto the cold, hard tiles below.

"You don't ever come into this house smelling of another man, you hear me?"

I nodded quickly. "I'm sorry. I won't."

I knew what would come next. I'd seen it all too many times from my hiding spot beneath the covers of my trailer park bed. So when he spun me around and dragged his pajama pants down, I wasn't surprised.

But that didn't mean I wanted it to happen. "Caleb, no."

His fingers only gripped me harder, punishing for daring to refuse him.

I knew better than to say anything more. My face still stung from where he'd struck me. He was a man, bigger and stronger than I was. He was capable of worse than a slap.

I wanted his forgiveness. So I didn't make a sound when he roughly took me from behind.

It was over in less than a minute. He pulled from my body and ejaculated all over my back and ass. I bit down on my lip, refusing to make a sound because I knew that would only make things worse.

He staggered backward up the stairs, yanking his pants up as he went. "Now you smell like me again."

I nodded, not moving, even though his cum slid down the backs of my thighs. Any scrap of dignity I'd had was destroyed, so what did it matter? I waited until he stumbled back down the hall to his bedroom, the door slamming behind him.

It was only then that I gathered the beautiful dress from where it pooled around my feet, along with Nash's shirt and my ripped panties. I gathered them all up, shoving the entire bundle into the kitchen bin. In the downstairs guest bathroom, I cleaned myself up in the shower, scrubbing at my skin until every inch of me smelled like my honeysuckle shampoo and bodywash, and then made my way upstairs to Caleb's bedroom.

"Go to sleep, Bethany-Melissa," he said in clipped tones from his side of the bed. "It's three in the morning, and you have work in a few hours."

I nodded, padding naked across his bedroom to slip in beside him.

I normally slept in his T-shirts, but tonight, I didn't dare ask for one.

And he didn't offer. He rolled to his side so he was facing the other direction, and a moment later, his quiet snores filled the air.

I didn't sleep. I lay there until the sun came up with silent tears streaming down my face. Both for the brother I'd lost and for the piece of me that Caleb had just taken.

5

BLISS

*I*n the brightly colored space of the childcare center, the night before seemed a million miles away. Caleb had been gone when I'd woken up, and I'd dressed for work slowly, carefully putting on more makeup than I normally did to hide the angry red mark across my cheek.

I couldn't have a bunch of three- and four-year-old's seeing that. They'd already asked questions about everything, and my slightly swollen eye was going to be hard enough to explain.

It would have been smarter to call in sick, but I needed to work. I loved my job, and being surrounded by smiling, happy, if sometimes grimy, faces was exactly where I needed to be after a night I'd rather forget.

"Miss Bethany? Did you know that dinosaurs can eat people?"

I grinned down at Kellan, a boy I'd had at the center since he was a baby. "I bet you're right. If dinosaurs were alive today, they'd definitely try to chomp up little boys who didn't eat their vegetables. That wouldn't be you though, would it?"

"No way! I always eat my vegetables!"

I ruffled his hair, even though I doubted it. "Good man. You know some dinosaurs really liked vegetables too. They're called herbivores."

Kellan launched into a detailed description of all the herbivores he knew, but the buzzing noise of the center's doorbell nabbed my attention. There was a security gate around the entrance to the expensive Providence daycare, and outside of parent pick-up and drop-off times, we kept it locked so all visitors needed to be buzzed in. I wandered over to the video monitor, expecting to see the weathered face of our postman, Ernie, but took a step back when a pair of dark-brown, unfamiliar eyes stared right into the camera, so close the rest of his face seemed out of proportion.

I scanned the grainy, distorted image, but there was no child with him for a late drop-off. I pressed the intercom button. "Good morning, sir. May I help you?"

He cleared his throat. "Good morning to you also. My name is Vincent Atwood. I have an appointment in..." The man glanced at his watch. "Three minutes and forty-seven seconds."

I dropped my finger from the intercom button and called out to one of my co-workers. "Sarah? Do you have any meetings booked this morning?"

She jostled a baby an inch higher on her hip and led the toddler hanging off her leg toward a table set up for painting. "Nope, not me. Must have been Josie."

I frowned. "She isn't due in this morning."

Sarah shrugged, distracted by the baby trying to crawl out of her arms, across the table, and into the paint pots.

I put my finger to the buzzer again, unwilling to let a strange man into the center unless I could verify his reason for being here. "My apologies, sir. I'm just trying to track down the person your appointment is with, and then we'll be right with you."

He nodded into the camera. "I'm happy to wait. I'm still early by one minute and twenty-three seconds."

The corner of my mouth lifted at the odd, overly polite remark. "Ah, okay. Thank you. Won't be long."

I ducked into the educator's office and snagged the phone from my boss's desk. Punching in her cell number, I waited for her to pick up while I cradled the phone between my ear and shoulder and watched the man on the monitor.

"Who's calling with an emergency? Bethany or Sarah? And believe me, it better be an emergency to be interrupting me on my day off."

I stifled the urge to roll my eyes at the older woman's accusations. Like I would call her on her day off just for fun. "Hi, Josie. It's Bethany-Melissa. I'm sorry to interrupt, but we have a man named Vincent here. He says he has an appointment with you in..." I glanced at the monitor. "Probably about thirty-three seconds by now."

"What?" Josie asked. But before I could explain further, she groaned. "Oh shit. I scheduled a job interview before I decided to take today off. I completely forgot about that."

I cringed. "Should I ask him to reschedule then?"

"No, no. Can you just do the interview, please?"

I raised an eyebrow. "I've never done that before.

Shouldn't I just ask him to come back when you're here?" Nerves picked up in my stomach at the thought of doing something like that with no warning or practice.

"You'll be fine. You're the one who'll have to work with him anyway. We really need a male educator. After that center on Braidwood Road opened with three male staff members, that's all I've heard parents talk about. I don't want anyone accusing us of not being inclusive. Or not providing male role models. That would just open a whole can of worms I do not have time for. He's the only male who applied for the position, so unless he's a serial killer, just hire him, okay?"

"How would I know if he's a serial killer? Are there questions for that?"

Josie laughed. "Just ask him."

I let out a giggle at the thought of asking someone that in a job interview.

Josie sobered. "No, seriously. I've already done all the background checks. He's clean as a whistle. Just take his résumé, ask him a few questions about his previous experience, and then tell him he can start tomorrow."

I nodded, even though she couldn't see me. "Got it."

I hung up, even though I really wasn't sure I had it at all. My stomach swirled with nerves, and I took a deep breath to steady them. Straightening my blouse, I pulled my shoulders back and strode to the front of the center, letting myself out of the door and into the gated area that separated the center entrance from the parking lot.

The man lifted his gaze, and I sucked in a deep breath.

Holy shit.

The man was gorgeous. His hair was longer on top

but neatly styled back with some sort of product. His shoulders were broad, nicely set off by a crisp white button-down that contrasted with his olive skin. The days were starting to get colder, but he'd clearly spent some time outside during the summer months. His deep-brown eyes caught mine, and I stopped abruptly.

The monitor had really not done him justice. In person, Vincent Atwood was incredibly attractive and not grainy and distorted at all.

Just as quickly as the surge of attraction had come, guilt swamped me. Caleb's accusations of being a whore and a slut rushed into my head. Even though I never would have done anything about it, thinking another man attractive, even if only for a moment, wasn't okay. Caleb had made that very clear last night.

There wouldn't be a repeat of that.

"Would you like to come inside?" I asked stiffly. "I'm Bethany-Melissa." I unlocked the gate for him and stepped aside, flattening myself against it so he could get by me without actually touching me.

Vincent cocked his head. "You aren't the woman I spoke with on the phone."

I let my gaze fix on the shrubbery just over his left shoulder, rather than on his handsome face. "No. That would have been the center's owner and director, Josie. She's unavailable this morning, unfortunately, so I'll be conducting your interview."

"Very well, then. Should we go inside?"

"Please. After you."

Vincent nodded and stepped into the center, while I quickly locked the gate again. He waited for me just inside the door. A slight smile had formed at the corner of his mouth as he surveyed the busy room full of noisy kids. Sarah called out a welcome greeting from the back of the room, but she had her hands full with the painting table.

Vincent glanced over at me. "Is it just the two of you taking care of all these children?"

I nodded. "We're a little short-staffed. Which is hopefully where you come in. We really need a new staff member. Do you want to come through to the office and we'll start the interview?"

Kellan ran from the other side of the room, a Spider-Man figurine clutched in his hand. "Hey, Bethy! Spider-Man can fly!" Kellan launched himself at me but tripped on the leg of a little chair in the process. He stumbled forward, careening straight for the floor.

On instinct, I reached to steady him, but Vincent's reflexes were quicker. He caught Kellan by the back of his shirt and hoisted him up into the air so his nose didn't smash into the floor. Gently, he put the boy back down on his feet with a soft smile. "Looks like you tried to outdo Spider-Man with your jumping skills. You landed it too, right on your feet. Well done."

Kellan grinned, despite the fact he'd nearly just face-planted, and shoved the figurine toward Vincent. "He can jump right up on the roof! Do you like Spider-Man, mister?"

Vincent crouched so he and Kellan were the same height. "Yes. I do. I have another little friend—his name is Ripley—who likes Spider-Man, so I watched all the movies and read all the comics."

"My mom said I'm only allowed to watch the cartoon. You want to play Spider-Man with me?"

Vincent glanced up at me from the floor, though his words were directed at Kellan. "I do. But I'm not sure if I'm allowed to."

I'd never interviewed someone for a daycare position before, but despite the fact I'd had a formal, sit-down interview when I'd applied for the job here, I couldn't think of a better way of getting to know someone than watching them interact with a child.

I pointed to a table. "How about we do the interview out here? You and Kellan can play Spider-Man, and maybe, once you've defeated the baddies, we can talk through any questions you might have."

Vincent nodded and went to the closest empty table, dragging a chair out. Kellan went to sit in it, but Vincent gently put his hand on the little boy's shoulder. "Wait a moment. We always pull seats out for ladies first."

Kellan stared up at him, his fair eyebrows pulled together in confusion, but Vincent guided him behind the chair, helping Kellan place his chubby hands on the backrest to hold it for me.

I couldn't help but smile at the sweet, old-fashioned gesture. It wasn't something I would have ever expected, or even thought to teach the kids, but I had to admit, it was kind of nice.

I smiled at Kellan. "Well, thank you, sweet sir. What a gentleman you are."

Vincent and Kellan both beamed at me.

"Now do we sit?" Kellan whisper-shouted at Vincent.

I covered a giggle while Vincent pulled a second chair out for Kellan. "Yes, little friend. Now we sit. Let's find out what Spider-Man is up to today. Perhaps he has some citizens who require saving?" Vincent took some Barbie dolls from a set of labeled drawers behind him and placed them on the table.

Kellan's big round eyes turned squinty. "Citizens?"

"People," I interpreted for him.

"Oh. Why didn't you say so? Spider-Man to the rescue!"

Kellan crashed his figurine with the Barbies, and Vincent found some other toys to add to the game. Within minutes, the two of them drew the attention of several other kids, until Vincent led a full table in a make-believe, role-playing game. He guided their creativity and encouraged their ideas, no matter how crazy they were. I gave up on the notion of actually asking him any formal questions and just sat back to watch.

Sarah swung by on her way to the baby changing table and leaned down to murmur in my ear, "He's good."

I nodded.

Everything was going well, and I was pleased that I could confidently tell Josie that Vincent would be a great addition to the team.

A sob suddenly formed in my throat out of nowhere. And a rush of emotion sent water welling in my eyes.

No. No, no, no. I'd promised myself this morning that I wasn't going to bring last night to work. I couldn't think about it here. I'd been actively pushing it out of my brain all morning, and succeeding, but I'd let my guard down, watching Vincent with the kids.

I'd stopped fighting it for one moment, and that was all the trauma needed to worm its way through my defenses.

I fought to swallow it down, but it was a losing battle.

Vincent's head snapped up from the middle of his game, his gaze instantly attentive to me. He glanced at Sarah, busy with the babies, and then at his little posse of four-year-olds.

I sucked in a wobbly breath and stood quickly, excusing myself and scurrying for the safety of the office where I could fall apart for a second.

I closed the door behind me and kept my back to it while the tears spilled over my cheeks. The ache spread across my chest, as well as the guilt, and the shame. It all attacked me at once, seeing its chance to bring me down, and pouncing on it.

The door opened quietly behind me, bumping me out of the way. I swiped furiously at my eyes, not wanting Sarah to see me cry.

"You're upset."

I choked and spun around, only to find myself staring up at Vincent rather than Sarah. In the small office, I realized how tall he was, but it was his expression that nearly undid me.

Instead of the awkward, disingenuous sympathy a stranger would have normally shown, Vincent's eyes were dark and angry. His gaze focused hard on me, taking in my tears that had probably smudged my eyeliner. They lingered on my cheekbone, and I quickly raised a hand to cover the bruising that might have been exposed by my running makeup.

I forced a fake smile, but I couldn't hold it. The tears kept coming.

Vincent stood glued to his spot, not saying a word, but not looking for an escape either. In the silence, the story burst from my chest. "I'm so sorry. My brother died last night, and I haven't had time to process it."

Vincent didn't utter a sound. So I just kept going.

"I saw his body. It was horrible, and I don't know how to keep the image out of my mind. He didn't just die, you see. He was murdered. It was graphic and sickening and...I'm so very sorry. I don't know what's gotten into me."

I wiped my fingers beneath my eyes once more and gulped in hicuppy breath. "You have the job, by the way. You're great with the kids. They already love you. When can you start? I mean, if you still want the job? I promise, this is a one-off. I do not make a habit of having break-downs at work."

Vincent's gaze flickered over my face, continually landing on my hand covering my cheek.

He knew.

I could tell from the look in his eyes.

"Thank you for the job offer," he said stiffly.

The silence rang out between us.

"But...you don't want it? I truly am sorry about all this. I can't blame you for wanting to run far, far away right now. I understand I look like a complete crazy person—"

"You don't. Crazy people...do not look like you. You just look sad."

I nodded.

"I can start tomorrow. Or today, if you need to take the rest of the day off. I could stay."

"No, please. You're so kind to offer, but tomorrow will be fine. I'm fine."

"People who say they're fine generally aren't fine."

He had a point I couldn't argue with. "Tomorrow is fine," I repeated.

"Very well. Tomorrow then. It's been very nice to meet you, Bethany-Melissa." He held out his hand for me to shake.

I didn't want to take his hand. After last night, I was second-guessing any contact with a man, but it would have been incredibly rude for me to ignore his offered handshake.

I put my hand in his.

His fingers squeezed around mine gently, and he pulled me in a step, so we were all up in each other's space. With his mouth at my ear, he whispered so softly I'd later think I imagined it.

"Whoever did that to your face doesn't deserve to breathe."

6

VINCENT

I'd thought I was immune to tears.

I'd seen so many of them as people cried at my feet, begging me to spare their lives. Some slid down cheeks silently, dripping off their chins. Some people gulped and choked while they pleaded and bargained. Others bawled angry tears and screamed obscenities at me, the water leaking from their eyes a by-product of their rage.

None ever affected me. No matter the person. No matter the reason.

None until hers.

In a car I'd stolen and stripped of any identifying features, I waited. At six on the dot, two women emerged from the childcare center, several buildings down from where I was parked now. Bethany-Melissa's auburn hair stood out; the reddish-brown color so much more interesting than Sarah's mousy brown.

The two women stood chatting, which was bizarre to

me. They'd just spent the entire day together, what could they possibly still have to talk about?

I didn't enjoy speaking more than was absolutely necessary. There were already too many words in the world. It was a constant babble of nothingness that I had no desire to add to.

But I liked her voice. It was softer than most. Gentler.

When I'd seen what someone had done to her face, the anger inside me had raged, burning higher with every millimeter of bruising her tears had uncovered.

She finally raised a hand in a wave, and she and Sarah parted ways, Sarah trotting to a waiting taxi and Bethany-Melissa getting into a shiny white hatchback. The days had been getting shorter lately, ever since the end of summer, and I used the sinking sun to my advantage, waiting until she was driving into the blinding beams of light peeking over the horizon before pulling out to follow her.

I wasn't surprised when she stuck to the streets of Providence. Her car might have been small, but it was an expensive European brand. She'd had neatly manicured fingernails when she'd taken my hand earlier, like she had the money to go to a salon regularly, and her shoes had been Italian leather.

It all spoke of money. A lot of money. More money than she should earn as a preschool teacher.

I noticed details. Details told me everything I needed to know about a person in under a minute.

A vital skill when you needed to kill them.

Not that I did that anymore.

New leaves had been turned over. New goals written down in the leatherbound book I kept in my bedside drawer, the one a therapist had made me start in the psych ward of the prison. It was the one thing I'd taken with me before I'd checked out.

Without their permission.

Even weeks later, I was still slightly annoyed my escape hadn't made the news. It would have made the cat-and-mouse game I liked to play with the police a little more interesting, but alas, it seemed it was not to be.

I couldn't blame the new warden. I wouldn't have wanted an escaped prisoner on my record either. It reeked of incompetence, and that was something a man of any profession should fear.

Even ones in my line of work.

I kept low in my seat, sticking several cars behind Bethany-Melissa, though she had no reason to suspect I'd be following her. I doubted she was checking her rearview mirror for someone stalking her.

Which wasn't very smart.

I'd talk to her about that. Once we were acquaintances, of course.

She pulled into the driveway of a large house in Providence, and I wrinkled my nose at it. Distasteful thing. Clearly designed by an architect to be edgy and modern. To me, it just looked pretentious.

It didn't fit her. Despite her expensive shoes.

I parked several houses away, slumping in my seat some more, even though I'd chosen a car with the darkest window tint I could find. So even if she had glanced in my direction, she probably wouldn't have noticed me.

I needn't have worried. The moment she stepped out of her car, the front door to the house opened, and a man stepped out.

I sat up, the fine hairs on the back of my neck prickling with awareness.

He was attractive in his gray suit and neat haircut. Handsome in a movie star way, with too-white teeth and hair that he probably had highlighted every six weeks.

In his arms was the biggest bunch of flowers I'd ever seen.

My upper lip curled. With one look, I knew exactly who he was. Not his name or his age or how much money his bank account held. But enough to know the sort of man he was beneath it all.

His insides reeked of jet-black darkness.

They were apology flowers. I could see it in the way he swept Bethany-Melissa into his arms, thrusting them into her face while her body remained a rigid, unmoving board. She made no attempt to take them, backing away from his touch so quickly I was sure she hadn't even consciously thought about it.

He let her go, but his wide smile betrayed his true personality. It morphed into something more like a shark with a mouthful of pointed, dagger-like teeth ready to rip the skin from her bones.

It was clear an argument had started from her lack of enthusiasm over his gift. His shoulders drew up toward his ears, stiff and tense. All the fake charm from a moment earlier disintegrating into a seething anger that had clearly not been buried too deeply.

She reached for the flowers, but he jerked them out of her reach, spitting words at her too low for me to hear, even when I cracked the window open an inch.

I rolled my head on my neck when the darkness inside me swirled and grew, just begging to be unleashed.

"Not yet."

Nothing good came from being unprepared. Nothing good came from moving too quickly and losing control.

The darkness had its place in my life, but keeping it under control was key. Because once it was out, I couldn't always get it back in.

She was crying again. I could tell by the shakes in her shoulders, and the boyfriend realized he was making a scene. His gaze darted to the houses around them, before he stepped in close to her and thrust the flowers into her arms.

She took them this time and then watched while he got inside his sleek black car. It zoomed backward out of the driveway at an extremely unsafe speed.

I ground my teeth when she jumped back like she was afraid he might hit her.

There were rules in my family about who we could kill. Killing women wasn't off the table. Not if they deserved it. But I drew the line at children, even though we'd had contracts for those jobs before. The thought curdled my stomach. Children could change.

Adults couldn't.

Which didn't bode well for this new leaf I was supposed to be turning over.

I could be the exception.

Doubtful, the darkness whispered.

"Shut up."

Bethany-Melissa watched her boyfriend drive away. Her gaze lingered on my car for a moment, and my breath hitched, even knowing she couldn't see me inside. I waited for her to walk into the house, but once she'd disappeared, I turned the engine on. Making a U-turn, I drove in the same direction the boyfriend had and quickly caught him at the nearest stop sign.

I sat behind him, staring at his personalized number plates.

CALE8.

"So either your name is Caleb or you like kale but can't spell," I muttered to myself. "As much as I'd like to assume you're an ignoramus, you're probably not if you managed to obtain a job that pays enough to live in that ridiculous-looking house that cost more money than you have sense. So, hello, Caleb. I'd say it's nice to meet you, except you have no idea I'm following you, do you?"

Caleb pulled out into the flow of traffic, and I followed, not bothering to leave a gap, because he had no idea who I was. I trailed him closely through the streets of Providence, only dropping back when I found myself in Saint View. The last rays of the setting sun disappeared into darkness, and the intermittent streetlamps did little to light the night around me.

I didn't mind that. I liked the darkness.

Ahead, Caleb picked up the pace until he was ten miles over the speed limit.

"Where are you going in such a rush, Caleb with an eight instead of a B? Off to abuse some more women?"

I didn't want to draw more attention to myself than necessary, but I needed information, and I wasn't going to get that by losing him now. I put my foot down on the accelerator.

A tiny flash of white up ahead had both me and Caleb slamming on the brakes. His car screeched over the blacktop, his wheels locking up as his slid along the road.

But it was too little, too late, his reflexes too slow to avoid the collision.

I sucked in a breath when a tiny white body hit the front of his car and went skittering across the road, coming to a stop as it hit the gutter.

Caleb's door opened. He put one foot down on the road and leaned on his doorframe. "Fucking bastard cunt dog!" he shouted, staring over at the unmoving mass. "What did you do that for?"

My fingers tightened on the steering wheel, forcing me to stay seated.

Caleb got back in his car, and it lurched off into the darkness once more.

I let him go. The chase was over. My evening now had a different mission.

I pulled my car to the side of the road and got out, walking quietly to the little white dog Caleb had hit. It was probably some kid's pet. I'd check the tags and take him home so they could have closure.

A yelp of pain cut through my entire being. I lurched into a jog and stared down at the creature.

Big brown eyes stared up at me, and a tiny bark escaped through a bloodied mouth.

I squatted beside her, looking the dog over and noting that she was actually female. "You're still alive, but Caleb just left you to suffer on the side of the road." I shook my head. "And they call me a psychopath."

The barks turned into whimpers as I put my hand to her black nose and let her sniff me. "How about we make a deal, little dog? I'll pick you up and get you some help, but you promise not to bite me. Blink if you agree to the terms of this arrangement."

She blinked. Several times.

"Very well."

I gently slipped my hands beneath her battered and broken body and carried the animal to my car. I placed her gingerly on the passenger seat before running around to my side and getting behind the wheel.

She looked up at me silently, putting her full trust in me.

"That's probably foolish, Little Dog. I'm the bad guy, don't you know?"

7

BLISS

I wasn't sure whether Caleb's flowers were an apology for getting drunk, hitting me, or forcing himself on me. He'd taken me by complete surprise with the huge bouquet, and I'd responded badly.

I should have just said thank you and accepted them with a smile.

Instead, my entire body had locked up at the sight of him, a terrified tremble picking up in my limbs that hadn't stopped until he'd driven away.

I let myself inside Caleb's place, carrying the flowers toward the kitchen so I could get a vase.

I only made it as far as the living room.

"Oh my God." I dropped the flowers at my feet as I took in the normally spotless room.

It was like a florist had exploded inside. Rose petals were scattered everywhere, all over the floor and couch. A bottle of champagne sat chilling in an ice bucket, condensation droplets clinging to the sides. Two wine glasses sat propped beside it, along with a tray of chocolate-dipped strawberries.

But it was the small square box in the middle of the table that elicited a gasp from my throat. Numb from head to toe, I crossed the room and ran my fingers over the blue-and-gold embossing.

I glanced back to the front door, as if Caleb might burst in at any minute, pluck the box from my fingers, and drop down on one knee in front of me.

Like he'd clearly been planning to do.

Before I'd gone and ruined it all.

You ruin everything, Bliss. Everything.

Once upon a time, that had been my mother's voice in my head. But somewhere over the years, it had become my own. She was right. I did ruin everything.

I lifted the lid on the box and stared down at the huge diamond, set on a band of shining gold. It was the most beautiful ring I'd ever seen. Even more stunning than the one that had been up for auction last night.

Last night.

How had that only been a day ago? It felt like a lifetime.

I could fix this. I had to. This was what I'd been hoping to happen for months. My father would be thrilled. It couldn't be all over. Caleb would come back. We'd talk, and kiss, and this would all go away. I'd make it up to him in the way he liked best.

I plucked the ring from its cushioned bed of silk and pushed it onto the fourth finger on my left hand.

It was slightly too small, pinching at my skin, but I ignored it. "Yes," I whispered to the empty room. "Come home, Caleb, so I can say yes."

Nash was wrong. Caleb and I did love each other. He'd proved it. Now I had to do the same.

I didn't have the time nor the money to get Caleb a ring. The money I earned from the childcare center barely covered the payments on the car I couldn't afford but had bought to keep up appearances. The rest of it disappeared into trying to keep myself attractive enough that Caleb would continue to want me. Regular hair coloring and cuts. Manicures. Pedicures. Laser hair removal and skin treatments. He seemed to be willing to overlook the fact I wasn't skinny. It wasn't like I didn't try. I'd spent thousands on diets and gyms and personal trainers. None of it had ever worked because I could never curb my eating.

Years of expensive therapy had explained why. All my formative years, I'd had to fight for food. My brain was hardwired to eat as much and as fast as possible. Being hungry triggered all those bad memories, so I'd spent years trying to ensure I never was, just to avoid going back there in my head.

Caleb had wanted me anyway, even when every other man looked past me, in favor of women like Sandra, who lived on lemon water and lettuce and had the physique to prove it.

My love language was food. Although I didn't have much to offer Caleb, I could give him that.

With the ring tight on my finger, I headed for the kitchen, collecting the fallen bunch of flowers from the floor. I located a heavy glass vase in one of the cupboards, filled it with water, and arranged the flowers as artfully as I could before setting them to one side on the countertop.

The refrigerator was well stocked, as always. I

surveyed the contents, looking over the clean shelves full of fresh fruits and vegetables, expensive cuts of meat from a specialty butcher, and a wide selection of cheeses, yogurt, and a bar of chocolate.

Deciding on steak, because it was Caleb's favorite, I got busy. I rolled up the sleeves of my blouse, catching sight once more of the massive ring now attached to my finger. My heart thumped harder. I was determined to make all of this up to Caleb. I chopped and prepared an array of vegetables, setting them on to sauté, then got busy whipping up a red wine sauce. The steaks panfried while I carefully watched a timer to ensure they would be perfectly medium rare, just how Caleb liked it. I'd always preferred mine well done but had started eating mine the same way Caleb did, because he'd claimed well-done steak was classless.

The sauce bubbled on the stove, and I rescued it before it could burn, while darting looks toward the front of the house every time a set of headlights flashed by. None of them stopped in the driveway though, much to my chagrin.

When the meal was ready and there was no sign of Caleb, I sent him off a quick text message.

Bethany-Melissa: *I'm sorry. Please come home. I've made dinner.*

I put my phone back in my purse and cast a critical eye over the meal I'd made.

It wasn't enough.

Not when he'd gone to all this trouble to propose, and I'd ruined it all.

I bit my lip, then ran upstairs, rifling through the

drawer Caleb had cleaned out for me when I'd started sleeping over.

At the back was a set of lacy red lingerie I'd bought a month ago and hadn't yet had the guts to wear. Tonight I would. Tonight, I would be his present.

I stripped my clothes, trying not to notice the stretch marks on my breasts and tummy. Or the cellulite on my thighs. I pulled on the one-piece, gasping at the rub of silky lace between my thighs and over my nipples. I added the matching robe, tying the belt at my waist but letting it show off my boobs. They were full and round, and I knew Caleb liked them.

I didn't dare look in the full-length mirror though, sure I would chicken out if I did. Instead, I went back downstairs to wait.

And wait some more.

The food went cold. The champagne turned warm. My calls to Caleb's cell went unanswered.

Eventually, when it became clear he wouldn't be returning, I cleaned up the kitchen, feeling foolish for doing such a task in two-hundred-dollar underwear. I popped the cork on the champagne and drank while I cleaned, because what sadder, more pathetic end to the day was there than getting drunk alone?

At midnight, I slipped beneath the sheets on Caleb's bed and let sleep take me.

I woke with fingers around my throat.

The rush of terror and adrenaline was so strong it would have knocked me over if I hadn't already been lying down. I tried to scream, clutching the wrists of the black figure hovering over me. On instinct, I kicked and thrashed, fighting to get air into my lungs, but the man only squeezed harder.

Frantically, I reached an arm out for Caleb, but the bed beside me was empty and cold. My voice wouldn't work. Even with my mouth open, no sound came out.

I stared up at the man, his face and hair completely concealed by a black mask and hoodie. His arms shook with the force of his grip, and his anger seeped from every movement. He picked me up by the neck and slammed my head down hard into the mattress.

"Shut up and listen, you stupid bitch. We had a deal, and that doesn't end just because Axel is dead. His debt is now yours, and there's another six months on his contract."

His fingers eased up the tiniest of fractions, and I sucked in a stinging breath that seared my lungs. I couldn't even speak; I was too busy trying to gulp down air. My eyes burned, but the man showed no remorse. Terror clawed through my body, but I no longer tried to move. It was pointless. If this man wanted to hurt me, then he would. Caleb's house was huge. The neighbors wouldn't hear me scream, and I had to assume Caleb wasn't home if this stranger had made it all the way up to the bedroom.

"What debt?" I rasped out around my swelling throat.

"Twenty thousand a month, and your club keeps its drug supply."

My club? Drug supply? I shook my head. "You've got the wrong person. Axel didn't leave me the club."

"Think again, princess. You're already two days late. I'm a patient man, but I don't run credit. You've got 'til the end of the month because you're new. You'll owe double by then. Last month, and this month. Forty K. Any longer, I charge interest."

Despite the mask that concealed his features, his gaze ran over my body. His fingers trailed down from my neck, between my breasts, barely concealed in the see-through lingerie I'd put on for Caleb. I froze, hating his touch but unable to do anything to stop it. A sob built in my chest, threatening to burst free the lower his finger moved.

It stopped right above my mound, and the man shook his head. "Pretty little cunt you have there, all wrapped up in red just for me. I almost hope you don't come up with the money, just so I can take my interest from it."

The man backed off, moving through the shadows of the bedroom to the doorway, and then disappeared through it.

The sob burst from my chest, no longer able to be concealed. I scrambled to the door, slamming it closed and locking it before sliding to the floor, where my tears took over.

All I could feel was betrayal. And anger. At Caleb for not being here. At my brother for dying.

"What did you do, Axel? What the hell have you got me into?"

8

BLISS

I woke up to the door ramming against my back and Caleb swearing from the hallway.

"What the fuck, Bethany? Open the door."

I blinked in the morning light flooding through the large windows. He shoved the door again, and it slammed into my spine with a painful thud.

"Wait," I called. "Hang on a moment."

I scrubbed a hand over my face, realizing I'd fallen asleep on the thick carpet, too scared to get up and move anywhere for fear the masked man would come back. I stumbled to my feet, only to be hit by the door again when Caleb ignored my warnings and pushed on it, storming his way into the room.

He stopped dead and stared at me. "Are you joking?"

I blinked at the aggression in his tone. "What?"

"What are you wearing?"

I glanced down at myself. The sexy outfit I'd put on to impress him was now a hot mess. My boobs were falling out, one strap was hanging off my shoulder, and I knew my mascara had to be smudged all over my face. My hair undoubtedly looked like a bird had slept in it. "I'm sorry," I murmured quietly.

"Was he here?"

I glanced up sharply. "Who?"

Caleb took two steps toward me, the menace in his eyes clear. "Flannel shirt guy?"

It took me half a moment to realize he meant Nash. "What? No! Of course not. Why would you say that?"

His gaze raked over my breasts and belly, but instead of making me feel sexy, it just felt cheap. I tugged the coverup across my front, needing someplace to hide.

"You've never worn that for me before."

I put my hand on his chest, trying to defuse a little of his anger. This whole thing had been a huge misunderstanding. If he'd just let me explain...

Both of our gazes drew to the ring on my finger. "It's beautiful," I whispered.

He stepped away harshly, like my touch offended him.

I rushed to explain. "There was no other man, Caleb. Only you. I made us dinner and put..." I gestured to myself. "All of this on. For you! It was supposed to be a surprise, but then you didn't come home. Where were you?"

"Out." He made no attempt to clarify.

My stomach churned with nausea as I took in his appearance for the first time. His hair was a disheveled mess. He wore the same suit he'd been wearing when he'd left the house yesterday, but now it was crumpled, his tie hanging loose. His eyes were bloodshot, and my gaze narrowed in on his lips. Were they pinker than normal? And swollen?

Like he'd spent a long time kissing someone else last night.

I hovered a hand over my mouth, knowing he'd been with someone else all night, while I'd been here, cooking and begging for his forgiveness.

Caleb turned away, like he could see the realization in my head. "Does June work for you?"

My heart ached. "June? For what?"

"The wedding."

I stared at him.

We both knew what he'd done last night. I wasn't even sure he'd been trying to hide it.

It was payback for what he thought I'd done with Nash. I'd hurt him, and humiliated him, so he hurt and humiliated me back.

The ring on my finger represented everything I needed in life. Wealth. Stability. Caleb would give me children to love and care for. We'd never be hungry or have to sleep in a bed ridden with fleas.

Even after growing up in my father's house in Providence, those core needs were never far from my mind. I couldn't depend on my father anymore. He'd made it very clear six months ago that he no longer had the means to support me. Left to my own devices, I knew it wouldn't be long before I was back in the trailer park. I heard its whispers. I heard the way it called me home.

Back to where I belonged.

I needed this marriage to Caleb if I wanted to avoid the life my mother had fallen into.

"June will work," I said quietly. "Perhaps it could be a beach wedding."

Caleb nodded. "Plan whatever you want. You'll move

your things in as soon as it's done. Let your father know."
He stalked into the en suite bathroom, the door closing
with a bang behind him.

I flinched at the sharp noise, wrapping my arms
around myself.

The ring taunted me with its tightness. A mocking
sign that although I was a newly engaged woman, none
of it fit quite right.

I called in sick to work, leaving a message on
the center answering machine that I was
unwell and needed a day off, but not to worry because I'd
be back the next day. I didn't want Josie or Sarah
concerned about me. I felt bad enough leaving them
short-staffed, though at least Vincent was due to start
today.

I needed to go to the police and report the intruder.
So I drove into the main street of town, where the station
was, and spoke to the receptionist behind the plexiglass.
She took my details, then told me to have a seat and that
someone would be out in a moment to take my
statement.

The electric doors flew open on my way to the waiting
area, letting in a blast of fresh air from outside that was
most welcome. I inhaled deeply, eyeing the man who
walked in. He had a black motorcycle cut over a tight
white T-shirt, and when he glanced down at me, my
breath faltered in my lungs over the green of his eyes.
They were so vibrant they were almost catlike.

"Hey, cutie," he said to me with a grin, continuing on his way to the reception desk.

I was sure I was blushing. I took a seat and stared at his back while he spoke to the woman behind the desk. His cut was embroidered with the image of a hooded demon with a scythe clutched in his skeletal fingers and letters that spelled out his club name. Saint View Slayers.

He was clearly known to the receptionist, because she instantly buzzed the security doors open to allow him to meet an officer waiting on the other side. "Go on through, War. They've been waiting for you."

He glanced in my direction once more and gave me a wink before disappearing with the officer.

I sank into my seat as the doors slid closed behind him. The hard plastic chairs had to have been wiped down recently, because the pine scent of antiseptic hung in the air, and it wrinkled my nose. Attractive man distraction over, I nervously drummed my fingers on the armrest while rehearsing in my head what I needed to say. I'd gone home and dressed carefully for this, making sure I looked neat and presentable. I'd covered my cleavage with a smart button-down shirt. I hadn't dared tell Caleb what had happened, for fear of him knowing another man had seen me in the underwear I'd worn for him. A big part of me questioned whether he'd even believe me. He hadn't believed me when I'd tried to explain about Nash's shirt, and he'd punished me for it afterward.

I couldn't have him do that again.

The nerves picked up in my belly, and as a middle-aged officer called my name, I faltered, realizing I couldn't report this after all.

The cops would go to Caleb's house and search for the entry point. What if they couldn't find one? I'd seen nothing out of the ordinary when I'd checked the doors for any sign of a break-in. The man had worn gloves. There'd be no fingerprints. They'd question Caleb. Maybe even suspect him.

I could already feel the rage that would rise in Caleb.

A tremble rolled down my spine.

The officer paused in the middle of the room, waiting for me to follow him. But when I didn't move, he called me again. "Miss? Did you still want to report something?"

He was staring at me with a calculating look on his face, and I suddenly felt like he could see through the carefully crafted makeup and outfit and right into my soul. The scared little girl, who'd lived in a trailer park and never knew where her next meal was coming from, felt very close to the surface.

He'd think I'd committed a crime. They already had all my details. I'd given them to the receptionist. Coming here and then changing my mind would make me appear guilty. I could see it all over his face.

I forced myself onto my feet, trying to think fast. "Not report a crime exactly," I confessed. "More like checking up on one."

He nodded and held a hand out. "After you, then. First door on your left."

I fought the urge to run and made my gait slower and steadier than normal. Down the hall, we entered a little room, bare of anything but a desk and two chairs. I hesitated, waiting for the officer to indicate which chair was mine, and when he pointed to the one on the opposite side of the desk, I sank down into it, grateful for the fact the desk hid the tremble in my legs.

I'd had it drilled into my head as a kid that the police were the enemy. They weren't there to help. Not ever. If you had a problem in the hood, we dealt with it ourselves. Nobody wanted the cops hanging around anymore than they already did.

"What can I help you with today, Miss Arthur?"

"My brother, Axel, was murdered two nights ago in Saint View. I asked to be informed of progress on his case, but as yet, nobody has contacted me."

The officer raised one bushy eyebrow. "If nobody has called you, that's because there's nothing to call about."

I stared at him. "A man was shot at point-blank range. Murdered on his front porch. There must be something to report."

The officer opened the cover on an iPad and poked at it a few times with his stubby finger. "Surname the same as yours?"

"No. It's Fuller."

"You married?"

"No. Not yet. Engaged." The word sort of stuck in my throat uncomfortably.

"So he's not your real brother then?"

I frowned at the condescending tone. "Excuse me?"

"You'd have the same surname if you were real siblings."

I didn't owe the man an explanation, and yet I found myself defending my relationship with my brother. When we'd been kids, it hadn't mattered one iota that Axel and I had different dads. Neither had been in the picture until I was six, and we were both lumped with our useless, drug-addicted hooker of a mother. There was enough shared trauma there to bond any two people, even if they didn't share an ounce of DNA. "We have different fathers. Same mother."

"Axel Fuller. Date of birth... Date of death..."

I confirmed the dates with a nod, trying not to stumble over the death date. I didn't think I would ever be able to say it out loud. Every time I thought about Axel being gone, all I had were regrets that I'd let him push me away.

"Oh." The officer thumbed through the screen without offering me a peep at it. "Looks like his case has been closed."

I sucked in a shocked breath. "You arrested someone?"

"No. It was classified as gang-related violence."

"Gang-related... Axel wasn't in a gang."

"Sources say otherwise."

"What sources?"

"I'm not at liberty to say, I'm afraid."

I shook my head. None of this made any sense. I would have known if Axel was in a gang...wouldn't I?

Not if he'd joined in the last few years.

"Miss, it sounds like you didn't know your brother quite as well as you think you did."

He wasn't wrong. Whether Axel had been in a gang or not, there'd been things he'd kept from me. Things that were apparently big enough to get him killed.

"Do you want some Goldfish crackers?"

My throat suddenly went dry, a lump forming that I couldn't swallow down. "So, you don't investigate gang-related deaths?"

The officer shook his head. "That's above our paygrade, I'm afraid. Those cases get sent on to the Gang Task Force."

"And they investigate?"

The man looked me in the eye. "I'll be straight with you, sweetheart. You seem like a nice lady. I'm not gonna blow smoke up your skirt. Your brother was a gang-banger, and his case isn't going to be a priority."

My fingers clenched around the tabletop. "That's unacceptable."

The man shrugged, closing his laptop. "It's just the way it is."

Axel's warning played over and over in my head. "What if it's not gang-related? What if it had been me, shot in the head on my front lawn in Providence?"

The man's eyes narrowed. "Do you believe you're in danger, miss?"

I wanted to say yes. I wanted to tell him about the man in my bedroom last night, but something stopped me.

My mother had gone to the police once. She'd dragged me along with her, telling me not to say a word unless I wanted her handprint on my behind. I'd been there when she'd reported Jerry as a pimp. When she'd accused him of forcing her into prostitution, and of raping her.

I'd been there when the officers had told her they'd investigate. And I'd been there when Jerry paid them off and came home to beat my mother to within an inch of her life.

We hadn't eaten for three days after that. She'd been too hurt to get off the floor for two of them.

Snitches got stitches.

It was a playground taunt but one that was all too real where I'd come from.

I couldn't say anything to the cops. I had no real information to give them anyway.

I needed to know more about who I was dealing with. I needed to know what my brother was involved with, and how it now affected me.

I needed to find his killer, because clearly, the police weren't even going to try.

9

BLISS

*P*sychos was only marginally less terrifying in the middle of the day. The parking lot was empty of all but a handful of cars, but the one I was looking for was parked in the same spot it had sat two nights prior.

At the door with the terrifying sharp-toothed clown logo, I took a deep breath and pushed through.

There were no burly bodyguards on the other side this time, which was a relief because I didn't like either of them.

The floor was sticky beneath my shoes, and I walked gingerly across it toward the bar, my shoes making a ripping noise as I pried them off the gummy floor. It was easier to move today. Only a few patrons milled around the room—two guys with motorcycle club cuts stood at a pool table, while other men sat on chairs watching a football game on a big-screen TV. It was still a dive bar, but with the blinds pulled open and sunshine streaming in from outside, it wasn't nearly as intimidating as I knew it could be.

"Get outta town. Disney, that you?"

I spun around to find Rebel standing with a tray of drinks resting on her jutted-out hip. She grinned at me, her many ear piercings shining in the natural light. Her pixie haircut was adorable, and her eyes looked huge, edged with dark makeup. She wore more clothes today, her skirt still short, but her shirt covered her breasts and belly. Doc Martens were laced up her calves. It was a distinct downgrade in sexiness than the piece she'd worn on Sunday night, but even still, it was a world away from the conservative blouse and slacks I'd chosen for the day.

I gave the woman a tentative smile and raised my hand in a half wave, grateful at least for her smiling face. "Hi. Yes. Me again."

"Minus the ball gown."

I smoothed my hands down over my shirt and laughed awkwardly. "Uh, yes. They aren't exactly my everyday attire."

"They're my never day attire, so you still got me beat. Looked good on you though. I'd wear ball gowns all day every day if I had the tits to pull them off." She gestured at her quite flat chest. "But as you can see, the big guy upstairs did not bless me in that department."

"Who needs tits when you got booty!" one of the guys yelled from the table nearby, who had clearly been eaves-dropping on our conversation.

Warmth heated my cheeks. I was embarrassed to have been overheard, but Rebel grinned at the older man with a long gray beard and pumped her fist in the air. "Damn straight! You know where it's at!"

She shook her hips, and the old man gave her a genuinely warm smile, which she returned easily.

She leaned in close to my ear. "That's Gunner. He's here every day. Sweet old bugger. Tries to play it cool for his biker buddies, but I know he's got a couple of little grandkids who he loves more than life itself. If you get him alone, he'll show you pictures of them and tell you all about how they can count to fucking five. Nobody cares, but we listen and say nice things anyway."

I could picture it. The man did seem a bit like a giant teddy bear with his broad shoulders and rounded belly. A teddy bear who could potentially pull a gun or a knife on you at any minute, of course, but I'm sure he saved that for when the grandkids weren't around.

Rebel nudged me with her elbow, drawing my attention back to her. Her face had sobered. "Hey, uh...I'm..." Her tough-girl, punk-princess exterior wobbled for a second, and she pressed white teeth into her bottom lip while she composed herself. "I'm really sorry about your brother. He was one of the good ones."

My eyes instantly filled with tears at her assessment of him. I'd always known it, despite what the cops thought, but it meant something to me that other people had as well. There weren't many good ones in Saint View, but Axel had absolutely been one of them. Whatever he'd gotten himself into in the last few years, he'd always be the brother who'd saved me even when he couldn't save himself.

I nodded at Rebel, and the both of us stared at each other while we tried to fight back tears. She recovered quicker than I did and clutched my arm, digging her long, painted fingernails into my skin. The bite of pain shocked the urge to cry out of me, giving me something else to focus on.

"Sorry." She released my arm and dropped her voice low enough that the guys around us wouldn't hear over the drone of the television. "Can't cry in here, even over Axel. You show them any sign of weakness, and that'll be the end of you." She shifted the drink tray back to both arms. "If you're going to run this joint, you gotta earn their respect."

Her words were a sucker punch to my stomach. "If I'm—wait, what?"

But Rebel was already sashaying away to deliver her drinks, leaving me gaping after her.

Run the joint?

I turned stiffly.

Nash stood behind the bar, watching me carefully. I hadn't even noticed him until then. My gaze met his, and he cocked his head to one side. He motioned me over to him with a wriggle of two fingers.

I went.

He leaned forward, elbows on the bar top as I approached.

"Figured you'd be back."

"You did?"

"You do own the place now."

The shock was less this time, now that I'd heard it twice. "Does everybody but me know that?"

Nash's forehead furrowed. "What do you mean? Isn't that why you're here? The lawyer spoke to you, right? He was here yesterday, asking for you."

"Only if the lawyer makes house calls in the middle of

the night and delivers the contents of wills while pinning you to the bed by your throat."

Nash blanched and reared back. "What the fuck, Bliss?"

I hadn't meant to say that. Those damn tears threatened to spill over once more. I blinked hard, willing them away. I'd heard Rebel's warning, but besides that, I was so tired of crying.

Nash took one look at my watering eyes though, and jumped the bar, landing on his feet in front of me. He put a finger beneath my chin and tilted it up, his gaze searching my face.

I hadn't come here to spill everything to him. I'd come for answers, but just like he'd been when I was a kid, Nash was a safe haven. Even still, Rebel was right. I needed to grow a backbone. I'd cried more in the past three days than I had in years. It had to stop.

If I numbed everything out, then I wouldn't have to feel it.

I just had to get to a place where that was even possible. And right now, with last night's fear still trembling through my limbs, and my heart broken for my brother, numbness felt a long way away.

Nash took in everything I was trying to hide but couldn't. "Do you want some coffee?"

I laughed, pulling away from his touch, knowing Caleb wouldn't want me near him like this. "You sell coffee here?" This didn't seem like a coffee and cake sort of establishment. More like beer, cigarettes, and bar fights.

"Not good stuff. But I know somewhere that does."

Without waiting for me to agree, he leaned over the

bar top, reaching beneath the other side for his wallet and keys. His shirt rode up a bit as he stretched, and my gaze strayed to his jean-clad ass.

"Enjoying the scenery there, Dis?" Rebel whispered, swinging by with her now-empty tray and tossing it onto the bar.

Heat flushed my cheeks, and I shot her a dirty look, even though Nash didn't acknowledge that he'd heard anything. Still, I was embarrassed. Nash's ass wasn't anything I should have been observing with another man's ring on my finger.

Nash straightened with his wallet and keys in his hand. "You ready? I'll drive."

I didn't trust myself to answer, but Nash wasn't waiting for one. He put his hand to my lower back and herded me toward the parking lot. "Mind the fort," he called to Rebel. "Don't fucking drink on the job."

Rebel's tears had been safely locked away, and her sass was back. "At least not 'til you get back and join in, right? Should I have shots ready to go?"

Nash just shook his head and kept walking. "You're fired."

She laughed louder. "You ain't the boss anymore, Boss Man. Damn, gonna have to get a new nickname for you now."

"You could just call me Nash, you know? Like everyone else. Since it's my name and all."

"Where's the fun in that? Everyone needs a good nick-name. Right, Disney?"

I wasn't sure. I hadn't gone by a nickname in a very long time. Until I'd moved in with my father, I hadn't even known my legal name was Bethany-Melissa. I'd only ever been Bliss until that point. My father had hated that nickname. He'd said it sounded cheap and classless, just like my mother.

He'd insisted on calling me Bethany-Melissa ever since, and he'd stiffly correct anyone who even tried shortening it to anything else. I was never Beth in his presence. Or even just Bethany. I couldn't even fathom what he'd make of Rebel calling me Disney.

I doubted he'd ever get the chance to school her on the correct use of my name though. My father would likely perish on the spot if he stepped inside Psychos.

Nash pulled the door open for me, then did the same with the door on his Jeep.

"Ah, thank you," I murmured. "You don't have to do that though. I'm not a princess."

"Rebel seems to think otherwise."

He closed the door and jogged around to his side, sliding behind the steering wheel.

The interior of his car was old and tattered but clean enough. The seats were faded, and mine had a small tear in the fabric, but the floormats had been vacuumed recently, and there was nothing but a soft-looking gray sweatshirt on the back seat. I busied myself by gazing around and out the window, all too aware that I'd again found myself alone with a man Caleb wouldn't approve of.

But I needed to talk to Nash. And I needed some sort of beverage to do that. A glass of red wine might have been my first choice if he hadn't pointed out the hour. So coffee would have to do.

Neither of us spoke during the car ride, but it was only a few minutes' drive to a diner on the main strip.

Nash parked in front of it, and I got out quickly before he could come and open the door for me.

"You remember this place?"

I stepped through the door ahead of him, gaze bouncing around the brown leather booths and cream floor tiles. "No. Should I?"

He shrugged. "Probably not. It's had a facelift since you lived here."

"My mother never took me anywhere to eat. Me eating was never high on her priority list."

He didn't comment on that bleak statement. He probably already knew, since he'd been there to witness it firsthand. He pointed at a booth in a back corner. "That's my regular table."

I made a beeline for it, Nash so close behind me I was sure I could feel his body heat through the thin material of my blouse. I scurried across one side, hoping he wouldn't sit beside me.

He didn't. He took the seat opposite, watching me in the same quiet way he always had. That was almost worse because it meant I had nowhere to focus but right on him.

I didn't want to notice how attractive he'd become. It was better to try to keep him in that big brother box, where he'd firmly sat until I'd walked back into his life.

My back was to the waitresses behind the glass counter that showed off an array of pies and cakes, but Nash waved to someone, and a moment later, two mugs of steaming-hot coffee were placed in front of us.

Grateful for something to do with my hands, I raised my mug to my mouth to take a sip.

"Careful," Nash warned. "They make it hot around here."

Warning heeded, I blew gently across the top of the brown liquid, clearing some of the steam rising from it.

Nash didn't touch his mug. His hands remained flat on the tabletop. "So, you want to tell me what the hell happened last night?"

I lifted one shoulder. "There's not much to say, other than what I told you at the bar. Someone broke into my fiancé's house and informed me, rather impolitely and abruptly, that since I now owned Psychos, I also owned its drug debt. Twenty thousand for last month and another twenty thousand for this month."

Nash's mouth flattened out into a thin line, but that was his only reaction. "Okay. Don't worry about it. I'll take care of it."

No way was that a satisfactory response. "Excuse me if I don't just take your word for it when some drug lord plans to take the payment out on me if I don't cough up the money."

His gaze narrowed. "I'm not gonna fucking let that happen, Bliss."

I instinctively knew he was telling the truth. But it wasn't enough. "I still need to know."

He finally nodded. "Fine. Technically, it's not Psychos that has the debt. The bar runs at a tidy, legal profit. Everything is above board. We pay our employees above minimum wage and we pay taxes. Everything is on the up and up."

Dread gathered in the pit of my stomach. "Why do I sense a 'but' coming?"

Nash took a sip of his steaming coffee and winced.

"Fuck, that's still really hot." He set it back down. His gaze raised to meet mine.

I didn't turn away. I needed to know everything he knew so I knew what on earth I was going to do next. "Nash, please, just tell me."

"I don't want to upset you again."

I hated that he thought me weak. I knew I'd done nothing to make him think otherwise, what with all the tears and falling apart in his arms the other night, but I hated it anyway. I didn't want to be like that.

Not with him.

I was already powerless in my father's house, and in Caleb's. Bethany-Melissa was weak-willed.

But once upon a time, Bliss had been a fighter.

When Nash called me that, it made me want to be stronger. "Tell me everything. I mean it. Every single little thing about Psychos and my brother. Stop sugarcoating it. I want to know it all."

He groaned, sipping his coffee again. "There's a reason Axel pushed you away the last few years. This shit isn't for a girl like you."

There it was again. Him thinking I wasn't strong enough. I sat back and crossed my arms over my chest. "Respectfully, Nash, you don't know what sort of girl I am. You haven't known me for a very long time."

"Axel didn't want you involved in any of this."

I lost my patience. "Well, maybe he should have thought of that before he went and got himself killed, leaving a bar and illegal debts and God only knows what else to me!"

Nash raised an amused eyebrow, his mouth curving

into a half-smile. "Well, shit. There's some spitfire hood rat still left beneath that uptown exterior, huh?"

I tried not to let on that the outburst had actually caused me physical pain and I was once again battling back tears. My heart ached over the fact my brother hadn't wanted me involved. "How come he didn't just leave the bar to you if he didn't want me around? Rebel already calls you Boss Man."

"I manage the place. But Axel didn't have a will, so the lawyer said his property gets split between his next of kin. You know your mother isn't gonna step up and claim anything legally. She can't. She's had warrants out for her arrest for years. And even if she did come forward, do you really see her coming in every day and working behind the bar? That just leaves you. I won't be surprised when your mom comes out of the woodwork, looking to take her cut once you sell the place, of course, but she can't do that legally without getting herself thrown in jail for a lifetime of selling sex."

I blew out a slow breath. "I didn't know any of that. About my mom and the warrants, I mean."

"How long has it been since you've seen her?"

I had no idea. "A decade maybe? Not since the last time she came to my school, looking for money. The headmaster called the cops, but she took off before they got there. Not before calling me a bitch in front of all my school friends because I had nothing to give her. It was the most mortifying day of my life."

The whispers and gossip after her appearance had been rife, as had the bullying. I suspected my father had found her and paid her off or threatened her with worse if she ever showed up again, because she hadn't. She'd slipped right out of my life as easily as when my father had paid her to take full custody of me in the first place.

But it was why I'd never told Caleb about Axel or my mother or the way I'd grown up. People with money didn't easily accept those who grew up without it. Even my father never talked about them, so neither did I. Bliss and everything she'd known was buried the day I'd become Bethany-Melissa.

Nash tapped his fingers, studying me. There was no sign of sympathy on his face.

I bristled. "What?"

"No, nothing."

"Say it. You clearly want to say something."

"Is that 'poor little rich girl' story seriously the worst thing that happened to you?" He held up a hand before I could answer. "Forget it. Sorry. I'm glad it is. It was what Axel and I wanted for you. It was why we fought so hard to get you out in the first place."

I didn't know what to say to that, other than to try to steer the conversation back to the facts. We'd gotten too personal too quickly. I wasn't that child he remembered, and he wasn't the boy I'd known either. "Could you tell me the things Axel didn't want me to know, please?"

Nash noticed the cool change in my voice. Something frosted over in his expression, too. "Psychos is more than just a bar. There's other things we run there. On certain nights."

"So, what? You have poker tournaments or something? Open mic nights?"

Nash sighed. "Shit. You really are sheltered. Do you really think we need twenty K a month of party drugs for a fucking poker tournament? Come to the club on Friday night. Late. You won't believe me unless I show you."

Before I could protest, he put down some bills on the table and pushed to his feet, heading for the doors, making it clear the conversation was over.

I had no choice but to follow him or be left behind without a ride.

10

VINCENT

"*I*'m worried, Little Dog."

Little Dog looked over at me from the plush bed I'd bought her at the pet store. It had taken me thirty minutes to choose the right one. I'd pushed and prodded at all of the different options, frowning at some that were too hard and would hurt Little Dog's broken leg, and others that were made from a horrible, cheap, scratchy material that would rub on her grazes and cuts. Eventually, I'd decided on one that was too big for the tiny, helpless creature, but it was made from a soft material and thickly padded. It was pink, just like the cast on her front leg.

The same agonizing had been done over a collar, feed and water bowls, and a selection of dog toys. Although she was not in any sort of shape to be playing just yet. Soon, though, when her leg healed.

She couldn't walk very well, but she wagged her tail at my voice, like she was trying to participate in the conversation.

I shifted in my bed, rolling onto my side, and propping myself up on one elbow so we faced each other. "Bethany-Melissa wasn't at work yesterday. Her friends at the daycare center said she was sick, but when I drove past her house, her small white car wasn't there."

Little Dog cocked her head to one side.

I mimicked the action. "Are you wondering about the fact you're a little white dog, and she has a little white car? Perhaps you're meant to be her dog? That would mean you'd have to live with Caleb with an eight instead of a B, though, and I'll remove his testicles with a rusty blade before I let him near you again."

I sighed and fell onto my back to stare at the ceiling, giving up on talking to the animal but not on talking in general. "I don't like that she's ill. If he's willing to hit her, he's not taking care of her when she's sick."

There was still two hours before I needed to get up for work, but I'd been worried about it all night, and sleep had almost completely evaded me. "She should have someone making her chicken soup."

I sat upright at the idea. There was chicken in my refrigerator.

I could make her soup.

Before I even had the chance to move though, my front door crashed open downstairs, cracking off the wall behind it.

I was on my feet half a second later and flat against the wall between my bedroom door and Little Dog's bed on the floor. I looked down at her and pressed a finger to my lips, willing her to be quiet.

I needn't have worried. She hadn't barked once since I'd rescued her. She didn't start now. She just struggled onto her back, offering me her belly to scratch.

I frowned at her. "You're a terrible guard dog," I murmured.

But then there were footsteps on the stairs, and all my attention focused on the door. I didn't have a weapon, but I'd never needed one. There was plenty I could do with bare hands and an urge to kill.

Not that I had that urge. Of course. My hands were not shaking with the urge to wrap them around someone's throat while the life drained out of them.

I didn't do that.

Anymore.

But if someone was in my house, they clearly wanted to die, so...

"Vincent! Please tell me you are not still in bed. It's after six!"

My shoulders fell as my bedroom door swung open. "Good morning, Mother."

She glanced over at me like she'd been expecting me to be behind the door, waiting to strangle her. Her gaze flickered down my body, then she quickly clapped a hand over her eyes. "Vincent, for goodness' sake. Put some clothing on. Of all the things for a mother to have to have to see first thing in the morning, your penis is not one of them."

I shook my head, stalking to the closet and pulling out a robe to cover my nakedness. "Perhaps if you didn't barge into my house like you own it—"

"I do own it."

"Reasonable argument." I pushed my arms into the sleeves and tugged the robe closed, fastening it with the belt. "However, I would argue that since you don't actually live within these four walls, perhaps you could try knocking? Especially at dawn, when I'm likely to be still in bed."

"Or you could wear pajamas."

I scrunched my face. "I'd prefer not to, thank you."

She waved a hand around, dismissing the conversation. "I came to ask you—oh my! What is that, and why is it in my house?"

"Again, it's not your house. And it's a little dog."

"It's a huge rat."

Little Dog whimpered at my mother's aggressive tone, and I quickly went to pick her up. "Don't speak to her like that, please. She's had a very tiresome few days."

My mother winced away from Little Dog like she might suddenly turn savage and try to claw her eyes out. "Here." She held out a bag.

I eyed it, already knowing what was very likely inside. "No."

Mother raised one perfectly groomed eyebrow. They were thicker now than I remembered them as a child. Like an ugly, thick caterpillar, just congregating with his friend above her eyes.

"No? You don't even know what I was going to ask you."

I put Little Dog down on my bed, and she immediately snuggled into the softness of my comforter. I frowned. Perhaps I should have bought her one of her own? Did they make comforters for dogs? I really didn't know. I hadn't had a pet for a very long time. "Mother, I do know what you're going to ask me. Or at least a variation of it, because it's the same thing you've been asking me ever since you brought me my first bag when I was twelve years old."

"I might have just bought you ice cream at the store."

I glanced over at the bag. "Chocolate?"

She shrugged. "No, it's a job bag. You were right." She leaned over and patted the side of my face. "Next time, I'll bring ice cream too, deal?"

I shook my head, opening the bag and peering inside. As usual, it was a muddle of items. Things that had been fleeced from the intended victim either by whoever had hired us, or my father when he'd been doing initial surveillance. My mother's handwriting filled a sheet of white paper, and I pulled it out, skimming over it.

"No." I put it back in the bag and held it out to her. "I told you when I got out of prison that I wasn't doing it anymore. I have other plans now."

She rolled her eyes dramatically. "Oh yes, of course. Silly me. The grand plan! How could I forget?"

I nodded. "Good. We're in agreement."

She shook her head. "My goodness. I'd forgotten how literal you are. Vincent. You do realize how ridiculous your plan is, don't you?"

I straightened my shoulders. "Why do you think that? Other people have done it. My friend Heath from the prison? He has a family now. A woman. Two other men. A little boy, and they have a baby on the way. He's happy."

My mother's eyes bulged. "A woman and *two* other men? What on earth kind of people did you meet in that jail?"

I didn't answer. I was well aware that Heath's arrangement wasn't conventional, but the connection he had to the people he shared a life with were fascinating to me. I cared for all of them deeply.

Well, Officer Pritchard and the lawyer, Liam, less than Mae and Heath. But even I'd seen the way the four of them didn't quite work with one missing. And then there was Ripley, their boy.

I smiled just thinking about my little friend, safe with his family. I hoped to see them again soon. After the police gave up on watching their property for any sign of me, that was.

"I want a family, Mother. A wife and a baby. I haven't changed my mind on that. I didn't start working at the daycare for fun, you know. I need to make sure I can be a good father." I thought that over for a second, Bethany-Melissa springing to mind. "And a good husband."

"So you'll marry someone from within our circle. The Montgomerys have that daughter. You know, the one who's always twisting a knife blade around in her fingers?"

I scrunched my face. "Sounds like a recipe for disaster. Two people who like knives in one house."

"Or you could look at it as having something in common." She clapped her hands abruptly, so loudly that Little Dog jumped. "I know! I'll ask her to help you with the hit."

I thrust the bag at her again. "Ask her to do the hit herself. Because I don't want it."

"Vincent, I'd really prefer it if you were just agreeable and didn't make me resort to..." Mother's gaze flickered to Little Dog. "Other measures."

I ground my teeth. "If you so much as touch my dog..."

The sweetness in her voice was fake. "I wouldn't dream of it. But, sweetheart, I really need you to take the hit. For me. One last time."

I blew out a long breath, wishing she'd just leave. But I knew she wouldn't. Not unless I did what she wanted. "This is the last one. Swear it."

She put her hand on her heart and solemnly swore, "Last one. I promise."

We both knew it wouldn't be. It never was.

The daycare was already bustling when I got there at eight, but I spotted the only person I was truly interested in right away. Bethany-Melissa's auburn hair stood out against the rest of the room, filled with various shades of brown, black, and blond.

That and the fact she was three feet taller than most of the occupants.

"Good morning, Mr. Vincent," a small voice sang out at my feet.

I crouched, offering Kellan a high five. "How are you today, my friend? Shall we play some more Spider-Man?"

The little boy cheered and grabbed my hand, pulling me through the room. We passed Bethany-Melissa trying to pry a two-year-old from her mother's leg so the woman could go to work, but she gave me a distracted smile.

Kellan tugged at my hand, guiding me to sit at the table with him. But instead of getting out toys, he pinned me with a look, his face completely serious. "Can I tell you a secret?"

I nodded. "Of course. I'm good at keeping secrets. I have many I've never told anyone."

Because telling people you had a body count in the hundreds was never polite dinner conversation. Especially when you weren't talking about people you'd slept with.

"I think Miss Befany-Melissa is pretty. I'm going to ask her to be my girlfriend."

I raised an eyebrow. "Want to know a secret of mine?"

The boy's eyes went big. He nodded and leaned in closer, putting his little hand on my arm.

"I think she's very pretty too. But for the sake of our two-day-old friendship, I'll step aside. You make sure you treat her well though."

Kellan grinned. "I'll bring her flowers every day. And take out the trash."

Kellan was everything I liked about children. He reminded me of Ripley. I glanced over at Bethany-Melissa, who swung the now smiling toddler around while his mom made a quick getaway.

She caught me watching her and made her way over, a big smile on her attentive face.

Kellan was right. She was very pretty.

Too pretty really. It was hard to focus on anything but her.

"What are you two boys chatting about all secret-like over here?" She swayed as she stood smiling over us. The toddler on her hip seemed to appreciate it. He'd laid his head on her shoulder and was snuggled into her neck.

I nudged Kellan. "Go on. Ask her."

Kellan's eyes went wide. He shook his head viciously and then zoomed off like he was the Road Runner. The toddler in Bethany-Melissa's arms struggled to get down and chase after him. She set him down, and the two boys disappeared into the fray of the room. "What was that about?" She sat next to me.

Her scent washed over me. Something sweet and delicious. I suddenly understood why the toddler had pressed his face into her neck.

I had an urge to do the same.

But like many of my urges, I stifled it. "Secret boy things."

She raised an eyebrow. "I'm good at keeping secrets."

"So am I."

She laughed, and the sound was like a bell tinkling. Beneath the desk, I gripped my thigh, digging my fingernails in sharply. "There is one secret I might need to tell you though..."

She raised an eyebrow. "Do tell."

I stood. "It's one that you really need to see."

"Why do people keep saying that to me?"

Her voice was such a low murmur I wasn't sure I'd heard properly. "I beg your pardon?"

She shook her head, and her ponytail swished. "It's nothing. Let's see your secret."

"We need to go outside for a moment."

Bethany-Melissa scanned the room. "There's not many kids here yet. We won't be missed for a moment. If you're quick."

"I will be."

We ducked outside, and I jogged to my car and pointed through the window. "Look."

Little Dog had a setup fit for a queen on the back seat. Treats, food, water, and of course, her fluffy pink dog bed.

I'd left all the windows down a bit so she'd have enough air.

Bethany-Melissa squealed. "Oh my God, is this your dog? She's so cute!" But then she spotted the cast, or maybe the cuts and grazes. "What happened? Is she okay?"

"I've only just adopted her. She was hit by a car I was driving behind on Monday night."

Bethany-Melissa clapped a hand over her mouth, her eyes going wide in horror. "No!"

"He left her for dead on the side of the road." The evil part of me whispered something in my ear, and I couldn't resist his demands to repeat it out loud. "I would have reported it to the police, but I only caught half the number plate. C-A-L-E...but I didn't quite get the rest of it."

The color drained out of Bethany-Melissa's face. "Cale... The last number wasn't an eight, was it?"

Yes.

"Might have been. Why?"

"Never mind. The main thing is she's okay." She glanced up at me. "We can't leave her in the car all day though."

I frowned. "I left the windows down."

"Why didn't you just leave her at home?"

"There's no one there. I didn't want her to be lonely, and I can at least have lunch with her if she's here."

She smiled. "That's very sweet."

I shrugged. "I haven't had a pet for a really long time. I'm not really sure what to do with them. My last dog died when I was seven."

"Oh. I'm sorry."

"We never forgave my mother for that."

Bethany-Melissa's eyebrows furrowed together. "Excuse me?"

"She killed my dog." Which was the real reason I'd been too scared to leave Little Dog at home today. I'd promised my mother I'd do the hit, but I knew her. Loving something, or worse, someone, was a weakness when it came to her. It didn't matter who it was, woman, child, or helpless rescue dog. If hurting that thing, or even killing it, meant she could control me, then she'd do whatever it took. I had a lifetime of stories to back up my claims. Which was why if I wanted a wife and a family, and to leave the family business behind me, then I had to get my mother to agree to it.

Bethany-Melissa's horrified expression made me realize I'd said too much.

"It was an accident," I assured her.

Doubtful.

"She was backing the car out of our driveway when he ran out."

Her horrified expression morphed into something more like sympathy. "Oh. That's so sad. I bet she felt awful."

I knew better than to tell her how my mother had looked me in the eye as she'd run down our dog without an ounce of remorse.

Like mother, like son. I might have liked animals more than she did, but remorse wasn't something either of us did well.

I had to get the crazy from someone.

11

BLISS

*A*s the week wore on, my anxiety levels crept up. Caleb had been busy with work all week, but that wasn't uncommon. We often only saw each other on weekends, so I spent my evenings at my father's house, eating dinner with him and Nichelle and the kids. The three of us adults pasted on fake smiles so the kids didn't know there was a problem.

My father and Nichelle were worried about money and the fact we'd very likely lose this house soon. I was worried about money too, but I wished it were only the bank who was looking for me.

My nightly ritual had become checking and rechecking the locks on the doors and then lying awake in my wing of the house, listening for any sound that was out of place.

But nothing happened. There were no more masked figures in the bedroom, threatening me with bodily harm if I didn't produce the money.

The money I still had no idea how I was going to get.

Nash had said not to worry about it, but that was easier said than done when it was me these guys were coming for if the cash wasn't delivered on time. I didn't want Nash doing something illegal to get the money and I was pretty sure he didn't have it just sitting in his bank account.

Between my car payments and the costs it took me to continue fitting in with Caleb and his friends, I'd been living week to week ever since my father had stopped supplementing my income with his credit card. I couldn't ask Dad for the money. I knew he didn't have it. If I asked Caleb for the money, he'd want to know why, and even if I could get around those questions, he'd ask why I didn't ask my father for the money. I couldn't do that to my dad. He'd be mortified if it got out how poorly his business was doing.

Caleb was a smart, savvy businessman who moved with the times. My father was the opposite, sticking to what he'd known, never innovating, never moving forward. My father had been so pitiful when he'd begged me not to reveal the extent of his business problems to Caleb, and I had never wanted to let my father down. Not after everything he'd done for me.

The only answer I could see was to sell Psychos as quickly as possible. Pay out Axel's debt, and if there was anything left, I could give it to my father.

Caleb would look after me, but I was worried about who would take care of Nichelle, Everett, and Verity. Nichelle hadn't worked a day in her life. She had no qualifications to fall back on. I could have gotten her a job at the childcare center but when I'd offered, she'd refused to admit there was a problem at all.

She was the proverbial ostrich sticking its head in the sand.

Nash had made out that Psychos had more to offer than it seemed from the outside, and his invitation to attend tonight had been playing over in the back of my mind. But I'd ultimately decided that going back there was foolish. Nash had already caused a rift in my relationship with Caleb. Unknowingly, of course. But it was still there. And it was something I needed to fix.

So after work on Friday, I said goodbye to Vincent, Josie, and Sarah, and drove into the city. I refused to let my mind wander to what was happening at Psychos later that night, and instead focused on the ring on my finger and driving to the man who'd given it to me. I knew he'd still be at work, but there were a lot of great little restaurants popping up around his building that I'd been looking forward to trying out.

I managed to get a parking spot half a block away from Caleb's building and quickly walked the rest of the way. The streetlights had come on, and my stomach rumbled in anticipation of a fancy meal in a nice restaurant.

In the lobby, the doorman smiled at me when I entered. "Miss Arthur. Good to see you again."

The man quickly walked to the elevator and pressed the button for me.

"It's nice to see you again, Jeremy. Do you have much planned for the weekend?"

"Yes, ma'am. My son has a baseball tournament."

The elevator binged its arrival, and I stepped inside. "I hope he does well."

Jeremy reached around and pressed the button for

Caleb's floor, without me telling him where I was going. "Me, too. He's been practicing hard. Enjoy your evening."

The doors slid closed, and I used the elevator mirrors to check my hair was neat and rub at the corner of my eye where my eyeliner had smudged. Caleb's building was huge, and his company owned the entire twenty-seventh floor. When the doors slid open, I came face-to-face with Caleb's elderly receptionist. Literally. The older woman and I stood nose to nose.

"Oh," she cried, jumping back a step. "Sorry, love. I wasn't expecting anyone to be there."

I gripped her arm to steady her. "No, I'm sorry for sneaking up on you. I was just coming to pick Caleb up for dinner. Were you leaving?"

Lindsay nodded, and I put a hand out to stop the doors from closing behind me.

"Yes, I already said goodbye to Mr. Black for the night. I've just been collecting my things. Dinner sounds lovely. It'll be good for that man to get out of the office for a little while. He's been here late every night this week."

I smiled at the fondness in her tone. "He works hard."

"Indeed he does. But don't let me hold you up. Do you remember the code for the security door?"

"I do. Zero-eight-seventeen." It was an easy one to remember, because it was Caleb's birthday.

"You got it. Enjoy your evening."

I wished her the same and let her pass me by into the elevator. Caleb's reception area was deluxe, just like everything else about him. Leather couches sat to my left and right, and in front of me was a long reception desk with a thick marble top. The company logo was etched into the wall behind in shiny gold lettering.

It was all very Caleb, reeking of money and class and quality. It was beautiful.

Our relationship would be too, once all this stuff with Axel was taken care of. Caleb and I would get back to normal, and then we could start planning our wedding.

I rounded the desk and punched the code into the security door. It opened with a quiet click, and I let myself in, making sure it was locked again behind me.

On the other side, the workspace was more like any other office. A myriad of desks in a big open space for low-level workers, and glass-walled offices around the perimeter for higher-up executives. Each had a view of the city and beyond into Providence and Saint View.

All the lights were still on, but predictably, all the lower-level workers had cleared out for the day, ready to start their weekend the moment the clock had hit five. But I knew Caleb would still be sitting behind his desk. He was always the last to leave.

A moan filtering through the office stopped me in my tracks, but I didn't hear it early enough to stop myself the heartache of seeing where the moan came from.

Through the glass walls of Caleb's office, I saw everything.

His shirt messed up and half unbuttoned. His tie undone, hanging loosely around his neck. His pants around his ankles while his business partner, Lucinda, bobbed over his dick.

Her shirt lay on the floor, her breasts pulled out of her lacy black bra and hanging while she sucked my fiancé's cock. Her moans around his erection, thrust deep into her mouth, and her rucked up skirt that showed off her panties, sent a wave of nausea through my system.

Caleb's gaze met mine.

He did a double take, jerking slightly when he realized someone was watching.

But then recognition dawned in his cold, blue eyes.

His hand slipped into Lucinda's hair, twisting a fistful of it around his fingers and controlling her head, pushing her deeper down over his cock while he thrust up into her mouth.

Her moans of pleasure only increased, encouraging him.

She had no idea anyone was watching.

He did. And he didn't care.

He fucked her mouth, staring at me, a vicious expression on his angry face.

Another punishment for something I hadn't even done.

His dick shone with his arousal and her saliva. Every upward movement of her mouth showed his thick erection, hard for her and not for me. He slammed his hips up and down, taking her roughly, until he grew tired of that and pushed her off, spinning her around so she faced the glass wall.

So she faced me.

Her eyes went wide. "Caleb! Bethany-Melissa is—"

Caleb was already behind her, yanking her panties aside and driving inside her.

Lucinda let out a yelp that was something between surprise and intense pleasure, her dark nipples pressed flat against the glass while he fucked her.

Revulsion swirled inside me, and I finally found control of my legs. I spun on my heel and ran for the exit,

Lucinda's porn star moans and Caleb's animalistic grunts following me the entire way.

I wouldn't cry. Not again. My eyes were dry when I slammed my finger against the elevator button, and they were still dry as I got back in my car, turned it around, and drove back home.

There was nothing left to cry over. He'd made it clear what our relationship was, and I hadn't listened. It was transactional. A farce. I'd be his trophy wife, the thing he showed off at the country club but never actually cared for. I'd have his surname and his money, but not his heart or his fidelity. If I married him, I'd be the hole he stuck his dick in at night in return for never having to work and the glamour being his wife would bring.

Once again, I was reminded that I would always be my mother's daughter.

I swapped sex for money and security. I just did it in more expensive clothes.

12

BLISS

I almost didn't hear the knock on the door of my living suite over the roar of pathetic despair that had cloaked me ever since I'd gotten home from the city. But then a little blond head poked through the doorway, and I knew I hadn't been imaging it.

"Bethany-Melissa? May I come in, please?"

I adored my sister and her sweet manners. "Of course you can."

"Mommy told me to come get you. There's someone at the door for you."

The smile fell straight off my face. "Who, Verity?"

The girl shrugged. "I don't know. Mommy just said to get you quick."

Nobody visited me at home, apart from Caleb and Sandra. Nichelle knew Sandra well and would have just sent her up to my rooms.

Caleb was probably still cleaning Lucinda's vagina off his dick.

With my heart hammering behind my chest, I

nodded. "Okay, good job. I'll go check. But hey, want to play a game?"

Verity's smile turned into a grin. "Yep!"

"Good. Hide-and-go-seek. First, find your brother and get him to play too. Then go hide. I'm going to see who's at the door, and then I'm coming to find you, okay?"

When Verity nodded, I dropped a kiss on her head. "Okay, go!"

She scuttled off to find Everett, while I grabbed my phone, dialed 911, and then shoved it deep in the pocket of the oversized cardigan I'd thrown on after I'd gotten home from walking in on Caleb's after-work sex date. My finger hovered over the call button, ready to press it at any minute if it was my masked friend. Or worse, some new debt collector Axel owed.

I took the stairs down to the grand entrance two at a time. The banister was dusty, since the cleaning staff had been let go, but that was the last thing on my mind. Nichelle stood in the open doorway, blocking someone outside from getting in.

"Nichelle? Is everything okay?" I could barely keep the wobble out of my voice.

Nichelle opened her mouth to answer me, but a voice from the other side of the threshold spoke up. "No, Disney. Everything is not okay. Could you please tell whoever this is that I know you? She seems to think I'm some sort of salesman, or worse, a Jehovah's Witness. I swear, lady, I met her at Psychos. I ain't here to try to save your soul. You rich folk don't have one anyway."

I put my hand on the huge, heavy wooden door and yanked it open. "Rebel?"

Rebel stood on the other side, an armful of clothes

and jewelry in her arms, and a makeup case on top. She raised one eyebrow at me. "Nice place, Dis. You gonna let me in or we just gonna stand out here giving all the neighbors a show?" She jerked her head toward the left. "The old bastard next door was checking out my ass when I was getting this stuff out of the trunk. Pervert."

Nichelle's mouth hung open, and she stared between Rebel and me like we were something in a museum that she couldn't quite work out. "You two know each other?"

I was almost as surprised as Nichelle was. But I ignored her question because it was clear I did indeed know the pixie with the foul mouth on the front step. "What are you doing here? How did you even know where I lived?"

"Nash and Nash."

When I just blinked at her dumbly, she elaborated. "Nash thought you might need some help getting ready for tonight. So he sent me." She did a cute little curtsy. "Your own personal dressing, hair, and makeup service." She glanced at Nichelle. "But your guard dog won't let me in." She leered at Nichelle. "Woof."

Nichelle spun on her heel, and with a dirty glare at me, stormed off. I stared at Rebel. "Oh my God. You did not just do that?"

She shrugged. "She was looking at me with judgy rich person eyes. You gonna let me in or do I gotta bark at you too?"

I laughed and grabbed her arm, pulling her inside and up the stairs to my suite. "Oh, shoot. Wait. I gotta find the kids. Leave that stuff here in the doorway and come with me."

"You got kids?"

"Sibling kids."

I made a beeline for the large walk-in linen closet in the east wing, that was a favorite hiding spot. I dragged Rebel along with me, her eyes wide, and peering around at everything we passed. "Dis...you no shit live in a palace."

I shrugged. "I think a palace denotes royalty. This is just your regular, run-of-the-mill mansion."

"You could fit my entire apartment in this hallway."

It made me think of the tiny trailer I'd spent my early years in. It was even smaller than the hallway. It could have fit in the closet I found Everett and Verity in a moment later.

I used the distraction to not comment on Rebel's observation and chased the two kids out of the closet, grateful they'd actually listened and hid when I'd told them to. If the person at the door had been the guy with the mask...

I shuddered while we walked back to my rooms. That couldn't happen. Not here, with Verity and Everett around.

It was a wakeup call. And a realization that I needed to stay somewhere else until this was all taken care of.

Rebel peered over at me. "You cold? You're gonna have to get over that, because the outfits I brought with me do not have a lot of coverage. But it gets warm inside the club anyway."

"Nash was sweet to send you over, but I'm really not in the mood to go out. I've decided to sell Psychos, but the real estate people will handle everything. There's no need for me to get involved."

Rebel stared at me like I'd grown another head.

"You're selling it? Have you lost your mind? You'd make so much more money running it." Then a look of dawning realization spread across her face. "I suppose the money doesn't really mean anything when you already have enough to fill an Olympic-sized swimming pool."

If only she knew that the amount of money we truly had probably wouldn't overflow in a kiddie pool. "I don't think stale beer and the odd darts tournament really brings in much money. But hopefully the sale will be enough to pay out the debts."

She stared at me. "Okay, Nash was right. You really do need to come tonight. 'Cause you have clearly no idea what you're talking about."

"I saw the books. Nash sent them over for the real estate agent. Psychos makes money but nothing to get excited about."

She blew out a long breath as she retrieved her clothes, makeup case, and hair curler from the floor. The rush of air lifted her short bangs. "There's a lot more to Psychos than what's on those books, Dis." She opened the door to my suite, and I followed her inside. She gazed around and shook her head. "Jesus fuck. I've never seen anything like this. Where's your bathroom? You've probably got multiple, am I right?"

"Just one in my rooms, but really, Rebel. Some stuff went down tonight, and I'm not very good company..."

"What happened? Can't be so bad that a drink won't shake it off."

The horrible words sat on the tip of my tongue, scalding and hot. I'd said nothing about what I'd seen because when I thought about it, I had no one to tell. My father was out of the question. Nichelle was nice but uninterested. My friends, Sandra in particular, might have listened, but there would have been judgments behind it. Perhaps discussion on what I could do to keep him more interested, at least until we signed our marriage certificate.

This was just what men of Caleb's status did. I'd heard it over and over again from Sandra when she talked about her husband and his friends, who seemed like serial manwhores. I thought I was prepared for it. But watching Caleb screw that woman, him knowing full well I stood there watching and hurting, had been too much.

"I caught my fiancé having sex with his business partner earlier tonight."

Rebel flopped down on the couch. "Well, he's a fucking dickwad, isn't he? I bet she's a shrimp, right? Bangin' body. But got hit in the face with an ugly stick?"

For some reason, that was exactly what I needed to hear. No questions about what I'd been doing to keep him happy. No sympathetic pats on the arm or condescending, "That's just what men do, sweetie."

"Something like that. But does it matter what she looks like? He still cheated. My friends will all tell me to turn a blind eye. Not sure how I'm supposed to do that when he saw me and just kept going."

"He what? Oh hell no. Why would you look the other way? I'd chop his dick off and shove his balls so far up his ass he couldn't shit for a month."

I burst into laughter, and a moment later, Rebel joined me.

"Seriously, girl. Come out tonight. We'll get drunk and we'll show you what Psychos is really all about. If you still want to sell the place or forgive your asshole fiancé at the end of the night, then fine. But give us a shot. Nash wants you there...and I don't know if you noticed, but that man is fine as fuck. If he wanted me there, I would be there in nothing but my goddamn birthday suit and a bow. Best way to get over someone is to get under someone else."

Embarrassment flushed through me, remembering the way I'd checked out Nash's ass and how I'd noticed the way his shoulders filled out his T-shirt perfectly. "Nash is like my brother. Or my father. He's almost old enough to be."

Rebel shoved her hands on her hips and stared at me like I'd lost my mind. "Nash has eyes that pierce my soul, abs I could do my washing on, and a ten-inch cock."

I choked. "He does?"

There was no way Caleb's was ten inches. It probably wasn't even half that.

"Hearsay, of course. I haven't seen it. But Axel always gave him shit about it."

The mention of Axel's name had my heart clenching.

Rebel seemed to notice and put her hand on my leg. "Sorry, Dis. I shouldn't have brought his name up. It hurts, I know."

I fought down the emotion. "It's ridiculous. I hadn't seen him in years. I've been missing him that entire time. But now it's got a chokehold on me that won't let up."

"It'll get easier. I promise."

"Part of it is the way he died," I murmured. "The police aren't investigating. They've written it off as gang-related violence. But Axel wasn't like that. We grew up with all of that around us, and he and Nash always swore they were never gonna get involved."

Rebel turned away, busying herself with the clothes. "Come on, choose something to wear. I brought a whole heap of different dresses." She threw them at me, one after the other, until I was half buried beneath the pile.

I hadn't missed the abrupt conversation one-eighty.

But I let it go and held up the first dress I pulled off the top of the pile. It was a slinky red number. And about large enough for my pinky toe. "None of these are going to fit me. My left boob alone is as big as your head. You're a toothpick next to me."

Rebel glanced over at me. "You have a point. I'd give anything for your curves."

"I'd give anything to be a size two."

Rebel shook her head. "Women, man. We really are our own worst enemies. How about we both just say we're smoking hot?"

I smiled. "Deal. But I still can't wear your clothes. No amount of body positivity is going to fit me into your dress."

"So you're going to come?"

I guessed I was. "Yes, but I'm going to have to find something in my own wardrobe." I stood and tugged it open, eyeing the racks of clothing with a critical eye.

Rebel came up behind me and let out a low whistle. "It's like a clothing store in here." She stepped inside the walk-in closet and ran a hand along the multitude of dresses, pants, and tops I had hanging inside. "A really boring clothing store that my nanna probably wouldn't even shop in, but a clothing store nonetheless."

"Hey!"

She shot me a look. "Your ball gown the other night was smoking. You had killer cleavage. Where the hell are all the dresses like that?"

I bit my lip. "My fiancé bought me that dress. It's not something I would have chosen for myself. I tend to keep my outfits more conservative."

"There's conservative, and then there's boring. I hate to break it to you, babe, but your clothes? They're way too dull for what we're doing."

I groaned, flopping back down on the couch. "See? I don't belong there. Better I just stay home."

But Rebel took a black dress from the back of the closet, eyeing it carefully. "Are you sentimentally attached to this dress?"

I shook my head. "I don't even know when I bought that. I'm not sure I've ever worn it."

"Great. Got a pair of scissors?"

"Oh my God, why?" But even as I said it, I got up and crossed the room to my writing desk pushed against the living room wall. From the top drawer, I pulled a pair of stainless-steel scissors.

Rebel attacked the dress with a disturbing amount of glee. When she was done, she tossed it in my direction. "Put it on."

I went into the closet and shrugged off my cardigan and sweats and shimmied into the formfitting dress.

It now barely covered my ass and showed off more cleavage than even the blue dress had. Rebel cheered and clapped, but when I looked in the mirror, my eyes bulged. "I can't wear this! You can practically see my underwear!"

"Wear a cute pair and flash 'em on purpose."

I stared at her. "Nobody wants to see my flabby behind! It's not cute and pert like yours."

She rolled her eyes. "You have booty, and it's the sorta booty women pay money for. You'd be surprised who'll want to see it. But you're being overdramatic anyway. I can't see your underwear and I'll probably be the shortest person there. Plus, this will be modest compared to what other people are wearing."

A prickly heat spread across my skin while I watched my reflection. Despite the length of the skirt being about five inches less than I was comfortable with, I didn't dislike my appearance. My boobs looked great, thanks to the way the dress cinched beneath them. The bar would be dark. Perhaps no one would notice the cellulite on my thighs.

"Add a killer pair of heels, some hair and makeup, and we can be on our way."

She guided me to my vanity table and got to work on my hair. We were both silent for a moment, and I watched her work in the mirror. I'd never had a friend do my hair for me. I'd gone to hair salons with friends and let hairdressers do our hair, but never had one of my friends ever sat me down like this and given me a makeover.

Rebel concentrated on a lock of hair she twirled around a curler. "Dis, I like you. So there's something I think you need to know."

Uncomfortable embarrassment swirled inside me. I should have known better than to get too comfortable with someone I barely knew. "That doesn't sound good. This feels like the time my best friend told me that Oliver

Brimwell didn't actually want to date me and only asked me out because his friends dared him to."

She screwed up her face. "The people you hang out with all sound like assholes."

I didn't say anything because she was kind of right. Caleb being the biggest asshole of them all.

"No, I just know something about Axel. I wasn't the one who told the cops. I don't snitch. But someone else might have."

I twisted so we were facing each other. "What?"

"You ever heard of the Saint View Slayers?"

"Of course. The motorcycle club." They'd been the guys hanging out at Psychos the last time I'd been there.

"That's the one. Cops classify them as a gang."

I shrugged. "So? They are one."

She nodded. "They see it differently, but for all intents and purposes, you're right. Anyway. The reason the cops think Axel is gang affiliated is probably because of them."

"He was in an MC?"

She shook her head. "No. But I know he hung out with them. Went to their parties." She hesitated. "That's all I know for sure. But if he was hanging out with them socially, maybe he was doing other things with them…"

I mulled that over. "You know this for sure?"

"I saw him at a party with my own two eyes."

"What were you doing at an MC party?"

She grinned. "A guy?"

"Gunner?"

She burst into laughter and threw a makeup brush at me. "No! I know I said Nash is hot, and he's older. But there's a big difference from Nash's almost forty to Gunner's sixty-five, sis."

I let Rebel finish my makeup and then do her own. If Axel was in with the Slayers, then I needed to know more about them. If the cops were right and his death was at the hands of a gang member, then I wanted to know who. "Could you take me with you?" I asked suddenly.

"Where?"

"To the Slayers party? Next time they have one?"

She paused with her mascara wand halfway to her eye. "Ah, Dis. You don't know what you're asking. Let's just get you through Psychos tonight, okay? If you can handle that—"

"Why on earth wouldn't I be able to handle it?"

She went back to coating her eyelashes with thick, black goop. "You'll see."

13

BLISS

*T*here was a different vibe in the air at Psychos when Rebel and I arrived. It wasn't just the fact it was so late. Or rather, early. The clock had ticked over to midnight on the drive over from Providence, and I wasn't sure if it was that or the fact that Rebel kept calling me Disney, but I actually did feel a little like Cinderella out past her bedtime.

I was not planning on running out of here in tears, or losing my Jimmy Choos, though. I was over crying, and these heels had been expensive.

Outside the bar, a figure leaned on the wall, a lit cigarette dangling from his fingers.

Nash.

He dropped it on the ground when he saw us crossing the parking lot and stubbed it out with the toe of his boot. The night was lit only by the midnight stars, a fat full moon, and a couple of wall sconces creating puddles of light at Nash's back. But I didn't miss the way his gaze rolled over me. His eyes flared ever so slightly, then wandered down my body, slow and thick as molasses, despite the fact my coat hid the too-sexy dress Rebel had talked me into wearing.

My footsteps faltered, my ankle wobbling a little in my heels.

Rebel tucked her arm through mine, pressing herself close to my side. "Get your head up, honey. Strut like you have all the confidence in the world. You show intimidation in this place, and the sharks will circle."

A spear of worry stabbed through me. "Nash wouldn't..."

"Nash wouldn't hurt a fly. But if you can't even handle him looking at you in your coat, then we should turn around right now because you are not ready for what's going to happen inside."

I stopped. I could feel Nash's gaze as he came closer, but that was fine, because my worry was partly his fault anyway. "Can somebody please tell me what the hell is going on inside? You're freaking me the hell out. I feel like I'm the stupid, naïve girl being led to slaughter."

Nash frowned. "You really think I'd let you put yourself in danger?"

A little of the fear released its hold on me. I knew he wouldn't. "No."

He nodded, seemingly no longer insulted. "You'll be fine."

"Aren't you working?"

"Not tonight. Tonight I'm just your tour guide."

"But some of us do have to work. So I'm leaving her in your capable hands, Boss Man." Rebel skipped ahead a few steps, walking backward and grinning at him. "Behave yourself. Her dress is gonna knock your socks off, but she's had a shit of a night and she's Axel's baby sister, remember."

"Like I'd fucking forgotten. Get to work."

She saluted him and disappeared inside the building.

Nash focused down on me. "What happened tonight?"

I sighed. "Long story. Can we go inside? I need a drink if I'm going to rehash it again."

Nash put his hand to the small of my back, guiding me toward the entrance. The creepy clown didn't bother me quite as much tonight. It felt a little less sinister with Nash behind me.

He opened the door for me and ushered me inside. The two burly security guards were back. I still didn't get a good vibe from them, even though this time they kept their opinions to themselves. I wasn't sure if that was because I was with Nash or if they'd heard I now owned the club and could fire them if I wanted to.

Murmuring a greeting because I'd had manners drummed into me from age six, I went to move past them into the bar, but Nash caught my wrist.

Even though he was restraining me, his touch was gentle. His fingers were warm, though slightly rough, like he'd spent his life using them well. "Not that way."

I turned and gazed up at him, questions in my eyes.

Security bozo number one pulled aside the black curtain at his back, revealing a door I hadn't realized was there. He opened it, and a spill of chatter and slow, sultry music fell out. "Have a good night, boss."

Nash slapped hands with the men and then moved in behind me, his lips at my ear. "Stay close to me."

A shiver rolled down my spine, and I had no idea if it was because there was something possessive in his warning or if it was because his warm breath brushed over my neck.

We stepped into a dark coatroom, and the heavy door shut behind us. My mouth opened again to ask questions, but Nash shook his head.

"Just take it all in. We'll walk around for a bit, and then you can ask me all the questions you want." He motioned to the row of coats hanging to our left.

I was suddenly self-conscious and not sure I wanted to give mine up, even though the little room was pleasantly warm. But I didn't want him to think I was a prude either. I drew the coat down off my shoulders and passed it to him.

"Fucking hell, Rebel," he muttered, taking in my dress.

I ran my hands over it. "Is it not good? She said everyone would be wearing outfits like this."

He bit his lip and then shook his head. "No. It's perfect. You'll fit right in."

"I'm nervous," I admitted.

"You should be. This isn't a country club. But I think you already know that." Nash pushed aside a second curtain, revealing the room beyond.

I sucked in a deep breath at the scene that played out in front of me.

"Welcome to the other side of Psychos, Bliss. Axel bought out the whole building about six months ago."

I dragged my gaze away from the scene to stare up at him in horror. "To do what?" I hissed. "What the hell is this?"

Nash shrugged. "Exactly what it looks like. It's a sex club."

This was way over my head, and I suddenly knew exactly why both Rebel and Nash had refused to tell me what was going on until I was already here. If I'd known, I wouldn't have come. I took a step backward, searching for the safety of the coatroom and the exit. I wasn't doing this. I'd been out of place enough when Psychos was just a bar. In a sex club, I might as well have a neon sign over my head that screamed 'I don't belong.'

I was too vanilla. Too straitlaced. Too...boring.

I breathed too hard, and panic clawed up my throat.

None of this was me.

But Nash caught my arm once more, and dammit if his touch wasn't all I could think about. "This is why I didn't tell you before we got you here. Stop freaking out. Nothing will happen when you're with me, okay? We're not participating. We're just watching." He spun me around, gripping my arms tightly. "I'm never gonna let anything happen to you that you don't want to happen. Not in the club, not in the bar. Not anywhere I am. Ever. You got it? No one will touch you unless they have a death wish."

There was so much ferocity in his voice that I didn't even think to question him.

"This is just your chance to understand what's yours now. You want to sell this place? Fine. We pack all this up like it never existed. Or..."

"Or what?" I whispered.

"Let's worry about that after I've shown you what you own. Come on."

He picked up my hand and led me out of the doorway. Like a timid lamb, I followed him into the fray.

I'd never seen anything like it. The big open room was twice the size of the Psychos bar, completely concealed on the other side of the wall. Red and gold lights swirled around the space, piercing the darkness. It left plenty of shadowy corners for I could only imagine what.

Throughout, huge gold performance cages had crowds of people around them. As Nash walked me slowly in the direction of one of them, I gasped at what was going on inside. The woman was completely naked, her lithe body oiled and glinting in lights that seemed to be built in to the cage roof and floor. She writhed on a bed made up only with a black silk sheet, her hands roaming her body, skimming her hips, gripping her breasts, her back arched, imitating sex.

I couldn't stop looking. There was something beautiful in her actions that was mesmerizing. It was almost like a dance. She had the sort of body I'd always wanted but could never diet long enough to achieve.

"You okay?" Nash asked quietly, watching me instead of the woman.

"It gets worse, doesn't it?"

A twinkle of mischief sparkled in his eyes. "Or better, depending on what you like."

I'd never even watched porn, so watching a live sex show was confronting. I wouldn't have ever thought it would be something I would like. It seemed cheap and classless, and yet there was a throbbing between my legs that said otherwise.

We moved to the next cage. This one held another naked woman but also a naked man. Their bodies again were toned and perfect, glistening with oil and shining in the lights. They had blindfolds across their eyes, and they stood at the very edges of the cage where the onlookers could participate.

I glanced at Nash. "You can...touch?"

He nodded. "Yes."

"Anywhere?"

"The performers will step back from anyone touching them in a way they don't like, and security is on standby to throw anyone out at one word from them. But for the most part, yes. You can touch them anywhere. Want to have a go?"

I shook my head quickly, and Nash chuckled. But I didn't move. My gaze was glued to the performers. Two women on the outside worked the man's body. Their hands reached through the bars, one jerking his erect cock, the other playing with his balls. A man stroked his abs and hips and thigh. Whatever he could get his hands on.

The female performer stood sideways to us, a man's fingers thrusting in and out of her core. Another man squeezed her ass, his fingers dipping between her crack while she rocked her hips. Breathy moans fell from her soft lips, like she was on the verge of coming.

I turned away quickly. That throbbing between my legs turned into a pulse that was hard to ignore. My panties grew damp.

"Do you want to keep going?" Nash asked.

"Yes." The word sounded almost like a moan.

I was less surprised by the third cage. Again, it was filled with a naked couple. The man had his face buried between the woman's thighs, licking her for everyone around them to see. They acted like they didn't even see the people watching them.

It was dirty and hot and beautiful all at once.

A topless waitress swung by, her breasts small, high and tight, a black choker around her throat

"Want a drink, Disney?"

I gaped at Rebel in nothing but her panties.

She grinned at me. "Now you know why I didn't need a dress for the night." She offered the tray of drinks to me again. "Take one, you look like you need it."

I took a glass of champagne, but my worry for my new friend drowned out the desire to drink. "Are you okay with this? They aren't..." I dropped my voice. "Forcing you, are they?"

"No way. Nash and Axel would never have someone working here who didn't want to."

"So you want to do this?" I had to be sure.

Rebel's bright-red lipstick gleamed around her white teeth. "Truthfully, Dis? I've never loved a job more than I love this one. The money is aces, and I kinda get off on guys watching me, all while knowing they can't have me."

Nash folded his arms across his chest. "Nobody here touches the staff. How much or how little the waitresses wear is up to them. Rebel could wear a dress if she wanted—"

"But the tips are better if you're at least semi naked."

Nash nodded. "Can't argue with that. Most of our waitresses are happy to work in their underwear, or less."

"I get groped more when I'm fully clothed and working at the bar," Rebel said with a shrug. "In here, they wouldn't dare."

The uncomfortableness in my chest eased a bit,

knowing Rebel was here and dressed as she was because she wanted to be, and not because anyone was forcing her.

She jerked her head toward the fourth cage. "Have you checked out Tiff and her guys yet? They were putting on quite the show just before."

"We were getting there, but Bliss looked like she needed a drink."

He wasn't wrong. I swallowed several mouthfuls of the bubbly liquid, surprised at the quality of it. "I want to see."

Rebel bumped me with her hip. "Atta girl."

Nash let me lead the way, and I joined the group gathered around the fourth cage.

"Holy shit," I murmured. I didn't swear much, but it was warranted in this case.

The woman—Tiff—had three guys with her. All of them were big, buff-looking men. They had Tiff tied in a standing star position, silk ties around her wrists and ankles, the other ends tied to the bars on the cage. Again, there wasn't a stitch of clothing between them. One of the guys kissed her deeply, plunging his tongue into her mouth while he held the back of her head. He'd gathered her long blond hair up in his fist and used it to guide her. His other hand tweaked and teased her nipple.

The second man knelt at her feet, worshipping her clit with his tongue. He used one hand to jerk the cock of the guy kissing her. While the third man gripped her hips, fucking her from behind. The three of them moved in perfect unison, dicks erect and gleaming with precum. All of it so overtly sexual I should have turned away, except I couldn't.

"Want to know something interesting about those four?" Nash's big body pressed to my back, hard and warm.

I nodded, mesmerized by the orgy.

"They're together outside of work. The four of them live together and are in a committed relationship."

I turned big eyes on Nash. "Why on earth would they do this then?"

"Because they get off on people watching? Or 'cause the money is really good? Probably a bit of both."

I breathed out, my legs feeling like they might give out at any time.

Nash took my hand and led me toward a couch in a darkened corner. "Come sit down for a minute. You seem like you need a breather and another drink before we go any farther."

I gaped at him as I sat, the black leather beneath my ass smooth and cool. "There's more than just this one room?"

He laughed. "Yeah, Blissy girl. There's more. But I think you probably get the idea now. Right?"

"I own a sex club. Yeah, right. I got it. Not words I ever expected to be saying, but here we are."

He chuckled. "It doesn't run every night, and none of this is legal. As far as the cops are aware, the Psychos bar is the only business run in this building, and all of this is storage. During the day, we make it look like just that. This takes effort and work to set up, and everybody who comes in signs a non-disclosure agreement that we take very seriously. What happens in Psychos, stays in Psychos. This place is invite only, and there's an expensive cover charge every time we run it."

I nodded, my head filling and then overspilling with the information. "I didn't sign one."

"You own the place, Bliss. If it goes down, you're going down with it."

I grimaced, watching Rebel sashay by, only for Nash to nab her and take two more drinks. He handed me one, and I sipped it gratefully.

"You're not making any of this sound very appealing. Why would you put yourself at this sort of risk?"

He shook his head. "I wouldn't. This was all Axel's show. And I suspect that this is what got him killed."

"You think someone from one of these parties killed him?"

He raised one shoulder, noncommittally. "I don't know, but it's a valid theory and one the cops can't pursue because they don't know about this side of the business. But there were definitely people who didn't like Axel running this place. Or didn't like that they were never on the invite list."

"You don't think it was the man who paid me a visit then?"

Nash shook his head. "No, I think that was one of Axel's suppliers. I intend on finding out who that is, but it's not like he kept a written record of who supplies him with the performers, as well as...all the other entertainment offered here."

"Prostitutes?"

He shook his head. "Axel was always pretty clear on that. Everybody pays a cover charge, but nobody pays for sex. What people do in dark corners or the private rooms? That's entirely up to them. But nobody pays for it.

Drugs, on the other hand, are freely accessible and can be bought at the bar."

"So this sex club I own is basically also a drug dealership?"

"You could put it that way."

I let my head fall back against the couch. "This is bad, Nash!"

He bit his lip. "Look, I'm not gonna lie and say I wasn't against all this from the beginning. But Axel was a smart businessman, despite his upbringing. This side of Psychos makes a mint, Bliss. Life-changing sorta money. The kind where you do this for a few years, and it sets you and your kids up for life."

I shook my head. "It all sounds super simple when you put it like that. But it's illegal."

"It's minimum fifty thousand profit a night."

I gaped at him. "A night? How many nights a week does this run?"

"Depends on the month. Mostly only one night a month, but there's been the odd occasion where we've done two or even three."

"You're telling me this place can make a hundred and fifty thousand dollars profit in a month? Only being open three nights?"

Nash nodded. "Between the cover charge, the drugs, and all the add-ons people can purchase, it's a lot of money. We can fit a lot of people in here, and as word spreads about us, more and more people try to get on the list. The fact no one is allowed to say what happens in here makes it all the more appealing, I think. People want to find out for themselves. It's all word-of-mouth marketing. Very underground and hush-hush. I thought Axel was crazy when he first started talking about it, but fucking hell, it works. There's three hundred and something on the list tonight, and that's not even capacity." He eyed me carefully. "But it comes with risk, Bliss. Don't get blinded by the dollar signs."

It was too late. The thought of having money like that was mind-blowing. My own money. Not my father's. Not Caleb's. It was something I'd never thought possible for myself.

"Six months. The guy in my room the other night. He said his contract with Axel lasted another six months. If I sold Psychos now—"

"You probably wouldn't get enough to pay him out. Psychos the bar is worth next to nothing. We don't own the building. Just the business. We pay rent for the entire space, and that contract would need to be paid out too. As well as our alcohol tabs and utility bills. I can't imagine anyone really wanting to come in and take over a place that smells faintly of piss and spilled beer." He shrugged. "But I guess you wouldn't really need to worry about that. You could just sell a diamond earring or something to cover the shortfall."

I didn't tell him that all my diamonds were actually cubic zirconia. I'd already pawned the only set of true diamonds I owned. I hadn't gotten nearly as much as I'd hoped for them either.

Nash's intense gaze flickered over my face. "So, what's it gonna be, Blissy girl? You selling up shop to the highest bidder? Or you walking in your brother's footsteps and becoming one of us?"

My father had raised me to do the right thing. That

meant selling Psychos and going to the police about the illegal goings-on and the masked man in my bedroom.

But even as I considered that, the hood rat in me knew that going to the cops would only make things worse as well as leaving me with more debts to pay.

There was a third option. I could look at this as an opportunity for something more. It might not have been the business I'd dreamed of owning. But it was already mine. It could provide for me and help pay off some of my father's debts so he could get back on his feet. He could hire a business manager to get his company back on track, and Everett and Verity wouldn't have to leave their private schools. I could pay for them to continue getting the very best education.

I wanted that for them. I never wanted them to suffer hunger or neglect the way I had when we'd had no money. I didn't want them to lose the safety and security they had now. I didn't want them knowing there was any other way to live than the privileged lives they'd had so far.

I could take away that pain before they even felt it.

"I'm in," I told Nash, knowing there was no other real option. "I'm one of you."

14

NASH

"*P*ut your eyes back in your head, Boss Man."

Rebel nudged me with her elbow as she collected our empty glasses. Bliss had announced she was going to the bathroom, and I'd watched her walk every step of the way, her rounded ass swaying as she strode away.

"Huh?"

"Don't play dumb. I'm standing right in front of you with my tits out and see-through panties, but all you have eyes for is Disney. I could literally shake my tatas right in front of your face right now and you wouldn't have even noticed."

"Please don't do that."

She snorted on her laughter. "Admit it. You like her."

"Of course I like her. She's a good kid."

She huffed on a laugh. "She's not a kid, Nash. She's twenty-five."

"Exactly. She's a kid."

"Just because you act like you're eighty doesn't actually mean you are, you know? You aren't that much older than her."

"I'm nearly forty. I was having sex before she was even born."

"Don't blame her because you're a slut!"

I sniggered.

"I've got to get these glasses back to the bar. But if you don't want her realizing you've got the hots for her curves, then you might want to stop panting over her like a slobbery dog. And for fuck's sake, do something about the boner."

I rolled my eyes. "We're at a sex club. Everybody has a boner."

"Yeah, but yours basically leans in her direction every time she's near you."

"Why haven't I fired you yet?"

"Because you love my tiny tits?"

Right now, I wasn't interested in anyone's tits. I wasn't looking to date. I wasn't even really looking for a fuck, though that would probably come soon enough.

But it wouldn't be with Bliss.

Axel wouldn't have stood for it. And even though he wasn't here now, I would respect that.

She might have agreed to join our crew and keep our doors open, and for that I was grateful. If she'd sold the place, I would have been out of a job that earned me more money than I'd ever make anywhere else, and so would my team. Rebel and the rest of them were the only family I'd ever had. And I was going to do everything in my power to make sure they all had roofs over their heads, money in their wallets, and food on their tables.

A big body dropped into Bliss's empty seat and draped an arm over the back of the couch.

I glanced over at him. "War."

"Nash."

His jean-clad leg skimmed mine. There was plenty of couch on the other side of him, but he made no move to shuffle over.

I didn't comment on it. "How's the MC? Your dad talked you into running the place yet?"

He grinned. "Nope. And he won't. Being VP is a lot more fun than being pres. All the power, none of the responsibility, you know?"

I didn't really, because despite knowing War for several years, I'd never had any interest in joining his motorcycle club. I only had a vague idea how the hierarchy worked, but enough to know that with his old man as president, War was next in line for the Saint View Slayers' throne.

Except he'd never wanted it, much to his old man's dismay. They'd all been coming to Psychos for as long as I could remember, and you picked up snippets of conversation here and there. You could learn a lot about people by listening to what they said in front of bartenders.

"How's business? I heard about Axel. That's a tough blow, man. I'd like to come to his funeral."

I nodded. "He would have appreciated that. Can't do much on that front 'til the cops release his body though."

War nodded solemnly, but then a wide grin spread across his face. "So, who's the hottie you've been following all around the club like you're as attached as her shadow?"

"She's Axel's sister. She owns the place now. Giving her the grand tour."

He raised an eyebrow. "No fucking shit?"

"No fucking shit."

"So...you can't go there. Bro code and all that. But there's nothing stopping me, right?"

I ground my molars. I liked War. I liked everyone really, and people liked me. It paid to be easygoing sometimes. But I wasn't sure I wanted him anywhere near Bliss.

I didn't feel very easygoing when I thought about her with another man. Even though I knew she had a fiancé, he was just some nameless, faceless idea that could easily be ignored. War was right there in front of me, with his shit-eating grin that ladies loved and biceps that could crack walnuts.

I was also well aware it wasn't my place to make decisions for her. And that while I was fifteen years older, I wasn't her father.

So when she came back from the bathroom, even though I didn't like it, I introduced her to the man who'd stolen her seat.

"War, this is Bliss. Bliss, War. War is VP of the local motorcycle club."

War slid over, giving Bliss back her seat.

Recognition dawned in her expression.

He winked at her. "Hey again, cutie."

She perched on the edge of the couch. "The Slayers MC?"

"That's the one." War's grin was so lazily charming I had a sudden urge to punch him in the face.

He ran his tongue across his bottom lip. "Cute name, by the way. That short for something?"

"Bethany-Melissa. Bliss is a family nickname."

I probably should have been happy she included me in her family, but I wasn't.

"So what should I call you?" War asked.

"You could just call me Bethany-Melissa."

"That's a mouthful."

"Rebel's been calling me Disney."

He screwed up his face. "What the fuck for?"

She laughed. "Long story. It involves a ball gown."

"I'm listening."

She gave him a warm smile and filled him in, and I was sure I saw War fall in love with her. If that were even possible for a man like him. Fall in lust, at the very least.

He was into her. There was no doubt about that.

"Bliss is engaged," I blurted out.

The woman was right in the middle of a story that had absolutely nothing to do with her fiancé. Fuck me. I might as well have stuck a tag on my chest that read, "Hi, my name is Cockblock."

War and Bliss both looked over at me.

"That true, pretty girl?"

Bliss practically preened under his compliments, and I stared at her. What the hell was she doing? Surely his flattery wasn't doing things for her?

"True. But I did walk in on him trying to find his tiny dick in another woman's vagina earlier tonight, so... there's that."

"You what?" I choked. A red-hot rage washed over me out of nowhere. "You didn't tell me that."

"You were too busy telling me I owned a sex club. Caleb's infidelity seemed somewhat irrelevant."

It wasn't irrelevant. Because even though she was putting on an 'I don't care' front, she had to care.

"You want me to kill him?" War asked casually, as if he killed people every other day.

I didn't take it as a joke because I knew there was a good chance War had taken a life or two in his time.

Bliss did, though. She laughed. "I'll give you his name and details later then, shall I?"

War leaned in, resting his elbow on his knee. The move brought him closer into Bliss's personal space, but she didn't move back.

"Anytime, baby. Offer is always there."

My fingers dug into the plush leather couch, fingernails stabbing into the fabric while I fought for something to say to steer this conversation around and to get War to disappear and forget that Bliss existed.

"War!"

All three of us sitting on the couch snapped our heads up at the shout from across the room. It was loud enough to be heard over the music, the chatter, and the occasional moan or cry as someone came.

Solomon struggled with an intruder in the doorway who'd managed to get through the door and the coatroom and into the main lounge area.

I recognized him. He was War's best friend, Hawk. The two of them regularly spent their evenings at Psychos, happily chatting Rebel up when she'd let them. Hawk had come to this side of Psychos a couple of times in the past, and I knew him well enough, so even though he wasn't on the list for tonight, I signaled to Solomon to let him in.

Solomon seemed like he'd rather run Hawk's head into the brick wall. But it wasn't a good idea. Hawk was a big guy, and he'd probably give Solomon a run for his money. The two of them were already creating a scene, and a fight was not the sort of entertainment we were trying to provide here.

Solomon backed up at my signal, letting Hawk go, and stepping back into the shadows he'd exploded from. Hawk shot him a dirty look and straightened his cut on his way to War's side.

"Hawk. Meet BM." War cringed and then laughed. "Okay, shit. Bowel Movement is not a fitting nickname for you, sweetheart.

Bliss laughed. "Anything is better than BM." She smiled up at Hawk and extended a hand to him. "I'm Bethany-Melissa. Or Bliss. Or Disney. Take your pick."

Her hand dropped back to her lap when Hawk completely ignored her.

He stared down at War, his face taut.

War seemed to notice at the same time I did. He sat up straight, his voice suddenly low and deadly. "Talk. What's happened?"

Hawk shook his head. "I swear, man. I came to find you as soon as I heard... It's your parents."

Even with Bliss between us, the tension that froze War's body was evident. His jaw went so rigid he could barely get words out.

A sick, dark feeling washed over me, like I knew what was coming before Hawk even said anything.

Hawk's expression was anguished, and he had to

swallow thickly before he could answer. "Their car went over the cliff up on Saint View Point. They got your mom out. She's not conscious, but she's alive."

Bliss let out a gasp, and despite the fact they'd only just met, her hand landed on War's leg in an attempt to comfort him.

If he noticed, he didn't say anything. His gaze was locked on Hawk, waiting for him to deliver the rest of the news. "And my old man?"

"He's dead. Murdered execution style. Gunshot to the head."

15

BLISS

I stayed at Psychos until the very last guest left around five in the morning. And then I stood in the parking lot, staring at the black square building, backlit by a rising sun, and saw it in a whole new light.

In the space of one night, it had morphed from a slightly terrifying dive bar to an empire.

One that I owned.

I'd never had control of anything in my life. I'd spent six years bending and breaking beneath my mother's mood swings and Jerry's abuse. I'd spent my school years desperately trying to fit with kids who'd grown-up with silver spoons in their mouths. I'd spent my adult life so far cocooned in my father's wealth, and then Caleb's.

All of it had come with a price.

All of it had left me weak. Useless. Unable to stand on my own two feet.

"You seem like a woman whose just made a life-changing decision," Nash mused from his perch on the hood of his Jeep. His long legs dangled over the headlights, and he lay back, resting on his elbows. The morning sunrise kissed his skin, and I tried not to notice how good he looked in it, despite the fact we'd been up all night.

I had no doubt I did not look even half as attractive. My feet ached, and the urge to sleep was there in the back of my mind. It was just held at bay by the pure excitement of everything I'd seen. Everything I owned. Everything I could be.

"I know Axel didn't want me involved in this. But what you've built..."

"Isn't too shabby for a couple of hood rat kids?"

"Yeah. That."

I turned away from the building and stood in front of Nash. "Thank you for showing me. And sticking with me all night. I know I was the kid sister cramping your style."

"You're fine. I didn't feel like playing anyway."

"Do you normally...participate? There were a lot of beautiful women in there..."

His gaze clashed with mine. "There were. Sometimes I join in. Sometimes I just watch."

My breath caught in my throat, because for a second, I had a full-blown mental image of Nash in the middle of the club, a woman on her knees in front of him, finding out if his cock was really as big as Rebel had claimed it to be.

The woman was me.

Nash jumped down off the hood of his Jeep and went to the passenger side, opening the door for me again. "Come on. I'll take you home. You must be tired."

I couldn't look at him. I clambered into the seat with the elegance of a walrus and drew my seat belt across my chest, fastening it while he jogged around to his side.

He glanced at me. "You're not going back to Caleb's place, I assume."

"Not a chance."

"Good girl. Back to your dad's then?"

"Yes, please."

Nash filled the trip with idle conversation, but I did little more than make "Mmm" and "Oh" noises of confirmation while he talked.

I had to be a bit drunk. Or maybe the incense inside the club had me stoned. Or maybe it was just the fact I'd spent five hours watching people have sex while not a single person had touched me.

All I could think about was the ache inside me, my slick panties, and the fact that Nash Sorensen had turned into a very attractive man.

All the more reason not to look at him. He was too old for me. He saw me as a younger sister.

But my clit didn't care. She was sporting a lady boner that made it hard to concentrate when he and I were in such an enclosed space.

He parked his car at the front of my house, and I practically dove out the door, calling my thanks for the ride and telling him I'd stop in at Psychos on Monday after work to talk things through some more.

I didn't stick around for a confirmation. I ran into the house, desperate to be alone.

The house was silent, as one would expect at this early time of morning, and I pulled my heels off to take the stairs two at a time on bare feet. The moment I got into my suite, I closed and locked the door, leaning against it hard, slightly winded either from the short sprint or maybe just from the night overall.

With my heartrate slowing now that there wasn't six feet of gorgeous, rugged, clearly experienced man sitting next to me, I made my way to my closet, depositing my heels in their designated spot. At the end of the large space, my full-length mirror displayed my reflection.

My eyes were big, and my auburn hair was wild and messed up, like I'd had a great night of sex.

You wish, the throbbing in my clit practically yelled.

I stripped the black dress off, leaving it on a puddle in the floor, unsure whether I'd want to keep it when it was really just not me.

My bra and panties followed, until I stood naked. I quickly turned away, not wanting to see my reflection. I'd heard what Rebel had said, about being envious of my curves, but when I stood in front of a mirror, all I saw were the parts of me I didn't like. The cellulite. The tummy rolls. The wobble in my thighs.

I turned off the light and tucked myself into bed, but my brain wouldn't shut off. It kept playing scenes from the night, always ending in the imagined one where I kneeled at Nash's feet, pure desire in his eyes.

I ran my hands over my body, touching my full breasts and squeezing my nipples. Pleasure shot through me and I worked the tips into stiff peaks that were ripe for his mouth.

If I closed my eyes and let myself float back to the club, I could almost see Nash leaning forward and yanking down the front of my dress to expose my breasts. They grew heavy in my hands, needy and desperate for his touch.

My core ached.

I gave myself up to the fantasy and leaned into it.

Nash's cock was as big as Rebel had said it would be. Thick and hard, not because of the scent of sex in the air around us or the performers in their cages. But because I leaned over his lap and wrapped my lips around the blunt head.

His hands dove into my hair, and he murmured his approval. "Take me deep, Bliss. Let me feel you."

I squeezed my nipples hard enough to mimic clamps, then dropped one hand to my clit.

I spread my legs. In the fantasy, I did the same.

Hands moved up my thighs, another man settling in behind me. I glanced over my shoulder to find War staring at me with an intensity that burned my body alive. With no care that we were in a room full of people or that I had my lips wrapped around Nash's cock, War rucked my skirt up around my waist and lowered my panties.

His eyes flared with desire as he took a handful of my ass, while his other hand spread my folds. "Look at your pretty cunt, baby girl. You're wet and dripping, just creaming yourself for my dick."

His words in my head were coarse and dirty, but when I touched myself, pushing my fingers between my folds, I was soaked.

It was almost too much to bear. I was already right on the verge after hours of sex around me. Putting War and Nash together in a fantasy was too much. I rubbed my clit and rode my fingers. I added a third, trying to emulate the thickness I craved, and eventually, I pulled my vibrator out of my top drawer and let that take the place of my fingers.

I pressed the vibrator against my clit before sliding it

lower to fill the ache inside me. My hips bucked right off the bed as an orgasm barreled down on me. It was too quick, but I couldn't bring myself to drag it out.

And Lord knew, I was used to a quick orgasm. I'd become a pro at it, quietly making myself come after every time Caleb and I had sex and he rolled over and went to sleep.

The moment the orgasm faded, embarrassment washed over me. Beneath the sheets, I was a sticky mess of my own making.

"You're an idiot, Bliss," I murmured to myself, dragging myself out of bed for a shower even though exhaustion was setting in.

I had no business fantasizing over anyone but Caleb. I was still engaged. The man's ring had been on my finger when I'd thrust it inside myself, desperate to fill the ache another man had woken up in me. Not just one man but two. I barely even knew War, and yet I'd let him into the most intimate parts of me during the fantasy. Nash was like a brother to me. Thinking of him in any other way would cause me nothing but complete and utter mortification.

But Caleb and I were done. The way he'd looked at me while he'd fucked Lucinda still sent chills down my spine. And owning Psychos made leaving him possible.

I'd have my own money. Not just the pittance the childcare center paid me. But real money.

Money meant opportunities.

Options.

Money meant I would never be forced into a marriage I didn't want, solely for the financial security the man could provide me.

I'd be everything my mother had never been.

I'd be free.

*T*here were seventeen missed calls on my phone when I woke up on Monday morning. They displayed above the twenty-three from the day before.

All of them Caleb.

I wasn't ready to speak to him. I knew what I had to do. I knew what I *wanted* to do. And yet I knew myself. I was easily swayed. A doormat.

I couldn't face Caleb until I was one-hundred-percent sure I wouldn't let him gaslight me into believing the entire thing was my fault.

I'd been ignoring him all weekend. I'd turned my phone off and stayed out of the house as much as I could. I'd taken myself shopping, to dinner, and then to a late movie. When I'd gotten home on Sunday night, Nichelle said Caleb had been by twice, looking for me.

I'd thanked her and told her I'd call him.

But I hadn't.

I knew I couldn't put it off much longer, and I would have to face the music later that day. But I needed to go to work first.

I dug through my closet because nothing felt right. Everything felt like Bethany-Melissa. Polished. Put together. The future wife of a successful businessman.

None of it felt like Bliss.

At the back, I found a pair of jeans I couldn't remember buying. I couldn't even remember the last time I'd worn denim at all. But I pulled them on, wincing a little at how tight they were, but once I had them buttoned, I grinned at my reflection. I found a black T-shirt in my drawer and partnered it with a jacket and a gray knitted scarf.

I wished I had a pair of Doc Martens like Rebel's, but I settled for a pair of white running shoes with the promise of scuffing them up a bit on my way into work so they weren't quite so blindingly white.

"Well," I said to my reflection. "That's new."

I liked it, though. It was casual and young, and I felt cute. The jeans made my ass look good.

It was a change to stare into the mirror and be able to say something nice about my body.

Feeling like a million bucks, even though the outfit probably cost less than a hundred, I jogged downstairs, grabbing a breakfast muffin and a banana from the kitchen before heading for my car.

I cranked up some music—some pop by a girl group Caleb hated because all their songs were squeaky and overexcited. I'd always thought they were catchy but had never said anything because of his disdain for them. Now I turned them up as loud as my car speakers would go and cruised to work with a smile.

Caleb's infidelity should have had me crying into my cereal for a week, and instead, it had given me everything I hadn't known I'd needed.

I turned into the daycare center's parking lot, and my smile widened as Vincent pulled in right behind me. I got out and went to his car, tapping on his window when he was still sitting behind the wheel.

He rolled the window down. "Good morning, Bethany-Melissa."

He was always very formal in the way he spoke. It was different, but I liked the guy. He was the sort of person who'd probably been labeled 'weird' as a kid, and I could relate to feeling like you didn't fit in. "Good morning, Vincent. Can I ask you something?"

He peered up at me, expression serious. "Yes."

"Can you call me Bliss?"

He blinked. "But your name is Bethany-Melissa."

"It is, but I don't think I want to go by that name anymore. And if you ram it all together and drop a few letters, you get Bliss."

He mulled the name over in his head for a moment.

"Haven't you got a nickname?" I asked. "Vinnie maybe?"

He grimaced. "I do, but it's not Vinnie. That's horrendous."

I giggled, making a mental note never to call him that since he clearly didn't like it. "What is it then?"

"Scythe."

I blinked.

Vincent just watched me.

It took me a moment to recover. In that moment, a kernel of worry opened up inside me. Last week he'd said something odd about his mother killing his dog. Now his nickname was Scythe? "Uh, that's an interesting one. Why?"

He held up his hand. On the back was a light-brown birthmark in a very distinct scythe shape. Relief crashed over me. The man was a little odd, but he was also cute and incredibly sweet with the kids. I'd clearly been watching too many episodes of *Dexter*. "Oh wow. That's uncanny. It could almost be a tattoo, it's so perfectly shaped."

Vincent nodded and got out of the car. He slammed the door behind me. "I'll call you Bliss, but Scythe isn't a nickname I advertise. I actually despise it."

I let out a laugh. "Understandable. Don't worry, I won't start calling you that. Might freak the kids out. And Josie. Kellan would probably love it though."

Vincent leaned against his car. "He would."

A yip from the back seat alerted me to Vincent's dog's presence. "How's Little Dog doing? She seems happy."

Vincent reached over the seat and retrieved the Jack Russel with the plastered-up leg. "Do you think so? I want her to be. She's a good dog. Josie said I could set up a bed for her in her office."

I widened my eyes at him. "Are you serious? She agreed to that?"

"Yes."

I couldn't imagine any sort of alternative universe where Josie would agree to such a thing. But she had gotten one glimpse of Vincent's biceps last week and let out a girly laugh I'd never heard before.

Perhaps all I needed to do to get on her good side was to be a young, handsome guy who clearly worked out. I reached over and patted Little Dog's soft ears. "Well, the kids are going to love you. And I bet you'll love them, you sweet girl—"

The screech of tires pulling into the driveway halted our conversation.

"Watch out!" Vincent stepped in front of me quicker than I'd ever seen anyone move, one arm reaching around and holding me to his back, the other clutching Little Dog to his solid chest.

I breathed in deep, trying to calm the adrenaline spike that had come from nearly being run over. I peeped around Vincent's back, accidentally breathing in the delicious, clean, man scent of him.

Holy Batman, he smelled way too good. Maybe I was still hardwired for sex after the weekend, but being pressed against him wasn't the worst way to start the day, even if it was because one of the kid's parents couldn't drive.

But then I registered the car and the man sitting behind the wheel, and all good feelings disintegrated.

Caleb's BMW stopped inches from us.

He got out of the driver's-side door, slamming it so hard I was surprised the glass didn't shatter.

I flinched.

Vincent tightened his grip on me, as if he'd sensed my fear. I'd almost let myself forget what Caleb was capable of. I'd let myself lock away the memory of him punishing me on the stairs for my supposed infidelity with Nash.

Now that night came back in full force, as well as the knowledge that he could do it all again if he wanted to.

Caleb's gaze clashed with mine. The seething anger in his eyes was as plain as day. His jaw was rigid, his fingers clenched into fists. He didn't acknowledge Vincent. He just glared at me with all the hate in his cold heart. "Get in the car."

I couldn't say anything. Fear had seized my voice box. My fingers tightened in the back of Vincent's shirt that I hadn't even realized I was clutching.

Vincent cleared his throat. "I suggest you take your own advice, sir. Bliss won't be leaving with you."

Caleb let out a harsh laugh. "Bliss?" He took two steps forward, going eye to eye with Vincent. "That's my fiancée you're talking about. You'll address her by her given name." He spat the words in Vincent's face one at a time, marking each with a pause. "Bethany. Melissa."

Vincent went still. He and Caleb were probably quite similar in terms of build. Tall but not super solid. If I hadn't seen Vincent's biceps when he'd taken off his sweatshirt last week, I wouldn't have had any clue about the body he'd been hiding underneath his loose fitting clothes.

Caleb clearly assumed the same. Either that or he was just arrogant enough to think that Vincent would step aside at his command, like I would have.

"Bliss asked me to call her by her nickname. So I will."

Guilt swamped me hard and fast. I wasn't sure if it was because I'd dragged Vincent into this or because guilt and shame were just a regular state of being for me. It was my fault Caleb was mad. My fault he was here, making a scene.

"Vincent, it's okay. Let me go."

"No."

If Caleb had said it, I would have been terrified. But when Vincent refused to let me go, all I felt was the rush of relief and safety. I wanted to step into him closer and let him wrap his arms around me so I could bury my face in his chest.

Little Dog let out a growl and then launched into a series of angry barks.

Caleb snorted, his gaze rolling over Vincent from head to toe. "No? Did you actually just try to keep me from my future wife? You think your rat there is going to help you, little gay boy?"

A rush of anger roared through me at the condescending tone in Caleb's voice and the homophobic slur. I had no idea of Vincent's sexual orientation, and it wasn't any of my or Caleb's business. But Vincent was hardly a boy. Clearly younger than Caleb, yes. But nothing about Vincent was anything but all man.

Caleb just chose not to see it.

"Stop it, Caleb!" I hissed, trying not to draw any more attention to us. At any minute, a parent could drop off a child, or one could look out the window. I didn't want this to be the example I set for them. "I'm not your wife. And I'm not your fiancée either. Not after Friday night."

He raised one mocking eyebrow. "Have you told your father this?"

I hadn't, and he knew it.

"What about all your friends? All your father's work colleagues. Your stepmother and her family. Have you thought of the scandal it will cause?"

"It's not me who ended this relationship, Caleb. It's you."

"You stupid bitch," he hissed. "You stupid whore. You don't get a choice."

"I do get a choice." But the words sounded weak. I heard it and saw it in his expression. I needed something more. A final nail in the coffin of our relationship so he'd just leave me the hell alone. Maybe I was being petty, but I wanted to hurt him the way he'd hurt me. "I deserve better than this. I've realized there are men out there who will treat me right, so when I say we're done, I mean it. I'm moving on."

He laughed. "Bullshit. You fucking liar. Who else would want your ugly, fat ass?"

I crumpled under his insults. It wasn't anything I hadn't heard before. Whenever we argued, he brought up my weight. It was an insecurity he took great delight in pushing. And every time, it hurt more than any other barb.

"I do."

My head snapped to Vincent, but he had eyes for no one but Caleb. Vincent's body shuddered like he was visibly holding himself back.

I picked up the bone he'd thrown me and ran with it. "We have a date, Friday night at seven."

Vincent instantly nodded in agreement.

Caleb looked ready to explode. "We had an agreement, and if you don't hold up your end of the agreement, I will bury you. Your father won't ever get another contract. And I'll have your stepmother washing my dishes, while your brother and sister shine my fucking shoes. That's how far I will ruin you, Bethany-Melissa. I will not be publicly embarrassed by you. You don't want to try me."

In a heartbeat, I could see it all come true.

In the next I saw the opposite.

I saw myself turn Psychos into something bigger and better than it even was now. I saw me as the savior of my family, the one who brought home enough money that my father could retire.

Nichelle and my siblings would have everything they needed.

I wouldn't be beholden to any man.

Especially not a violent asshole like Caleb.

I struggled to pull his ring off, tugging at the too small band painfully until it slipped from my finger. I threw it at him. "Get in your car and drive away, Caleb. We're done. Do your worst."

The ring bounced off his chest and onto the ground at Vincent's feet.

Caleb gaped at me. "That's a thirty-thousand-dollar ring, Bethany-Melissa!" He crouched to pick it up.

The heel of Vincent's boot drove down on Caleb's fingers.

Nausea swirled my stomach at the crunch of breaking bone.

Caleb let out a blood-curdling scream, but Vincent didn't remove his foot. He ground down harder, twisting his heel slowly and deliberately, leaving Caleb howling.

I knew Josie was probably having a conniption inside the center. There was no possible way she hadn't heard Caleb's screams.

"Get off me! Get off!"

Vincent watched Caleb writhe on the ground for a moment before he squatted down beside him.

In his arms, Little Dog went crazy, barking, growling, and snapping at Caleb's face.

Vincent's voice was barely a murmur when he spoke. "When I get off your hand, you're going to take your cheap ring, get in your car, and then forget that Bliss ever existed. You say her name, I will end you. You think her name, I will hunt you down and put a bullet through your skull. You so much as accidentally drive past her on the street, and I will chase you down, gut you, and feed your intestines to my dog."

Vincent stood and removed his heavy boot from Caleb's mangled fingers.

I stared at Vincent's profile in shock.

Caleb scrambled backward until he hit his car. His cheeks blazed with red spots, and he clutched his fingers to his chest. Two were bent at very unnatural angles, and blood dripped down his arm, soaking the cuff of his button-down shirt. "You think you're so tough? Wait until you hear from my lawyer. Then we'll see if you're such a big man."

He got into the car, but his gaze narrowed in on me through the open window. "You'll be at the company dinner on Saturday night. You will smile. And then I'll fuck you in the coatroom like the dirty whore you are. I'm not scared of your bodyguard here. He'll be in jail by the end of the day. So don't think you can hide behind him."

Caleb spat out of the window, put his foot down on the accelerator, and sped through the parking lot with a squeal of tires and exhaust fumes.

Vincent watched him drive away and then turned to me. "We're late for work. Shall we go inside?"

All I could do was nod.

16

BLISS

*V*incent walked inside the daycare center like he and Caleb had just had a chat about the weather.

It took two hours for my fingers to stop trembling.

As predicted, Josie and Sarah had heard everything. They'd practically had their noses glued to the window when Vincent and I came inside. Vincent had greeted them in his usual formal way and then gotten straight to work, going over some number skills with Kellan and his little friends.

Josie had stared at him in a mixture of terror and awe. Sarah had swallowed thickly, whispered a hurried, "Are you okay?" But when I'd nodded, she'd scuttled off to the opposite side of the room, giving Vincent a clear berth.

Josie eventually got herself together enough to pin me with a solemn stare. "I have meetings this morning with two potential families. And then I'm taking a long lunch that will very likely involve alcohol after what I witnessed this morning. But when I return, we need to talk."

I could only imagine how that conversation was going to go down.

Josie got busy with her meetings, and I took my cue from Vincent and threw myself into teaching and playing with the roomful of preschoolers.

I didn't get a chance to talk to Vincent until Josie had seen out her visitors, shot both of us dirty looks, and then taken herself to lunch. As soon as she was gone, I set my group of kids up with Play-Doh and plastic shaping tools and snuck over to where Vincent had his kids, including Kellan, competing in an obstacle course he'd made in the outside play area. We stood side by side watching the kids chase each other around, letting their squeals and laughter wash over us.

"I want one," Vincent said eventually.

I glanced up at him. His dark-brown hair flopped across his forehead, and he brushed it back absently with the back of his hand.

"One what?"

"A child."

It didn't hugely surprise me. Most people who worked in this industry, male or female, really liked kids, and if they were young enough to not have any of their own, they were probably using the job to fill that 'clucky' void inside them. "You're good with them. They like you."

"I like them, too."

We went back to watching the kids.

"I'm really sorry about this morning," I said eventually. "Caleb..."

"Came to a center full of small children, your place of work, and threatened to end you. He also called Little

Dog a rat, which she is clearly not. I think that says all I really need to know about Caleb."

The frost rolling off Vincent was like opening the door to a freezer. But I instinctively knew it wasn't directed at me. I could practically still feel the warmth of his body as he'd held me at his back, putting himself in the firing line of Caleb's rage and insults.

I still remembered how good he smelled. That gentle cologne was intoxicating even now. "I just wanted to say thank you. For what you did. And for what you said."

Who else would want your ugly, fat ass?"

"I do."

He'd said it with such conviction that Caleb had believed it. And so had I.

For all his uniqueness, Vincent was classically hand-some with his clean-shaven, chiseled jawline and dark features. He had an intense, broody quality to him that would draw the eye of any woman. But this softness inside him, his adoration for a group of kids he'd only known a week, and the way he'd put himself on the line for a woman he barely knew, was what made him truly attractive.

He put his hands in the pockets of his jeans. "I meant every word. He doesn't deserve to breathe the same air as you, Betha— Bliss. I would have made good on my threats then and there if there hadn't been a roomful of witnesses."

I blinked, realizing we were talking about two different things. I'd been talking about him telling Caleb he wanted me. He was talking about his threats to maim and disembowel.

A shiver rolled over me, but I tried to shake it off.

People said things like that all the time. Just because Vincent was a tad on the literal side, didn't mean that he'd really meant any of the things he'd said in the heat of the moment.

He'd protected me. Stuck up for me. I'd felt safe with him, and more than that, I liked him. A man who tenderly wiped toddler tears and listened to twenty-minute-long, rambling stories about Spider-Man and Disney Princesses was not anyone I needed to be worried about.

"Well, I appreciate the backup—"

"Kellan?" Vincent snagged the boy's arm as he ran past, quickly dropping down to his eye height.

"I'm playing, Mr. Vincent!"

"I know, little friend. But look at me for a moment."

I saw what Vincent had spotted. One of Kellan's eyes was half swollen shut. The skin around his lips had turned a rashy red.

"Are you feeling okay?" Vincent asked carefully.

Kellan rubbed at his swollen eye. "I'm fine."

He clearly wasn't fine at all.

My heart thumped harder while I racked my brain for Kellan's medical history. "I think he's had anaphylactic responses before. How long has he been like that?"

Vincent knew instantly. "He was normal when we came outside, so no longer than ten minutes."

"That eye is swelling fast then."

Vincent bundled Kellan into his arms. "Okay. We're off to get you some medicine. Everybody else inside to Miss Sarah. I think I heard her say she's getting the painting easels out."

The kids cheered and traipsed inside. Sarah looked

up at the sudden influx of little bodies, took one look at Kellan's face, and blanched white. "His eye…"

"We're on it." But I could already see where this reaction was heading. "Josie's at lunch. Get her back in and call that agency she gets temp workers from. We need someone to come out now because…"

I bit my lip, not wanting to say it out loud and scare Kellan.

But I could already see that this reaction was going to end with an ambulance. "Get him an antihistamine and have his EpiPen ready to go. Just in case he gets any worse."

But this wasn't my child. And I wasn't taking any chances when I was the most senior person here. I let Vincent walk ahead of me into the staff kitchen where we kept a locked medicine cabinet up high on the wall, out of reach of children. In Josie's office where Kellan couldn't hear me, I called 911, gave them the center's address, and told them we had a child with anaphylaxis who needed immediate attention.

Vincent had Kellan sitting on the kitchen counter when I got back in there, a bottle of kids' antihistamine with the lid off next to him, and an EpiPen clutched in his fingers.

"How is he?" I asked in a rush, trying to keep the panic at bay.

Kellan's eye was almost completely swollen shut. He was still talking and breathing okay, chattering away over the sound of a YouTube video on an iPad Vincent had given him, but there was no sign of the allergic reaction slowing down yet.

"I don't think that antihistamine is going to be enough," Vincent said quietly.

I eyed the EpiPen in his hand. "You ever used one of those? On a real-live person, I mean. Not just during first-aid training?"

I hadn't. And the prospect of holding Kellan down and stabbing him in his skinny leg was terrifying.

"I have a peanut allergy. I've had to jab myself more than once. It's not pleasant, so let's hope we don't have to do it to him."

For some reason, that made me feel a bit better. "I think his allergy is peanuts too. How did he even get any peanuts in here? The center is nut-free."

Vincent shook his head. "If he's particularly sensitive, it might have been that one of the other kids had peanuts before they came this morning and didn't wash their hands. Or maybe this is a new reaction. Something outside might have set him off."

"Could be pollen, or the grass? Maybe one of the trees in the yard, though none of them are new."

Vincent stared down at me. "Could be dog hair."

"Little Dog is still in Josie's office."

"None of the children have been in there, but her hair is probably on my clothes too." Vincent's mouth pulled into a grim line. "If this is my fault and something happens to him..."

I took his hand in mine and squeezed it.

He jumped, like I'd shocked him. His deep-brown gaze dropped to our joined hands. But then eventually he squeezed back.

The wail of the ambulance sirens had us both breathing

easier, and Vincent bundled Kellan and the iPad up, striding quickly out the main doors to meet the paramedics. I grabbed Kellan's bag from his cubbyhole and ran after them.

Kellan looked tiny, sitting on a long white stretcher while a paramedic checked him over.

The woman nodded once, then turned to us. "He's not too bad. You did the right thing, getting the antihistamine into him. I don't think we'll need the EpiPen, but I want to take him to the hospital for observation anyway. One of you can come with us."

Vincent opened his mouth, clearly ready to volunteer, and I knew Kellan would probably have preferred him over me, but in the absence of Josie, I was the senior member of the staff. Vincent had only worked here a week. It needed to be me.

I put my hand on Vincent's arm. "I need you to go call Kellan's parents and ask them to meet us at the hospital. And then I need you to help Sarah until the temp gets here, okay?"

Vincent seemed torn, his gaze glued to Kellan. But he eventually turned back to me and nodded. "You'll keep me updated?"

I nodded. "My number is in the staff files. Find it and text me your number, and I'll send updates when I can."

The paramedics had finished up their assessments and made way for me to get in with Kellan.

I smiled at him. "Hey, kiddo. Wave bye to Vincent. Aren't we lucky, going for a ride in an ambulance?"

The doors closed with a bang, and then in a wail of sirens, we left Vincent behind, staring after the ambulance helplessly.

*K*ellan was already looking better by the time we got to the hospital. The swelling in his eye hadn't gone down any, but it had seemed to stop growing. I ran along beside the stretcher, keeping up an endless stream of overly animated chatter to occupy him, until we found ourselves in a curtained-off bed in Emergency.

"This is the end of the road for us." The paramedic locked the wheel on Kellan's bed. "But he'll be just fine. The nurses and a doctor will be here in just a moment to get him going. High five, little dude. Thanks for being a top patient."

Kellan grinned and slapped his palm against the paramedic's. I thanked them profusely then climbed up on the bed with Kellan, who scrambled into my lap, and we watched YouTube until Josie, Kellan's frantic parents, and the doctor all arrived at once.

"Mrs. Simpson, I'm so sorry this happened! I was at lunch and then I got a call. I got here as soon as I could," Josie babbled, though no one was really paying attention to her, Kellan's parents too focused on him.

"Hi, Mommy! Miss Befany-Melissa and me got to go in a ambulance 'cause I got allergies again."

I gave his mother a weak smile, expecting her to yell at me, but she just ran her hand through Kellan's floppy blond hair, pushing it back off his forehead while she checked the swelling in his eye. She breathed out a sigh of relief. "Oh, thank goodness. This isn't too bad at all. He's had much worse reactions. He didn't need the EpiPen?"

I shook my head. "I was worried, but the paramedics said he was okay. He's had some antihistamine medicine though. I told the paramedics, and they gave him something else too, but I'm sure they'll tell you all about it."

I shuffled Kellan off my lap and slid off his bed, leaving him in his parents' and doctor's capable hands. I backed out of the curtain, and Josie followed me quickly, calling reassurances we'd write up a full report and check into the entire incident thoroughly.

Just a few feet down the hospital corridor, she yanked me aside into a quiet alcove. "What on earth happened?"

I filled her in, Josie's stunned expression turning to anger the more I spoke.

"So he was in Vincent's care? This is unacceptable."

I frowned. "Well, yes. But I was there too. One minute he was fine, the next minute his eye was blowing up like a balloon. We went through all the correct procedures. And the paramedics assured me Kellan will be just fine."

"That's hardly the point. This shouldn't have happened at all!"

I blinked. "Josie. We knew Kellan had allergies, and nobody knows what set him off. It's not like we fed him a peanut butter sandwich then sat and had a chat when he had a reaction."

Josie paced the tiny space. "This is my fault. I shouldn't have let you interview him. I should have been there to do it myself. I'm going to need to fire him. The Simpsons need to know we took fast and extreme measures to ensure their child's safety. Perhaps if we can get in front of it, they won't get on that damn Facebook group and tell all the other parents."

My mouth dropped open. "What? You can't fire Vincent. He was doing his job."

She whirled and stared at me. "And what was he doing this morning when he threatened to *gut* your fiancé, Bethany-Melissa! Sarah and I heard every word. He gives me the creeps."

"Since when? You were practically drooling over him a few days ago, acting the fool and flirting with him like you aren't a married mother of two with a husband at home."

Josie's eyes widened. I was sure mine had too, because even though it was true, I had not meant for all of that to come out.

I had definitely not meant for it to come out sounding slightly jealous. Vincent hadn't shown Josie any sort of interest other than professional. Even if he had, that wasn't my business.

I owed her an apology. What I'd said was completely out of line. "Josie, I'm sorry. I shouldn't have said that. But you really can't fire Vincent. He's very good at his job. What happened this morning was a personal matter. He was simply standing up for me."

But her features had frosted over, her shoulders and spine ramrod straight in her anger. "I've made my decision, thank you."

Anger on Vincent's behalf rose inside me. "Vincent's fast thinking might have saved that boy's life today. He was the one who noticed the reaction first. And he stood up for one of your employees, deescalating a potentially dangerous situation that could have easily spilled over into the daycare itself if he hadn't been there to keep Caleb out. But you're going to repay him by firing him?"

Guilt mixed with the anger. I wasn't letting Vincent go down for standing up for me. "Josie, if you fire Vincent, you might as well just fire me too. I was there for both incidents. Both were as much my fault as his. If not more in the case of Caleb. That's entirely on me."

I knew Josie wouldn't fire me. She didn't have enough staff to keep the place running if she lost both me and Vincent.

"I think that's for the best. You've been a good employee, Bethany-Melissa. But Caleb has already called and stated that he'll be spreading the word about what sort of person you are. Our children's fathers very likely run in the same circles as him. In light of what has happened today, I do think that terminating both yours and Vincent's employment is necessary."

I gaped at her. "You're seriously firing me?"

I'd never been fired from a job in my life. I was a model employee, always early in the mornings, always stayed back to help close, even though I didn't get paid for it. I was a rule-follower at heart. I did as I was told.

But of course, Caleb had tried to spin this morning's scene into something that portrayed him in a good light. Like the classic narcissist he was. Of course it was my fault. It always was. My hate for him doubled, then tripled, multiplying in on itself until it was almost all-consuming.

Josie took a few steps backward, like she could see the rage building. "If you have anything left at the center, I'll have it sent to you. I'd prefer if you didn't return."

I had to hold myself in place while the woman walked away, her kitten heels clicking on the linoleum floor.

A few deep breaths later, I was finally composed

enough to walk again. My phone buzzed with an incoming text, and I pulled it out. It was from an unknown number.

Is Kellan okay?

Another came in right behind it.

It's Vincent.

And then another a moment later.

Vincent Atwood. From Lilybugs Daycare.

I almost laughed. Like I was expecting messages from so many Vincents that I would need both his surname and place of employment to identify him. The poor guy was about to get railroaded by Josie, and he didn't even know it. I couldn't let him go in unprepared.

Bliss: *Kellan is fine. His parents arrived, and the doctor is with him. Josie is on the warpath, though. You're about to get fired.*

Vincent: *Oh. I see. That's unfortunate.*

Unfortunate indeed.

The beep of the hospital monitors had become a permanent fixture in my ears, and I was sure my ass was now molded in the shape of the uncomfortable, hard plastic chair I'd been sitting on for three days.

My brothers and sisters from the club had all come by. Aloha had smuggled me in two bottles of bourbon, which I'd been steadily sipping from like it was water. His old lady, Queenie, had tried a more traditional approach and had brought several hot meals up for me, wrapped carefully in insulated containers. They all sat untouched on a counter in my mother's hospital room, cold and forgotten because I wasn't hungry.

My mother was too pale. I'd never once seen her look so lifeless, small, and helpless.

Fancy Maynard and helpless didn't go together in one sentence. She would have knocked some heads together if anyone had ever so much as breathed the notion that she might not be fully capable of anything.

Except right now, she really wasn't. There were tubes

and machines keeping her alive, and she hadn't moved once since I'd rushed right out of Psychos and burst into the ER demanding to be taken to her.

A heavy hand came down on my shoulder.

I jumped, automatically reaching for my gun stashed in the back of my jeans.

"Settle," Hawk murmured. "It's me."

He'd been my best friend since we were little kids. Our old men were best friends too, and when Hawk and I had shot outta our mama's lady business just ten days apart, our best friend status had seemed inevitable.

He was the only person who knew the real me. Everything about me, from what sorta cereal I liked in the morning to the type of women I wanted on my cock in the evening.

"How you doing, brother?" he asked carefully.

"Fucking losing it. Didn't even hear you come in. You could have been one of the Sinners, and right now, I'd have a gun to the back of my head."

Or worse. If someone from the rival club wanted me dead, my brains could have been sprayed all over Fancy's crisp white hospital blankets.

First rule of this life. Be fucking aware of your surroundings.

Especially when there was clearly a hit out on your family.

Hawk tutted like he was a disappointed grandmother. "You need to go home. This shit ain't safe. We have the whole compound in lockdown. Everyone but you."

"Do what you want. Not leaving her. Not 'til I know she's gonna get better. Or she…"

Nobody needed to fill the silence. Fancy was either

still meant for this world, or she was leaving it along with my old man.

My gut knew the latter was more likely. The doctors had prepared me for it. I'd seen her deteriorate so quickly I was scared to turn away for fear she'd be gone when I looked back.

I still refused to believe it though.

"Stubborn jackass," Hawk muttered. But he didn't try to convince me again. He knew it was a losing battle. "I'm gonna go get us some coffee and some food, 'cause you smell worse than the floor of Psychos, and your face is fucking gaunt."

"That's a big word for you," I replied without any of my usual amusement. Hawk and I had been insulting each other for years. It was our love language, and an instinct, but I couldn't find the humor in it today.

Hawk clearly wasn't feeling it either. "I'll be back."

I nodded, fighting off a surge of exhaustion and the desire to lay my head down on the bed and rest. Instead, I watched him walk out the door and then focused on every other person walking by, just so I had something to do. Two doctors in white coats who were probably young enough to still be in diapers. A dozen nurses in their green scrubs, scurrying around like worker bees. Not one of them walked at a pace any slower than an easy jog.

A flash of auburn caught my eye, snagging my attention.

I'd only seen that specific color on a woman just two other times. "Hey!"

The woman stopped in her tracks and raised her head, glancing in my direction.

It was her. The stunner from Psychos the other night

who'd been hanging out with Nash. The same woman I'd noticed at the police station the other day when I'd been there paying off one of their officers. Fuck, she was a sweet little thing with her unusual-colored hair and pretty eyes.

"You remember me?" I asked, sitting up straighter.

She glanced around, like I might have been talking to someone else, but when there was clearly no one else around, she stepped forward into the doorway of my mother's room. "War, right?" Her gaze fell on my mother. "Oh no. Is this your mother?"

I had to look away from the sympathy on her face in order to answer her. "Yeah."

"She was in the car with your father when..." She bit her fat bottom lip, white teeth pressing into the juicy pink pillow.

I swallowed thickly. "When someone put a bullet in his head. She was in the passenger seat. The car went over the cliff at Saint View Point."

Bliss covered her mouth with her hand and took another step into the room. "That's...I don't even know what to say. Like something out of a movie. That stuff doesn't happen around here."

I laughed, but there was no humor in it. "Sweetheart, that shit happens around here all the time. You just don't hear about it on the six o'clock news, because people from Saint View ain't all upper-class white assholes in suits and expensive cars. You sure you're Axel's sister?"

Pink bloomed on her cheeks. "That sounded really naïve, didn't it? I swear, I'm not."

I shook my head. "If that shit hasn't touched you, then

you're lucky. 'Cause I wouldn't wish all of this..." I nodded toward my mom. "On anyone."

Her blue-eyed gaze rolled over me, and damn if I didn't like it, even though there was no heat or desire behind it. It dropped to my mother once more and then the empty seat on her side of the bed.

"You want to sit for a minute?" I asked her.

"Oh no. I should..." She paused, thinking her excuses over. "Actually, I have nowhere to be. I kinda just got fired."

"How does someone kinda get fired?"

She slumped down in the seat opposite me, my mother in her bed between us. "Okay, fine. I actually got fired. Just now, in the hospital corridor. I'm still processing that I don't have to go wipe snotty noses and change diapers for the rest of the day."

I made a face. "Sounds like a shit job anyway."

A hint of a smile pulled up the corner of her mouth. "I didn't mind it."

"Puts you in good stead for owning Psychos then. Plenty of piss and vomit to clean there, I'd think. Or worse, cum on the nights they have parties."

She grimaced. "You aren't making bar and sex club ownership sound appealing."

I chuckled. "Good coin though?"

She nodded. "That's what they tell me."

"I thought about running a few of my own, once upon a time."

She seemed interested in that. "But you didn't?"

I shook my head. "I don't really have the head for business. Too fucking irresponsible, as my pops would have said." I blew out a long breath, thinking of how much I'd disappointed the old prick in my thirty years. "I'm more of a partygoer than a host."

"Do you go to all of Psychos parties then?"

"Most. Axel knew how to put on a good time."

Her gaze flickered over me. "So you knew my brother well then?"

I shrugged a shoulder. "We weren't close, like him and Nash. But I knew him, yeah. Saint View ain't that big. And if someone ain't trying to kill or steal from you, you probably know them enough to have a beer with."

"I see. Rebel said she saw him at one of your parties recently."

I squinted at her. "Rebel's got a big mouth. What happens in the club ain't supposed to go a step out of it."

"Oh my God. Don't be upset with her. That's all she told me, I swear." She nibbled on a nail, her eyes huge and worried.

I sat back, folding my arms across my chest. "Don't look so worried. Rebel's a big girl, and she can handle herself."

"That's hardly reassuring. You won't...hurt her, will you?"

I blanched. "What kind of abusive asshole do you think I am?"

"You're the leader of an outlaw motorcycle gang."

I stared at her.

Leader.

President.

"Fuck," I swore under my breath. "Fucking fuck!"

Bliss jumped.

I put a placating hand up in a stop signal. "Shit, sorry. Not you. And not Rebel either. Don't stress your pretty little ass over it. I'll tell her to pull her head in, she'll come back with a smart-ass comment, and that'll be the end of it."

Bliss visibly relaxed, but curiosity still played out all over her face.

I just wanted to keep her here and talking. 'Cause while I didn't really want the company of any of my brothers and sisters in the club because their tiptoeing around me was too much, I was sick of my own poor company. "You just made me realize that I'm prez. Of the club, I mean. President. My pops is gone, and I was VP." I scrubbed my hands through my hair and groaned.

"You weren't expecting it."

I shrugged. "I mean, I know what this life is. Being prez makes you a target. I've known that since I was a boy. But fuck."

"You never think your parents are actually going to die, do you?"

"Yeah, that."

She nodded. "I really am sorry for your loss."

"Thanks."

She went to stand. "I should leave you two alone. I've overstayed my welcome."

"I liked the distraction."

She paused, and I let myself drink her in. Though she was dressed more casually today, it was easy to picture her back in that sexy black number she'd been wearing at the club.

"What?" she asked self-consciously.

I was too tired to come up with a lie. "I was thinking about how much I wanted to fuck you on Friday night."

Her mouth dropped open. "You...you what?"

I chuckled. "Ain't nobody ever said that to you?"

She laughed uncomfortably. "Ah, no. Definitely not."

"They think it. Trust me. You still got that fiancé?" I eyed her fingers. They were bare.

"No. I told him this morning that we're over. Gave back his ring."

"Good."

I wasn't exactly sure why it was good. Because her having a fiancé wouldn't have stopped me wanting her. But I guess it might have stopped her wanting me.

She looked down at her feet.

Where was the confident woman in deep-red lipstick from Friday night, who'd strutted around the club, not even noticing how many men stopped and stared at her? Me fucking included. "Come over to the clubhouse on Saturday night."

Her gaze darted to the door, like she was thinking about making a run for it. "Uh..."

"We have a party every Saturday night. You'll like it. Queenie's a good cook. We'll smoke some meat and hang out. Bring Rebel, since I need to spank her ass anyway."

She raised an eyebrow.

"I can spank yours too, if you like," I said with a chuckle.

I liked the shade of pink her cheeks took on. And fuck. Flirting with her gave me something to feel other than bleak, cold numbness. By the weekend, Fancy would either be better, or she'd be gone. Either way, I'd be looking to get drunk and laid.

I could do both without the pretty red-haired, blue-eyed stunner. But if I had her to think about all week, then it might just be bearable. "Come. I haven't got a proper nickname for you yet. So I need some more time with you to work one out."

"If I come, do I get final say in said nickname?"

"Oh, I plan on you coming, baby. Nickname or not."

She frowned at me like she was a fucking school-teacher and I was the misbehaving brat in the back row. "We both know what you're insinuating, War."

I laughed and held my hands up. "I meant nothing by it." The laughter was almost painful in my chest after barely breathing for the last few days. Bliss was fucking fresh air and sunshine. I wanted to suck her in and hold her inside me so the warmth could melt the ice. "Just come. To the *party*."

"Fine. I'll catch a lift with Rebel."

I sat back, suddenly feeling lighter than I had in days. It had been the same feeling I'd had when I'd seen her in the club.

It had been so long since I'd actually been interested in someone. Not just one of the club's girls who satisfied my biological desires on a nightly basis. None of them interested me one iota, apart from as a warm slit to stick my dick into.

None of them had hair like fire. They were all stick thin, so skinny their collarbones jutted out. Bliss was the opposite of that. I wanted to grab her ass while she rode me. I wanted her full tits in my face when I came in her sweet cunt.

When she backed out of the room, her cheeks were pink again.

I liked that look on her.

18

BLISS

I'd been planning to let myself mope on Tuesday. Too much had happened the day before, between the Vincent and Caleb showdown, an emergency trip to the hospital, losing my job, and then running into War. I needed a minute to process.

But at 8:00 a.m., the doors to my suite flew open and Nichelle strode in, peering at me beneath the pile of bedclothes. "You're still in bed? You do know what time it is, don't you?"

"I am, and I do."

"You're late for work."

"I got fired."

Nichelle's pretty blue eyes went round. "You what? You can't get fired!"

Despite the fact I was normally very patient with Nichelle, and even liked her most of the time, it was early, and she was screechy, and that plus an overall grumpy mood made me punchy. "I realize you've never been fired, since you've never worked a day in your life, but the general way it goes is the person getting fired doesn't actually get a say in it. So yes, I can get fired."

"David," Nichelle yelled out into the hallway.

I stared at her. "What are you doing? Tattling on me? I'm twenty-five, Nichelle."

She was only five years older. Not that she was acting like it.

I sighed. This was my fault for still living at home. But I hadn't wanted to rock the boat. All young women in my social circles lived at home until they were married. It was very old-fashioned, and many acted as if they just really believed in the sweet tradition of it all.

The reality was, so many of the women in my circles, like Nichelle, had no ambition other than marrying a rich man who would keep them in the lifestyle their fathers had brought them up in. To move out of home, they'd need a job. A very well-paying one if they were to keep up with the rest of their friends.

It was why I still lived at home. Even working full-time, I couldn't afford the lifestyle without the help of my father.

He arrived in the doorway, still dressed in his pajamas, his hair rumpled with sleep. He was slightly out of breath, like he'd actually run at the banshee-pitched shouting of his wife. "What is it?"

"Bethany-Melissa got fired from the daycare center."

Dad's grip on the door handle tightened. "Oh."

Nichelle stared at him. "Oh? That's all you're going to say? David, I know she's your little princess, but if you haven't noticed, our bank accounts are dry. We don't have the money to pay for her if she can't pay for herself."

Apparently, Nichelle was feeling punchy this morning too.

She spun back around to face me. "Don't be thinking you're just going to lie around here all day and sponge off us."

"Nichelle," my father warned. "Bethany-Melissa has never just laid around all day."

"Unlike some other people in this house," I murmured.

Nichelle shot me a dirty look. "I'm a stay-at-home parent. It's a very busy job."

I rolled my eyes. Me and the nanny were more parents to Everett and Verity than she'd been. She was just lucky, now that there was no money to pay a nanny, the two kids were in school from eight 'til four.

My father pinched the bridge of his nose. "Please don't argue. I don't have the energy for it. Nichelle, shouldn't the kids be on their way to school?"

She huffed off, and my father gazed down at me. "I don't like to put pressure on you, but you do know how precarious our situation is at the moment, don't you? When you marry Caleb, things will turn around for all of us, but until then..."

I sat up, pulling the sheet up around me. I hated the stress lines that had appeared on his face in the last six months, since everything had gone downhill for him. "You don't need to worry about me. I already got another job."

"You did? Where? Another childcare center?" He perched on the end of my bed, his eyes filled with pride. "I should have known. You've always been so responsible."

The day Nash and Axel had brought me to this house with a tiny Barbie backpack filled with the few things I owned, Axel had crouched so we were eye to eye. His big hands had gripped my skinny little shoulders, and he'd held me tight. "Be good, Bliss. Do whatever they tell you to do. Don't argue, okay? This is your big break. Your chance to get the hell out of Saint View. Don't give them any reason to send you back, okay? Promise me."

I would have done anything Axel asked of me. If he'd asked me to swallow razor blades or wrestle crocodiles, I would have done it without question. He and Nash were my big brothers and the only heroes I had.

So I'd done exactly as he'd said. I'd been quiet and good and never made any trouble.

I was still doing it now. I couldn't tell my father about Psychos. That pride in his eyes would have extinguished the moment the word fell out of my mouth.

I wanted to confide in him. I wanted to tell him all about Axel, and Nash, and the bar I now owned, and Caleb. But I couldn't add any more to his plate. Somewhere deep inside I was still the little girl, terrified of his rejection.

I'd have to tell my family eventually, but me leaving Caleb would be a huge blow to my father's hopes for getting the company back on track. Caleb wouldn't want to work with him now, but if Psychos party nights did as well as Nash had made out, then we wouldn't need Caleb. I could invest the money into Dad's company, if I could get enough of it. He'd looked after me. I wanted to look after him.

If that meant sex clubs and drugs, then so be it.

It was the only way.

I turned up at Psychos in the middle of the day, right in time for the lunch rush.

But when I walked inside, the bar was completely empty, except for Rebel sitting on the bar top, cracking a piece of gum between her teeth, her Doc Martens swinging.

She dragged her gaze away from the TV when my movement caught her attention. "Disney! What are you doing here? Shouldn't you be at your kiddie germ factory?" She jumped down off the bar and skipped over to hug me.

I hugged her back. "The kiddie germ factory is no more."

Her eyes went huge. "You blew it up?"

I snorted on my laughter. "What on earth? Who hurt you, Rebel? 'Cause it's really twisted that *that* is where your mind went."

Her shoulders relaxed a little, and she shook her head. "Trust me, you do not want to know about my hidden traumas and how they shaped my twisted mind. We'd be here all day. But just to clarify. You don't have a penchant for explosives that I should watch out for?"

"I can confirm that I do not have a stash of TNT in the trunk of my car. No."

She giggled. "Okay, so fine, maybe I shouldn't guess what happened to the daycare and you should just tell me."

"The truth is much less interesting. I got fired. So here I am, ready to work. Not that there seems to be much work to be had. It's dead in here."

Rebel's mouth dropped open. "You're gonna work? Here? With us?"

"Sure. Why not? I do own the place, so I figure I should probably get involved."

Rebel let out a screech of excitement and grabbed my hands, dancing around with me in excitement. "Oh my God, yes! We're gonna have the best time! You are gonna make so much money at the parties. Like, those guys are gonna take one look at your tits and they are gonna be shoving hundred-dollar bills in your cleavage."

It took me a moment to process what she'd said, but when I did, shock jolted through me. When I'd said I wanted to work here, I hadn't even considered the parties. I'd been thinking more about working here during the day, maybe getting some new meals on the menu and some lunchtime two-for-one specials.

The parties were a different kettle of fish altogether. I couldn't do those. Rebel had been fully nude by the time the party ended last weekend. So had half the room, both staff and guests, so it hadn't seemed out of place at all. But I couldn't do what she did.

"Bliss isn't doing that."

Nash's voice was hard and clipped. A barked-out command of authority.

Rebel and I both glanced over and found him leaning on the doorway of his office, his gaze pinned firmly on me.

"Uh, nobody asked you, Boss Man. Her club. She can work where she likes."

Nash didn't respond. His dark gaze never left mine. "No, Bliss."

Maybe I was still irritated from my earlier argument

with Nichelle. I was definitely still angry with Josie for dismissing me as easily as she had, even though I'd worked with her day in and day out for seven years and I'd almost thought us friends. I was definitely still furious with Caleb for more reasons than I could count on one hand.

Everybody in my life seemed to think they knew what was best for me. Even Axel and my father, though well-meaning, had stifled me. As had the fear. There was always so much fear, in everything I did, or didn't do.

"Be good, Bliss. Don't give them a reason to send you back."

"You'll be at my company dinner on Saturday night. You will smile."

"When you marry Caleb, things will turn around."

I couldn't let another man tell me what to do. Not even one who had my best interests at heart. "That's not your decision to make, Nash."

Quick as lightning, he was in front of me, towering over me, his glare hot. "Do you even know what you're saying? You saw one percent of what a Psychos party is."

One percent? I'd watched a woman get railed by three men while a crowd of people watched. I'd seen someone snort coke off a woman's inner thigh before licking her pussy like it was a chaser. What the hell else was there?

I wasn't going to ask and prove his point that I was in over my head. Instead, I straightened my shoulders and stood to my full height. "I want to learn this place from the ground up. From the cleaner and the cooks to what-ever else there is. You keep telling me I know nothing about the business—"

"You don't," he growled.

"All the more reason for me to find out. Like it or not,

Nash, I own this place. I'm your boss now, and you can either get on board or you can leave." My fingers trembled as the words fell out of my mouth. I tucked them into fists, praying he wouldn't notice.

"Dis," Rebel said quietly.

But Nash and I were too busy glaring at each other.

I wanted to back down, but I couldn't. Not if I wanted these people to respect me. I had to take my place, even if that meant coming down on Nash the way I was now.

I hated it.

But things had to change. Bethany-Melissa would get eaten alive here. I needed to be Bliss to survive. I needed Nash to stop looking at me like I was a child. And I needed to stop giving him reasons to do that.

Maybe if I were nude, with other men desiring me, Nash could no longer see me as anything but a grown woman.

He took another step in so my chest brushed his. "You grew up in private schools where your dress had to cover your knees. You probably had a fucking debutante ball, didn't you? Axel would roll over in his grave if I let you do this."

I stood my ground. "There is no letting me. You don't own me. And I'm not Axel's little sister anymore."

"So what? You're gonna start nude waitressing with Rebel? You gonna put on a show in a cage?"

I sucked in a deep breath. "If that's what I decide I want to do, then maybe I will. But the point is, it's my decision."

"It's a bad one." His gaze flickered over my face. For a second, it rested on my lips, but then he turned away, his expression tortured.

I wasn't letting him get out of it that easily. I was too annoyed with him. He was acting like my father. "What's it to be, Nash? You asked me if I was in, and I said yes. What about you though? You gonna stick around and help me turn this place into something even bigger and better than it is now? Or you gonna keep treating me like I don't have a brain of my own?"

Some of the fire went out of him. "I never meant it like that. I know how smart you are. You always were. I just feel like someone needs to watch out for you."

"We all watch out for each other," Rebel said quietly. "That's what family does."

I nodded.

Rebel and I both turned to Nash.

He breathed out heavily. "Yeah, fine. I'm in."

19

BLISS

*N*ichelle had barely spoken to me all week. But when she stuck her head into my room on Friday evening, she had the kids with her, so I pushed aside my annoyance with her and smiled brightly. "You guys all look nice. Where are you off to?"

"Dinner at the club. Do you want to come?" Everett asked in his little boy voice.

I glanced at Nichelle, knowing full well they couldn't afford a nice meal out. She shrugged. "Your father said we were going out and to come get you."

I shook my head. This meal would be going on their already near-to-the-limit credit card, I was sure, simply for the reason my father couldn't afford to fall off the social radar. He had to be seen out in public, especially at the club, which was where half of all of Providence's business deals seemed to take place. But I wasn't going to add to the financial burden by coming along, nor did I want to be anywhere Caleb might be. "Not tonight. I've had a long week and am excited to just sit at home in my sweats."

There were no parties at Psychos this weekend, much to my dismay. The cash register at the end of each day, just from the bar side, didn't paint a pretty picture. I'd said as much to Nash. The money from the last party, once costs were taken out and staff members paid, barely covered what I'd need to pay Axel's suppliers at the end of the month. We needed more of what was bringing in the big dollars if I wanted to pay out my family's debts as well as have money to live on.

Nash had frowned and told me it was risky. The more parties we had, the more chance there was of someone slipping up and word getting around to the wrong people. But my dwindling bank account was never too far from my mind.

Nash had insisted I take the weekend nights off though, since I'd scheduled myself to work the days. So once my dad, Nichelle, and the kids had all yelled out their goodbyes, the big door downstairs slamming behind them, I wandered into my bathroom with the intent of running myself the most luxurious bubble bath ever. I turned the faucet on to begin filling the tub, then went back to my room in search of my Kindle and some candles. "Wine," I muttered once I plonked them on the bathroom vanity. "A huge glass of wine needs to be in my hand."

The tub was massive, and plenty of room to go before the water would spill over, so I ran downstairs to the kitchen, grabbing a glass from a cabinet and a bottle from the refrigerator. I'd only been intending to have one drink, but then I shrugged and took the bottle with me.

A knock on the front door right as I passed it on my way to the stairs stopped me. I cringed, thinking of the filling bath, but it would only take a moment to get rid of whoever this was. I flung open the door.

"Good evening."

I gaped at Vincent standing on the other side of the doorway in a navy-blue suit with a crisp white shirt beneath the jacket. There was no tie, the neck of his shirt open and showing off the tan skin of his chest. His hair was slicked back neatly, and he had his hands in his pockets, which somehow just completed the casual yet stupidly attractive pose.

I tried to make my mouth move, but I was so shocked I could barely utter a sound. I'd noticed Vincent was attractive. I wasn't blind. But Vincent in a suit that fit him perfectly, with his deep-brown eyes watching me intently, was a whole new level of attractive.

It took him from *hey, here's a cute guy I work with*. To *holy fucking shit, throw me up against a wall and smack my ass*.

Heat rushed through me at the crude thought that was incredibly unlike me.

"Are you ready?" he asked.

My brain may as well have been flashing a 'the lights are on, but nobody is home' sign. "Ready for what?" I asked numbly.

"Our date. Am I early? You said Friday at seven, I believe?"

What the hell? It took me a minute to work out what was going on, but when I did... Oh Jesus. I'd told Caleb Vincent and I were dating. And now here he was. "Vincent, I didn't..."

What on earth was I saying? The man had protected me from my abusive ex. I'd gotten him fired. And yet he was here, looking like he'd just stepped out of the pages of a *GQ* magazine. He was clean, and fresh, and he smelled like heaven. After the grime of Psychos all week, whatever other plans I'd had went right out the window.

"Oh holy moly," I yelped, pushing the door open farther while taking off for the stairs. "My bath!" Without turning back, I yelled out to him. "Slight emergency, but come in!"

I thundered up the stairs and sprinted into my bathroom, catching the faucet maybe thirty seconds before it would have delivered enough water to overflow. I plunged a hand into the depths, pulling the plug, and perched on the edge while I caught my breath. "Well, that's what I get for drooling over the very attractive man. I nearly flood the bathroom as well as my panties."

"What are you doing?"

I jumped a mile, letting out a startled scream.

Vincent's eyes went wide, and he held out a placating hand. "I'm sorry. You said there was an emergency. I just wanted to make sure you were okay."

I shook my head, clutching a hand to my chest. Had he heard what I'd said? Oh good Lord, kill me now. "How the hell do you move so quietly?"

"Occupational necessity."

I squinted at him, then realized what he meant. "I never thought of it like that, but the ability to tiptoe out of the babies' room when you've just managed to get them all to sleep is a good talent to have. One I've mastered too."

He didn't answer. "Were you taking a bath?"

I shook my head. "Oh no. I was going to, but I need to get ready for our..." I couldn't say the word date. Vincent wasn't even close to in my league. He was the sort of good-looking that only dated Instagram influencers who lived in their bikinis and whose bodies were like Photoshop airbrushing come to life.

"Our date," Vincent supplied. He shrugged out of his jacket, tossing it on the closed toilet. "You should take your bath. I don't mind waiting."

I shook my head. "No, no, it's fine. I'm so sorry I'm running late. I don't want to hold us up any more than I already have."

He undid the button at his wrist and rolled his sleeve up. I tried not to drool at the corded ropes of muscle in his tanned forearm.

"It's no trouble. You're taking the bath." He took the plug from my hand and plunged his arm into the rapidly draining water, stopping it from emptying any further. Then he turned the faucet on, replacing the water that had been lost. "Do you like it hot?"

"I do."

He nodded, studiously upping the temperature and testing it with his fingers. "Bubbles?"

I almost laughed. This was so ridiculous. "Yes, please. There's a bottle on the ledge over there."

He leaned across the tub to retrieve the little purple bottle and squirted a measured amount carefully beneath the flow of water. It frothed up into soapy foam, a delicate honeysuckle scent wafting with the steam.

"No one has ever run me a bath before. Not a man, I mean. Well, I don't know. Maybe my dad did when I was little."

But I suspected it had always been my nanny.

"Why didn't your fiancé do this for you?"

I opened my mouth to answer but then realized I didn't have one. "I don't know. I never asked…"

"You didn't ask me either, and yet, I did it anyway."

He was right. If I hadn't already been swooning over Vincent in his suit, then I would have started over that simple act. Caleb had never done anything nice or sweet for me. Even when he'd bought me a dress, it wasn't for me. It was so I'd look good on his arm.

Vincent waved his hand around in the sudsy water, then nodded, like he was satisfied with his task. He stood, retrieving his jacket. "I'll wait in your sitting area."

"Or you could stay," I blurted out.

He froze.

So did I.

What the hell, Bliss? I rushed to fill the awkward silence. "I mean, once I'm in, I'll be covered by bubbles. You won't see anything… Or you could just…face the wall." I didn't know what the hell I was doing. "Or not. I'm sorry. I've had a couple of drinks already. Ignore me."

Liar. I hadn't had a sip. I was just stupidly awkward.

"Very well." He turned and faced the wall. "Get in."

I tried not to breathe too heavily. I'd lost my mind. Getting naked with the man just sitting right here. He could easily sneak a peek out of the corner of his eye while I was clambering like an elephant into the bath. I was tempted to leave my underwear on.

Except I already knew he wouldn't.

So I stripped, hiding my bra and panties beneath the rest of my clothes and then climbed into the bathtub.

It was the perfect temperature, and there were so

many bubbles that they provided more than enough cover. I needn't have been worried.

It was just the fact that I was naked, while he was fully clothed. Even if he wasn't peeking.

"Is the water okay?"

The water was heavenly. The exact perfect temperature, and it was like a welcoming hug after the week I'd had. He'd been right. I had needed this. "It's perfect."

He nodded. "Good. That pleases me."

"Did we have reservations anywhere? Am I making us late?"

"Not at all."

I sank a little deeper in the water. "Where are we going?"

"My place."

I blinked. "Uh...that's a little presumptuous of you..."

"What do you mean?"

Great. It wasn't presumptuous at all. Perhaps he just hadn't wanted to take me out in public. I cringed at the unwanted, ugly thought. "I just meant that normally guys only take you back to their place if they want...sex."

"Is that what you want me to want?"

Oh my God. I was suddenly really glad we weren't looking at each other because I was contemplating drowning myself. How did I answer that? If I said no, that would be horribly insulting. And a lie. If I said yes, though...I couldn't say yes. That was too forward.

Rebel would have said yes. I'd spent my whole week watching her flirt with guys at the bar. I envied the ease she had with everyone, while I fumbled over my words and hoped to be a ghost. I wanted people to see right through me, like I wasn't even there.

Most men did.

Vincent didn't.

"That's a really forward question for a first date," I whispered.

"Is it? I apologize then. I didn't intend to make you uncomfortable."

"You don't," I rushed. "You just took me by surprise."

"I make most people uncomfortable."

I frowned at that. I'd never felt uncomfortable with him. Curious by the odd things he said perhaps, but never uncomfortable. In fact, I clearly felt too comfortable if I was willing to get in a bath with him still in the room. Vincent had been nothing but polite and kind. He was good with kids. And he'd gone above and beyond with Caleb. Sure, maybe he'd been a little over the top with the graphic death threats, but I'd needed someone to say those things. Caleb had already proved himself willing to hurt me. And he wasn't the only one. I hadn't forgotten my midnight visitor's threats and demands.

I moved a few bubbles around strategically. "Not me."

He didn't say anything.

I wondered if he were smiling. "How was your week of unemployment?"

"Dull. Yours?"

"Busy. I kind of inherited a bar. So now I work there."

"You inherited it? It was a family business?"

"My brother owned it. He was killed recently. Now it's mine."

Vincent stiffened. "What was his name?"

"Axel Fuller."

"You have different surnames."

"Different fathers."

"How did he die?"

I sighed.

"I made you uncomfortable, didn't I?"

"It's just new. And still hard for me to talk about. I haven't even had the guts to really say it out loud to anyone. Except you."

"I remember you said he was murdered."

"Gunshot to the head. The cops say it was a gang-related thing."

"You don't believe that?"

"I don't know. It might have something to do with the business. Or his personal life. It's good Josie fired me really. It gives me the chance to dig around. See if there were other things going on. Even if it was gang-related, I want to see someone put away for his murder."

Vincent smoothed his palms over his thighs. "I have a family business too."

"Doing what?'

"Nothing I want to be involved in."

I paused, not pushing at that when I had plenty of my own family things I didn't want to be involved in. "Do you want to go to your place now?"

"For sex? Or for the dinner I prepared? Just so I know."

I wanted to laugh but I had a feeling he was being serious, and I didn't want to laugh *at* him. "How about dinner, and we'll see where the night takes us?"

20

VINCENT

"*W*ould you like the heater on? I have an outdoor one if you're chilly."

Bliss shook her head and smiled over at me. "No. I'm fine. Thank you."

"What about a glass of water? Or wine? Apple juice? Soft drink?"

She held up the one already in her hand. It was still three-quarters full. "Nope. Still good on that front too."

I nodded, wiping my palms on my pants. "Right. Good. Just sit right here. I'll go get the food."

"Okay. I can't wait to see what you've made. Thank you, Vincent. This is really lovely. Your home is gorgeous."

I glanced around my outdoor area critically. I'd spent the entire day scrubbing down the Mediterranean-style space that overlooked the large inground swimming pool. I'd set the table carefully with a white cloth and shining silverware. Fairy lights overhead reflected in Bliss's hair, turning it a fiery red.

I wanted her to like my house. I wanted her to have a good time.

I didn't know how to make sure that happened.

I scurried to the kitchen, pulling out all the appetizers I'd prepared earlier. A huge tray of cheeses and meats and specialty breads. I carried it back outside, where Bliss stared thoughtfully over the pool with her drink in her hand.

I placed the tray in front of her and then stood back to watch her face carefully.

"Oh wow. This is gorgeous." She smiled up at me.

She wasn't beaming though. I frowned. It wasn't enough. "Wait a moment. Please."

I scurried back inside, pulling a tray of warm finger food out of the oven. I slid it all onto a platter and carried that back out to her as well. "Here."

Her eyes widened. The two trays of food took up the entire tabletop. "This is enough food for a party. Are you expecting anyone else?"

"No. Just you." I hesitated. "I have other choices. Soup? And for main course I have steak or chicken. I could cook fish if you prefer? I bought some, just in case..."

She cocked her head to one side. "Are you a feeder?"

I squinted. "What does that mean?"

She laughed. "It's a love language. Feeding people brings you joy. Most often found in little old nonnas who bustle around their kitchens, trying to shove food into their grandchildren's mouths. But apparently also found in handsome, twenty-something men."

"I didn't know what you would like. So I made everything."

She reached out and took my hand. "Please sit down. We have more than enough food right now. I'm not fussy. I'll literally eat anything. But I want to eat it with you, not with you running back and forth to the kitchen every few moments."

I nodded. "I'm sorry. I've never been on a date."

"You mean you've never been asked on one?"

"No. I've never been on one."

She picked up a fork and speared a rolled-up piece of prosciutto. "How is that even possible when you look like that?"

I glanced down at myself. "When I look like what?"

Her laughter was so sweet. I liked it. I wanted her to laugh all the time, because it felt like it wormed its way inside me and chased away some of the darkness.

"Fishing for compliments, much?"

I hadn't been, but I didn't comment.

She picked up a napkin, running it through her fingers. "I just meant that you're clearly very attractive. It surprises me that you haven't dated many beautiful women. Did something happen? You didn't even date in high school?" She smiled. "You would have been that dark, mysterious, broody sort of guy that all the girls love, even though you know he's probably trouble, weren't you?"

She was joking, but there was definitely an air of curiosity to her statement.

"I can't remember most of my high school years," I admitted.

She cringed. "Oh wow. Drugs or alcohol?"

I shook my head. "Neither. I have a condition that

affects my memory. Sometimes it steals memories altogether, and sometimes it lasts for long periods of time."

"Oh wow. That must have made studying difficult."

"I was out of school a lot anyway. I had to work."

"In your family business? How old were you when you started working there?"

"About ten. Maybe eleven."

She nodded. "You didn't even really get a chance to be a kid. I know I live in a big fancy house now too, but I didn't always, so I do understand how it is. Not everybody has the luxury of getting a good education or completing high school when your basic needs are going unmet." She glanced around the house. "Looks like you're doing pretty well now though."

"My parents own it. I just rent it from them right now, until I work out where I'm going and what I'm doing."

"It's beautiful."

So was she. She was so incredibly pretty. I wasn't sure whether I should say that or not. I wanted to. Because it was always my first instinct, to say whatever I was thinking. But that had not always served me well in the past. I didn't like that I made people uncomfortable.

But it was what made me good at my job too.

I just didn't want Bliss to see me that way. I was trying so hard to be normal. Living in a normal house, in a normal suburb. Getting a normal job, though that hadn't worked out too well. But I would try again, even though real jobs seemed to pay a shockingly small pittance. Everything else I just wanted to leave behind.

I wanted to date a woman. I wanted to know what her skin felt like, soft and pliable beneath me in bed. I wanted to know what it would feel like to sink inside her body and have her welcome me there.

Scythe had all those memories. He kept them locked away from me, where I couldn't reach them. I desperately wanted some of my own. Some he couldn't take from me.

"So is it just you and your parents?" Bliss's gaze flickered from the smorgasbord to my face. Her fingers hovered uncertainly over the food so long that I picked up one of my favorite hot pastries and held it out to her.

She bit into it, murmuring her pleasure at the taste.

I liked that. "I have two sisters as well. Ophelia is older. Fawn is younger."

"What beautiful names."

I nodded. They were. "I don't see them though. Fawn left about a year ago. She wanted to make a clean break from the family and be her own person. Ophelia travels a lot. I never know where she is from one moment to the next."

"You must miss them."

"I do."

I missed Fawn's sweet innocence. And I missed Ophelia's loud voice and constant action. I missed them because their absence left me the sole focus of my parents. In particular, my mother. Despite being a tiny woman of five feet two inches, my mother had her own ways of getting what she wanted.

Always.

"Would you ever go visit Ophelia on her travels? I'd love to go traveling. I've never been outside the States, but I really want to go to France."

"I could take you. It's nice there."

Her eyebrows raised. "You've been?"

"A long time ago. For the family business. But I liked it when I was there. I'd like to go again." I'd like to go anywhere with her.

"I want to see the Eiffel Tower and the..."

Bliss continued on, listing out all the tourist hot spots. But a noise at the front of the house had caught my ear. I closed my eyes for a second, hyper-focusing in on it.

No.

No. No. No.

I pushed back from the table and shot to my feet, cutting Bliss off mid-sentence. "Will you excuse me for a moment, please? I need to take care of something."

Without waiting for her to answer, I spun on my heel and strode through the open doors, past the kitchen to the front of the house. I yanked open the door before the person on the other side even had a chance to knock. Not that they would have. Because they never did.

"Here he is, my boy." My father stood on the stoop; my mother's hand tucked into the crook of his arm. His dark-gray suit was stylish and expensive. My mother's long dress floated around her ankles.

"What are you doing here?" I demanded.

"We're here for dinner."

I blinked at the two of them. "You're...I have company."

"We know." My mother patted my arm. "We'd like to meet her. So here we are."

I stared blankly at them, my brain whirring. I had picked Bliss up. Her car wasn't sitting in my driveway. I most certainly hadn't told either of them that I had a date.

Which meant one of three things. They had my phone tapped. They were having me followed. Or they had cameras installed in my house.

I wouldn't have been surprised if it were all three.

I glanced back through the open-plan house and caught Bliss watching. I raised a hand in an awkward wave and then moved outside onto the step with my parents, closing the door firmly behind me. "I did the job you wanted me to do. I told you, that was the end."

My mother held her hands up. "We just came to meet your girlfriend. She's a pretty one, isn't she? All that beautiful long hair. Long enough to strangle someone with, isn't it?"

My fingers clenched into fists. "You're not meeting her. Not now. Not ever. I told you, I'm finished."

My father clapped a hand on my shoulder. "Now, now, Son. You are living in our house."

"I'll move out tomorrow."

My mother laughed, the sound nothing like when Bliss laughed. When Mother laughed it was like nails down a chalkboard. "And go where? You're a creature of habit, Vincent. New places make you uncomfortable. Which is why you're still hanging around here, despite the police manhunt focused on you."

"There's no hunt. I've scoured the newspapers and police scanners. The prison covered it up."

"Maybe so, but it would only take one little phone call from a concerned citizen..."

I ground my teeth. I couldn't go back to prison. I had friends who needed watching over. I'd met Mae, Heath, Liam, and Rowe while I was in jail. Their boy, Ripley, had become my friend after I'd escaped. They needed me, and I needed them, especially now that Mae was pregnant with a baby. I was laying low at the moment, watching from afar because I suspected the police were watching them in the hopes I'd turn up. And now there was Bliss...she needed watching as well. Even more than they did. They had each other. Bliss was all alone.

"You know I could just kill you at any time, Mother."

My father rolled his eyes.

Mother stepped up and cupped my cheek. "But you wouldn't. Because your Achilles' heel has always been people you love. Foolish as that is, since it makes you easy to manipulate."

She was right. It didn't matter that she was the master manipulator, the one who twisted everything into a threat. Even during the months and years when Scythe had controlled my body, he'd never laid a finger on my mother. Because we both loved her. It was ingrained. Built into our hardwiring. She was the one who'd put dinner in front of me every night. Who'd tucked me into bed and brushed my hair back off my face lovingly when other kids had been mean because I wasn't like them. She was the one who'd helped me escape the psych ward at the prison.

I didn't want to love her. It would have been a whole lot easier not to.

Because then I could have just snapped her goddamn neck and been done with it.

Her thumb smoothed over my skin. "Look. If you aren't ready to introduce us, then we'll leave."

She'd given up too easily.

My mother never gave up. Which meant that she

hadn't really come here with the intention of meeting Bliss. She'd merely come to remind me that she owned me. Because I did have soft spots.

And Bliss had rapidly become one.

21

BLISS

*V*incent sat down, his cheeks pink. "I'm very sorry about that. It was my parents. We need to talk about boundaries. Clearly."

I smiled, because from Vincent, that was almost a joke. "No problem at all. You could have invited them in. I wouldn't have minded."

"No."

He said it so sharply it was almost a bark. Okay then. I wasn't about to jump in the middle of their family squabbles.

Vincent peered around the outdoor area, squinting into the darkness and then tilting his head back to inspect the roof of the undercover area.

"What are you looking for?"

"A camera."

I raised an eyebrow. "Like, a security camera?"

"Something like that."

He was visibly agitated. He'd gone from sweet and relaxed to stiff and awkward. I was certain it wasn't something I'd done. Clearly, he'd had words with his parents and now he was lost in whatever had gone down with them. If this had been any other first date, I probably would have bailed.

But Vincent was different. He hadn't run away when my thing with Caleb had blown up in front of him.

He'd been a friend. I wanted to return the favor.

I put my fork down. "Can you take me somewhere?"

"Anywhere."

"Get your keys."

The drive was quick and quiet, Vincent still lost to whatever was going on with his parents. But when we pulled up at our destination, a smile flickered over his features. "I love ice cream."

"Have you been here before?"

"Not for a really long time."

"It's changed owners in the last few years, and it's even better than it was." I opened my car door. "Come on. Chocolate fixes everything. Even parent problems."

Vincent held the door open for me, and together we made our way to the counter where there were at least thirty different flavors of ice cream lined up behind a glass screen. There were a lot of other people around, which was unsurprising since it was a Friday night, so we joined the line, waiting for our turn to order.

A young couple in front of us—they couldn't have been any older than fourteen—had their arms wrapped around each other. He murmured something in her ear, and she tipped her head back and laughed. He took his opportunity to plant his mouth down on hers, stealing a kiss.

It was sloppy and awkward but also kind of sweet.

I nudged Vincent. "See what you were missing by not dating in high school?"

"Braces banging together and slobbering all over each other?"

I held in my giggle. That wasn't exactly the way I'd seen it. The romantic in me had turned it into something sweeter, but if I looked at it through his eyes, he was probably right. "You're right. High school dating is probably not the greatest. I never did much of it either."

The line inched forward, and we went with it.

Vincent gazing down from his much taller height. "How come?"

I shrugged. "Nobody wanted to hold hands with the fat chick, I guess."

It was less of a guess and more of a fact. I still remembered the day I'd overheard Sandra saying exactly that as she'd gossiped about me with another of our friends. I'd pretended I hadn't heard, but even now, a shot of pain speared through me. Those old rejections, though it had been a decade ago, clearly still had barbs that were holding on. It had set me up for a lifetime of putting up with men's bullshit, because I didn't feel worthy of being treated better. I'd dated a little in college, but both men had been assholes that I'd put up with until they'd inevitably lost interest in me and broke it off.

Vincent's fingers brushed mine.

My breath hitched. I gazed up at him, trying to determine if it had been deliberate or accidental.

His deep-brown eyes were hard to read but easy to drown in. His fingers brushed mine again, and then his pinky wrapped around mine.

I bit back a grin. "Vincent. Are you holding my hand?"

"I'm holding your finger. I wanted to hold your hand, but I wasn't sure if that was allowed on a first date, and I didn't want to be presumptuous."

I stared up into his impossibly handsome face, and my heart hammered behind my chest. "I don't know how you ever made anyone uncomfortable. You're incredibly sweet."

He didn't say anything.

My gaze kept flickering to his lips, and all I could do was think about kissing them.

He caught my gaze and cleared his throat. "You keep staring at my mouth."

"You noticed that, huh?"

"Why?"

I'd never been the one to initiate a kiss. I was always too terrified of rejection, even when I was in a relationship. But somehow, despite how attractive he was, I was the one with more experience between the two of us. If I wanted something to happen, it needed to come from me.

I wanted to kiss him.

"First kisses are allowed on first dates. That wouldn't be presumptuous."

He stepped in an inch. "Are you asking me to kiss you, Bliss?"

His voice turned deeper, and suddenly, I wasn't sure if the entire 'I don't date' thing was even true. Because Vincent was looking at me with a heat that made me want to swoon. It was definitely the heat that made me nod.

His hand cupped the side of my face, and he lowered his mouth to mine.

Vincent's kiss was soft and sweet, his lips gentle on mine.

My knees instantly went weak, but I pushed up on my toes, clutching his arms while the rest of the world around us ceased to exist. His fingers slid to the back of my head, holding me to him.

It was over too soon, a mere meeting of our mouths before he stepped back.

My head reeled at the connection such a simple, innocent kiss could create. I stared at him, shocked at how much I'd liked it when it had been so brief. He hadn't even used his tongue, and yet his fingers flexing in my hair and the press of his hard body beneath my hands promised so much more than he'd given.

The smile I gave him had to have been blinding, but I forced myself to look away, not wanting to seem too eager. "Thank you."

"For what? The kiss?"

I shrugged. "Yes. And for coming to my house tonight. For making me dinner. For holding my finger."

He smiled at me sheepishly. "Thank you for not feeling uncomfortable."

"What can I get you folks?"

Vincent and I looked up, and then moved forward to take our spot at the counter as the door behind us opened with a jingle of the bells.

Three young guys spilled in, their voices loud and slurred. They all wore football jerseys, and one started up a chant. "The Bears are number one. The Bears are number one."

Nobody joined in.

The young girl behind the counter gave me an apologetic grimace. "I'm sorry, what was that? One, two, or three scoops?"

"Just one, ple—"

"Oh! They got raspberry swirl. You guys see this? It's so fucking good." One of the drunk football players pushed his way to the front, slamming his hand against the glass top counter. "Fuck yeah, I can't wait to get that shit in my belly. Yo, girlie. Three scoops for me."

A mother with two little kids sitting in the booth to our left shot the men a dirty look.

I wrinkled my nose at the absolute stench of alcohol wafting off the guy who'd pushed in and was now standing way too close to me.

"There are children here," Vincent said quietly.

The man whipped around. "What was that, bro?"

Vincent quietly repeated himself. "I said, there are children here. You can't speak like that in the middle of a family venue."

The man's gaze rolled over Vincent's suit. "What's it to you? You ain't got no kids."

"I don't. But the lady just there does, and so does that family, and that one. Not only that, you just pushed in front of people who've been waiting their turn. And you were incredibly rude to this young woman who is just trying to do her job."

The drunk guy laughed like some sort of pig-hyena hybrid. "Oooh, guys. The line police are here. He's gonna arrest us for line-jumping."

The young girl behind the counter with an ice cream scoop in her hand, still waiting for me to choose a flavor, pointed at the drunk guy. "Walk yourself to the back of the line. I'm not serving you."

We'd drawn the attention of the entire room. There was no missing it, every person had their eyes glued to us. I cleared my throat uncomfortably.

"I'm a paying customer!" the man shouted. "You can't refuse service!"

"Actually, I can. Because you're drunk, cussing, and basically being rude. So now instead of walking yourself to the back of the line, you and your buddies can walk yourself right out of the shop."

The girl couldn't have been any older than sixteen, and yet she handled herself with complete grace and confidence that I envied.

The man clearly didn't feel the same way. "Fuck you, you stupid little bitch." His fingers curled into a fist, that he punched into the glass ice-cream cabinet.

The glass exploded, shattering everywhere. I jumped a mile, while the girl behind the counter screamed.

Vincent was on the man in a heartbeat, shoving him up against the wall, his hand around his throat.

The families around us gathered their children and scurried for the door.

"Call the police!" I shouted to the girl behind the counter. She grabbed a phone off the wall while I turned to help Vincent.

I had no idea what I was going to do. I didn't know how to fight. But I wasn't going to let him go up against three men by himself.

The other two guys rushed to help their friend.

"Behind you!"

But Vincent didn't seem to need my warning. As the

first of the guy's friends moved in, Vincent pulled the first one off the wall and spun him round, sending both men flying to the floor.

I stopped dead in my tracks.

So did the third guy.

Vincent snarled at him. "I suggest you don't come a step closer unless you want to end up like your friends on the floor there."

With huge eyes, the man held up his hands. "I'm good with remaining vertical."

"Like I thought." Vincent sucked in deep breaths, trying to calm the tremble in his fingers. He twisted his head to one side, his neck cracking audibly, and then turned to the girl behind the counter. "Are you okay?"

She nodded quickly, complete and utter fear in her eyes.

"Lock yourself in the storeroom until the police get here, okay?"

The girl's eyes were huge, but she agreed and scurried away.

Vincent waited until I heard the door lock, and then he stepped over the men, both bleeding on the floor. The one who'd punched the cabinet predictably had gashes and glass stuck in his arm and across his knuckles. They bled profusely while he howled. His friend lay beneath him, unconscious either from when his friend's head had collided with his or when they'd both gone down like a sack of potatoes. He'd hit the floor with a sickening thud, but he was still breathing. His chest rose and fell rhythmically.

Vincent grabbed my hand, no asking for permission

this time, and towed me to the parking lot and into his car. "Are you okay?" he asked.

"Fine. Jesus Christ, that guy was an asshole!"

Vincent nodded, shoving his key in the ignition.

I put my hand on his arm. "Wait. We should stay. The police will want a statement."

Vincent shook his head, pulling out of the parking lot and getting us onto the road. "I can't."

"Why not? You got an outstanding warrant out for your arrest?"

Vincent glanced at me, then back at the road. "That seemed more like a third-date conversation. I would have told you before the third-date sex. I swear."

I couldn't help it. I burst into laughter.

Vincent looked at me like I was crazy. "Are you having a mental breakdown? I don't think laughter is the correct response right now. Shouldn't you be screaming hysterically? Or trying to escape the man who just admitted to being wanted by the police?"

But I already trusted Vincent. Warrant or not, nothing was going to change my opinion of him, or the safety I felt when he was around. I shook my head. "My brother and his best friend have both been arrested at least twice. My mother did a one-year stint for prostitution when I was eleven. My stepfather is currently still in jail. My old neighbors when I lived at the trailer park had a meth lab... I'm not Providence born and bred. Your warrants don't scare me. But just out of interest, what's it for?"

Vincent put his foot down on the accelerator, leaving the ice-cream parlor behind us. "I dismissed myself from jail. Without permission."

I gaped at him. "You escaped? How is that even possible?"

"Is it supposed to be hard?"

I sniggered, but then I sobered. "Come work for me."

Vincent frowned. "What?"

"Come work for me at my bar. Do security. I want to feel safe there. And I feel safe when you're around. I know you like kids—"

"I like you more."

I warmed all over. "So is that a yes?"

He nodded solemnly. "It's a yes."

22

BLISS

The Saturday night crowd hadn't arrived yet when I pulled into Psychos' parking lot, but it was still early. Rebel finished at six, and I was picking her up with a back seat of shopping bags, ready to go back to her place and get ready for the Slayers party that night.

I'd had Vincent on my mind all day, and something inside me had wanted to ditch the party. But then I'd convinced myself that one nice night didn't equal a relationship. I wasn't doing anything wrong by accepting War's invitation. My intense and immediate attraction to War aside, Rebel had seen Axel hanging out with the Slayers. Somebody there had to know more than we did. They wouldn't tell the police, but maybe they'd tell me.

Unless it was the Slayers who'd killed him.

If that was the case, going to their compound tonight was a very stupid idea.

I let myself in, frowning at Solomon, the door guard, asleep on his chair. "Good to see I'm paying you to take a nap."

He didn't even stir. I shook my head. I'd assumed War's friend, Hawk, had gotten past Solomon at the sex party the other night after a hard-fought battle... Probably not if this was anything to judge by. He'd probably just walked on in, and Solomon had only chased him after the slam of the door woke him up.

I waved to Nash behind the bar, but Rebel was in the middle of explaining something to one of the other girls, and I didn't want to interrupt her training session. So I wandered behind the bar and into Nash's office, plonking down in his comfy chair. Nash glanced over and frowned at me, so just to needle him a little more, I stuck my feet up on the desk with a challenging grin aimed in his direction.

I could practically hear his teeth grinding.

It was almost hilarious. I needed to stake out the giant labyrinth of a building for a space that could be my own office, but I liked that Nash's was right in the center of everything.

My phone buzzed in the back pocket of my jeans, and I pulled it out quickly, hoping it was Vincent.

Caleb's name flashed on the screen.

I pushed it to voicemail.

The phone immediately lit up with another incoming call, which also got sent straight to voicemail.

The third call made it clear Caleb wasn't going away. I slammed my finger on the answer button. "What do you want?"

I'd never spoken to Caleb like that before. I'd never spoken to anyone with pure aggression and fierce anger in my voice.

"Where are you?"

"None of your business."

"You stupid little ho. I'm standing on your front step in a suit, ready to pick you up. Where the fuck are you, Bethany-Melissa? I'm coming to get you, and you'd better be ready by the time I get there."

"Go home, Caleb. I told you, we're done—"

"And I told you we weren't and that you needed to be by my side tonight."

I could picture it. Me, putting on a pretty dress, like I had every other time he'd told me to. We'd go to the country club, where he'd spend the entire night ignoring me, while he laughed and joked with his work colleagues. I'd smile dutifully at their sexist comments and pretend they weren't insulting.

Caleb didn't want to show up alone. People would ask where I was, and he would have to say I'd broken up with him. It was a bad look for a businessman in his thirties if he wanted to be taken seriously. It made him appear unsettled and untrustworthy if he didn't have a steady relationship to flaunt at such events, even though everybody in the room knew that married men cheated.

I don't know why I'd thought Caleb would be any different. But I knew what he was now, and I didn't care about his wounded pride. I was free from him, and I wasn't going back. Goddamn him for even thinking he could call me. "We're not together, Caleb! You don't get a say in what I do anymore!"

A shadow fell over me. Nash's eyes were fire, his entire body ready for a fight even though the fight was miles away, standing on my doorstep. "Is everything okay? The entire bar can hear you shouting."

"Who the fuck is that?" Caleb growled. "Is it him? The

piece of trash you're sleeping with?"

"Oh, if that isn't the pot calling the kettle black. Did you forget how your dick accidentally fell into Lucinda?"

"Because you're a frigid bitch who couldn't please a man if you had a guidebook by your side. You think he wants your used-up pussy? You think any man is going to want you when you don't even have the self-control to stop putting food in your fat fucking face? You ugly bitch, no man will ever want—"

Nash yanked the phone out of my hand. "You want to know where she is, rich boy? She's at my bar. Spread out naked on my desk. I stripped every piece of clothing from her body, and then I worshipped every inch of her. I erased every trace of you with my tongue. I went down on her, licking her sweet, wet, juicy pussy until she screamed my name loud enough for the entire bar to hear. My name, fuck boy. Not yours. Has she ever even uttered a sound when you fucked her with your tiny dick? You could never even get her wet, could you? And yet you call her frigid because you don't know how to please her. You're an embarrassment, Caleb. You're a little boy, with a small dick, trying to play with the men. She doesn't need you. She doesn't fucking need anyone."

He slammed his finger down on the red cancel call button.

I gaped at him.

His breath was ragged, his fingers clenched so hard around my phone I thought it might crack. His eyes were wide and wild, gaze darting around his office like Caleb might appear at any moment and challenge him.

All I could think about doing was kissing him.

His eyes turned downward, his expression morphing

into something more apologetic. "Fuck, Bliss. I'm sorry. But I could hear every word he said to you, and I just fucking lost it."

I couldn't even speak. My nipples had turned into stiff peaks at the thought of him laying me out naked on this desk and tongue-fucking me with an entire bar outside to hear every moan.

He squatted in front of me so we were more similar heights, his eyes filled with anguish. "Shit. You're mad. I didn't mean it, Bliss. I just know how men like him are. They don't back off until another man calls them on their bullshit."

The bubble broke.

I didn't mean it.

I cleared my throat. "No, thank you. I appreciate you standing up for me."

He rocked back on his heels, his expression changing to one of wary hesitation. "You aren't mad? I was kind of graphic. And out of line."

I shook my head. "No, it's fine. I get it. You said it in the heat of the moment." I pushed out of his chair and pocketed my phone. "Is Rebel done? We have plans."

"Yeah, I think she's just grabbing her coat." He stepped aside, leaving a wide berth for me to get by him without us touching. "Have a good night."

"Thanks. We will. You too."

I scurried by him, grabbing Rebel at the coatroom on my way out, and hustling her along with me.

"Hey." She jolted along at an almost jog since my legs were longer than hers. "You're the boss, Dis. You aren't supposed to be this keen to get your employee out the door."

"Did you just hear what happened with Nash and Caleb?"

Her face fell. "The whole bar heard, Dis. What Nash said—"

"I wasn't really naked on his desk, you know that, right?"

"Sure. I mean, the door was open. But I was kinda hot at the idea of it." She giggled, fanning her face with her fingers. "Aren't you?"

I was hot. I was so freaking hot I was sure you could relabel me an incinerator. The heat licked through my entire body, centering between my thighs.

The cool night air outside the bar was heavenly, and when I got in my car, I immediately put the window down, letting more of it in. My entire body felt too warm, my skin too tight.

Rebel watched me, laughter brewing on her lips. "Oh, Dis. You got it so bad, baby."

I couldn't even deny it. I just nodded.

She slapped my thigh. "Don't worry. Nash might be an idiot and sticking to his whole big brother act, but there's a clubhouse full of sinfully hot bikers at this party we're going to tonight, and I guarantee, at least one of them will not mind you taking out your sexual frustrations on them."

War's ruggedly handsome face flashed in my mind, and the heat inside me flared again.

I needed somewhere for it to go.

I needed to take my frustrations out on someone. I needed a release.

The sooner we got to the party the better.

23

BLISS

The Slayers' MC compound was like a mini jail on the outskirts of Saint View, the woods surrounding it on all four sides, and only a narrow private road making it accessible by car. The tall, barbed-wire-topped fence started at the turnoff, and we'd been driving for five minutes along the bumping lane, trying to get to the gate.

"Are you sure we're going the right way?" I asked Rebel for the third time. I peered out the window. There were a few houses here and there, their lights visible through the thick trees, but it wasn't like the road was signposted with a cheery "Welcome! Club entrance 200 yards on your left."

"I'm sure. The entrance is just up ahead. Listen, before we go in. Do you need a safe word?"

I gaped at her. "For what?"

"If you want out."

I swallowed thickly, nerves rocketing around my

stomach. Maybe I did need one. It couldn't hurt. "Sandwiches."

Rebel raised an eyebrow. "Okay then. Interesting choice, but sandwiches it is. You want out, just...make out like you're planning a picnic."

"Could I not just say, let's go?"

"Probably, but I don't think I need to explain to you where we are. These guys aren't always polite company. War runs a tight ship. He'd never let anyone get hurt, but he's not gonna protect you from crude language or a slap to the ass either, you know? You're probably gonna see stuff that doesn't happen at your five-course dinner parties."

A set of huge metal gates loomed ahead of us. The Slayers' logo right in the middle, a hooded demon with a scythe in its hand in the center.

It was almost as terrifying as Psychos' logo.

"Last chance to bail, Dis. You in or you out?"

"I'm in."

"That's my girl." She shimmied her slight shoulders with excitement. "We're gonna have the best night. These guys, Bliss. They're fucking hot. If the bad boy thing does it for you, that is."

I wasn't sure if it did or not. Caleb was certainly the complete opposite of a bad boy. And Vincent had a very clean-cut, preppy look about him too. Nash was definitely headed more toward bad boy in terms of his appearance, but Nash was nice right down to his very soul.

But there was no doubting I was attracted to War. I had been from the moment I'd seen him at the police station.

I stopped the car to pause at the gate, and a hooded

figure stepped from the shadows, his MC cut tight on his chest, a sawed-off shotgun in one hand.

A trickle of fear rolled down my spine at the huge, intimidating man walking our way. I had no idea what his name was, but it should have been Tree Trunk. Because he was as tall and as thick as one. Rebel stuck her head out the window and waved. "You wanna let us in, Fang? Just me."

"That ain't your car, Rebel. Who's with you?"

"Bliss Arthur? War invited her."

A look of recognition crossed the man's face, but he still bent down to peer through my open window.

"Ah, hi," I stuttered, completely intimidated by his size and scowl. "Nice to meet you."

He didn't answer, his gaze lingering on Rebel. He pulled a small flashlight from the inside pocket of his cut and shined it around the back seat. "Pop the trunk."

I pressed the little button on the dash, and Fang checked out the back. We waited quietly, and when he was done with his inspection, he slammed the trunk and tapped it twice.

"You're good to go. Have a nice night, ladies."

The gates opened with a shudder, letting out a creak of protest, but slowly swung inward. I inched the car forward, creeping inside. Once we were out of earshot, I turned big eyes on Rebel. "Well, he was kinda scary!"

Rebel glanced back over her shoulder where Fang had taken up his position in the dark again. "Fang? Nah, he's a pussy cat."

"More like a tiger. He's huge."

She wriggled her eyebrows suggestively. "He's huge everywhere."

"You've slept with him?"

She nodded. "He's an A-plus fuck too, Dis. If you want to take your frustrations out on him, I'd highly recommend it."

I shook my head quickly.

She shrugged. "Maybe I will then. It's been a while."

"How many of these guys have you slept with?" There was no judgment in the question. I was literally just curious.

She shrugged. "No idea, to be honest. I don't keep a little black book." She winked at me. "It kept running out of pages."

I laughed at her, envying her ease with her body and her sexuality. I wished I had half of her confidence. "My little black book would be more like a corner torn out of a page. Or however big you'd need to write down a whole three names."

"Three? Seriously, Dis? I had three on my list the night I lost my virginity."

My mouth dropped open. "You did not lose your virginity in a foursome!"

She laughed. "Okay, fine. It wasn't quite that bad. But three guys? What the hell are you rich people doing over there? Live a little! Are you even allowed to say blow job on your side of town? Or do the heavens open so lightning can strike you down."

"Not in polite company."

"Well, there ain't no polite company here tonight. You ready? 'Cause that's the clubhouse."

A huge rectangular building loomed ahead of us. It wasn't attractive and kind of reminded me of Psychos' imposing exterior. But unlike Psychos, a large roller door took up the entire front of the building. They had it up, light and people and music all spilling from inside.

I parked my car beside a row of bikes, extremely careful not to get too close for fear of knocking one of them down.

But Rebel sprang out of the car, and I quickly turned the engine off to run after her, not wanting to be left behind in the dark.

"Hey, Rebel's here," someone yelled from the thick of the party.

She was a bigger woman with a round face and a wide smile. Her dark hair was braided into tight strands and then wound on top of her head in a huge bun. Her gold hoop earrings gave her a gypsy vibe.

"Queenie!" Rebel trotted to her side and gave the woman a hug. Then she waved me over. "Q, this is Disney."

Queenie turned to me, a motherly smile on her face. "Disney? Your parents really dislike you or did you already pick yourself a road name?"

I wasn't sure what a road name was exactly, but I could guess. I was pretty sure War and Hawk and Fang didn't have those names on their birth certificates either. "I'm Bliss. Rebel's the only one who calls me Disney."

The woman nodded. "Nice to meet you. Is this your first time, sweetheart? War said Rebel was bringing someone. Didn't tell us any more than that though."

I wiped my sweaty palms on my jeans. "Yes, ma'am."

Queenie hooted. "Oh Lawd, she's got manners. Where the hell did War and Rebel find you? No need to ma'am anyone around here, sweet thing. Ain't nobody that formal. Come on, let me introduce you around

before you turn tail and run back to your car. We don't
bite."

"Unless you want us to!" a male voice called out.

"Shut up, you great lug," Queenie said to the man
sitting on an outdoor couch with a beer bottle balanced
between his fingers.

He tilted his head up as we walked behind him. "You
love me, my queen bee. Don't pretend you don't like it
when I bite you."

I went hot with awkwardness at their intimate talk.

But Queenie laughed and dropped a kiss on his
upturned face. "You know it."

I recognized Aloha from Psychos, and he did a double
take when he recognized me. "Bliss! Good to see you
here. You already met my woman, I see?"

"I did. She's very kindly introducing me around."
Which I was incredibly grateful for because Rebel
seemed to have disappeared into the crowd of people.

"Come on, sugar, let's keep going. You need to come
meet the rest of the girls if you want to hang here. The
boys will accept anything with tits and a warm pussy, but
it's the women you need to get on your side. They might
be tiny skinny scraps of things, but don't underestimate
how wily they can be." She grinned at my worried face.
"Not me, of course. I couldn't care less who hangs around
here, but I already locked my man down tight, and he
doesn't stray. The other girls are younger, and they have
their favorites amongst the guys. You don't want to step
on that if you want to keep them sweet."

I swallowed thickly. I'd just walked into a whole
different world with a whole new set of rules I hadn't
studied in advance.

Queenie waved at a few other people and introduced me to a couple of other guys, most who were already vaguely familiar, even if I hadn't spoken to them directly. I caught sight of Rebel for a moment, and she shot me a questioning thumbs-up, which I nodded to, even though I really wasn't one-hundred-percent comfortable, but then she disappeared again, so I kept following Queenie.

Inside, a long bar took up almost the entire right-hand wall. Two men with club cuts stood with the rows of alcohol at their backs, pouring drinks for the women who sat on the other side.

I was instantly awkward. They both wore tiny tight dresses that rode up their thighs. One had a skirt so short I could see her panties and I was pretty sure she knew it. Their long legs were toned and skinny and looked great in the impossibly tall high heels.

Queenie nudged me. "Don't be jealous. They might have tiny little bodies we ain't had since we were prepubescent, but they jealous of our titties."

She shook her own, and I grinned at her. I liked Queenie a lot.

"Siren, Kiki. Meet Bliss. She came in with Rebel."

Kiki jumped off her stool, wobbling over to us on her heels that she didn't seem to have much practice in. "Bliss! What a beautiful name!" She wrapped her skinny arms around me in a surprisingly strong hug.

Queenie frowned, then glanced over at the guys behind the bar. "She's toast, and it's not even nine. No more."

"Aw, Queenie!" Kiki complained, but it was clear there was no messing with Queenie's orders. She was obviously the mother hen, and she'd cut Kiki off.

Siren didn't get up off her seat to greet me. She just nodded coolly. I did the same back.

"You want a drink, Bliss?" one of the young guys behind the bar called out. He introduced himself as Ice and had long blond hair that curled around his collar.

I did. Badly. But I was also a little worried about fully relaxing in this place. Everyone had been kind and welcoming so far, but I hadn't forgotten that any one of them could be Axel's killer.

"Yeah, she wants a drink," a deep voice said at my back.

I glanced over my shoulder, though I knew exactly who it was.

War grinned down at me. "Hey, baby girl."

I couldn't help the grin that spread across my face. I didn't know what it was about him. Perhaps it was the protective way he'd sat at his mother's bedside while she was frail and helpless. Or maybe it was just my hormones intercepting the smart thoughts that were probably trying to warn me away from the leather-jacket-wearing, tatted-up, self-confessed bad boy. "Baby girl isn't a very creative nickname."

He grinned. "It's not, is it? I'll do better. But first, pick your poison. We got a party to have, and you can't be sober for it."

"Is that a club rule?"

"Nah, but I can tell you want one. And so do I." He put his hand on the small of my back and guided me over to the bar. "We aren't big on wine here. So it's beer or hard spirits. Scotch, bourbon, vodka, or tequila."

"Tequila."

He let out a chuckle. "Okay, okay. I wasn't expecting that, but good for you."

The guy behind the bar had already poured War a glass of scotch on ice, but War pushed it to the side. "Make it two. Nobody should do tequila shots alone."

"I'll have one as well," Siren called, sliding off her barstool and strutting over to stand at War's other side. She put a hand possessively on his arm. "How are you, baby? How's Fancy doing?"

War moved his hand subtly out of Siren's grip to pass a shot glass to me, while Ice behind the bar poured another for Siren. "Fancy is my mom," War explained.

I nodded. "How is she doing? Any change since I was there the other day?"

Siren's mouth fell open. "You were there? At the hospital?"

I glanced at War, unsure of why that was so shocking. "Um, yes?"

She glared at War. "You said you didn't want any visitors. Baby, I would have come right up."

It was pretty clear Siren was marking her territory. That tequila looked better by the second because I didn't want to be in the middle of their argument. They obviously had history, and I didn't want to be the cause of any problems. "I was at the hospital for other reasons. I just happened to run into him while I was—"

War cut me off with a glare in Siren's direction. "I would have called you up if I'd wanted you there. I didn't. So take the hint."

Secondhand embarrassment had me cringing. I was so uncomfortable with the whole thing, I searched around for Rebel, ready to shout, "Sandwiches!" even though I would look like a crazy person.

But Siren didn't seem to take any offense to War's complete rejection and dismissal. She shrugged, downed her shot, and strode off into the party.

War nudged me, drawing my attention back to him.

"Sorry about that. That was all for your benefit. She likes to try playing alpha dog when Fancy isn't around."

"Fancy is normally the alpha dog?"

He nodded. "Alpha bitch, I guess, technically. Pop was the prez, but he was so wrapped around Fancy's little finger. Totally pussy-whipped."

I smiled at the image of a big, burly biker, an older version of War, bowing to the commands of the little frail woman I'd seen in the hospital. "He must have loved her a lot."

"He did. But she loved him too. I almost hope she doesn't wake up, you know? I don't want to have to tell her he's gone."

"Is there any change in her condition?"

"No. But the doctors tell me that's a good thing. They thought she'd be dead by now, but she's hanging on tight, like the hellcat she is."

I ran a finger along the rim of my shot glass, letting it wobble beneath my touch. "She sounds like a strong woman."

"She is. Stronger than most men."

"I hope I get to meet her." I meant it. God knew I needed more strong women in my life.

He glanced over at me, his eyes warm. "I hope so too. But for tonight, no more talk about my mom. Okay? Surely, we have more interesting things to talk about."

I smiled. "Deal."

"Drink first."

I picked up my tequila shot and tossed it back, wincing when it burned down my throat. "Can I get a beer?" I asked Ice. "Please?"

He pushed one across the bar top while War watched me. "Tequila with a beer chaser. I like you." He motioned to Ice. "I don't want to see either of our beers empty for the rest of the night, capiche? And keep the shots coming." He raised his voice. "That goes for everyone. Queenie, quit cutting people off. We can cry over Prez next week. Tonight, we're celebrating the fact that Fancy is still with us. And that we're all still here. Together."

A cheer went up around the room, and War took my hand, leading me through the crowd to the center where four well-used, brown leather couches faced each other, a short square table in the middle. It was covered by beer bottles and ashtrays, cigarette butts all poking out of them. War's hand was warm around mine, and butterflies lit up in my stomach, even though I could feel Siren's scowl and other women's gazes on me.

One of them was Rebel's. I caught her eye as War towed me to the seats, and she raised an eyebrow, her gaze flickering to War's hand around mine. "Well, that's new. War holding someone's hand."

War looked over at her as he dropped down onto one of the couches, pulling me down to sit beside him. I tried to sit with a little space between us, but the couches were old, and War and I sank in together, our thighs pressing against each other.

He paused, eyeing her with a beer bottle halfway to his mouth. "I got a bone to pick with you, sunshine."

Rebel grinned at him. "Wouldn't be the first time."

"I hear you been talking about the club outside the club."

She shrugged, giving him a cheeky grin. "What is this, Fight Club? First rule of Fight Club—"

"You know the rules."

She sighed. "All I said to Bliss was that Axel hung out here sometimes. That's it. I didn't share any state secrets."

"That's only 'cause you don't know any."

"True."

He pointed the beer bottle at her. "You know there's punishments for breaking rules around here."

A flicker of worry lit up inside me. "She really didn't tell me anything."

But Rebel reached over and patted my arm. "Don't worry. It's fine. I knew the rules and I broke them."

War finally took a sip of his beer. "I told Bliss here I was gonna spank your ass."

Rebel let out a laugh. "Did you just? Not sure if that really counts as a punishment…"

Heat flushed my face.

"But now that Bliss is here, I ain't gonna be the one who does it. One of you other assholes is gonna have to step up."

There was a chorus of volunteers from the guys.

Rebel sniggered. "You're all a bunch of pervs."

"Ain't none of you touching her but me," Fang growled from the doorway.

I hadn't even seen him arrive at the party. For a huge man, he moved incredibly quietly.

War seemed surprised but nodded at him. "Fang has spoken, so unless any of you idiots are stupid enough to challenge him, looks like Fang gets the privilege of tanning our little friend's behind."

Fang moved through the room at what felt like a glacial pace, towering over every other man and woman. He sat on the couch opposite us and motioned for Rebel.

I gaped. "Wait. You were joking, right? He's not really going to spank her, is he?"

War leaned in, his mouth at my ear. "Yeah, baby girl. He is. But don't fret. I chose this punishment because I knew she'd like it. I'm well aware of Rebel's kinks."

"Because you…"

"Nah. I never went there. But you get to know what people like pretty quick when you hang out at sex parties with them. Watch."

Fang rubbed his hands over his thighs as Rebel practically skipped over to stand in front of him. She didn't seem to care at all that there was an entire room full of people about to watch him degrade her like this. I was half appalled with myself for just sitting there, and yet Rebel didn't look bothered at all. In fact, her chest rose and fell so rapidly she was almost panting.

"Get your pretty little ass across my lap."

Rebel giggled and lowered herself over his legs so her leather-skirt-covered ass was in the air and her face was pointed to the floor. "Spank me, Daddy," she said in a fake, high-pitched voice that had everyone laughing.

Everyone except Fang.

He lifted her skirt, exposing her almost bare ass to the room. She only wore a tiny pink thong beneath it, and the men erupted in cheers at the sight of it nestled between her cheeks.

Fang's big hands trailed up the backs of her thighs

and then beneath the hot-pink fabric. In one quick motion, he tore it.

"Fang! I fucking liked those panties!" Rebel struggled on his lap, trying to slap her palms across his chest.

He pinned her down. "Stop fucking moving." His palm cracked across her backside.

Another cheer went up from the room.

Rebel stopped moving and let out a moan.

Fang's hand rubbed over the instant red mark, soothing away the sting, before he did it again.

Rebel's moan was almost orgasmic.

I stared at the expression on her face while Fang massaged the globes of her ass, his fingers slipping between her thighs to touch her exposed pussy.

War laughed. "All right, all right, you two. Take it somewhere private. This isn't party night at Psychos."

Fang stood, picking up Rebel in his arms like she weighed nothing. His huge erection strained behind his jeans, and Rebel scrambled to wrap her arms and legs around him like she was climbing a tree. He gripped her bare ass, supporting her weight, and stormed through the party, kissing her deeply as he searched for an empty bedroom. Down the hall, a door banged, and Rebel's moans were drowned out by the conversation starting up again.

I didn't even know what to say. I'd never seen anything like that before, and I wasn't sure if I was completely appalled, embarrassed, or so incredibly turned on I was thinking about breaking a rule if that was how the punishments went.

I'd never had a man spank me.

But Rebel had looked like she was on the verge of an orgasm.

"Did you like that, baby girl?"

There was already a warm buzz building inside me from our first round of shots and the beer I'd mostly chugged. I didn't drink much so I knew it was all going to my head, but after that little show, I needed more. "I think I need another drink."

War chuckled. "Ice! More tequila!"

Ice brought over a tray of shots with lime and salt.

War's gaze met mine. "Did I tell you about the club rule where all tequila shots have to be done off someone else's body?"

"That didn't seem to be a rule earlier when we did them at the bar."

He winked at me. "I just made it up. I'm the prez now. I can do that."

"And if I say no?"

"You'd be breaking a club rule, and I'd have to punish you, just like we punished Rebel."

I was pretty sure Rebel was having the time of her life in Fang's room right now and thoroughly enjoying her bad behavior.

"Would you like it if I did that to you, baby girl?" he asked again.

My heart fluttered at the looks he kept shooting me. Being the center of his attention was heady.

"'Cause I'd really fucking like to have my palm on your ass and see your pink slit peeking through your thighs as I did it."

I let out an unsteady breath, feeling his words tingle right through my clit.

He put a shot in my hand and then tilted his head away from me. "Lick my neck."

I hesitated.

"For the shot, Bliss. I was only joking about punishing you. I ain't gonna do nothing you don't want."

But I did want. My clit was begging for it.

I leaned over so my face wasn't even an inch from his neck. I closed my eyes and breathed in his scent. Tobacco and leather and the faint sweetness of alcohol. I'd never realized how well they went together until I smelled it on him. I ran my tongue along his neck, delighting in the goosebumps that broke out in my wake.

He groaned. "Fuck, do it again."

I did.

I licked his neck once more, daring to turn it into an open-mouthed kiss against his skin.

Quicker than I would have thought possible, he was dragging me onto his lap. "Straddle me."

I knew there were other people watching, but I was too turned on by War and Fang and Rebel that I let myself pretend there wasn't. It wasn't like my ass was on display, like Rebel's had been. I swung my leg across War's lap, letting my knees dig into the couch on either side of his thighs. My core brushed against the noticeable bulge in his jeans, but I kept most of my weight in my knees, not wanting him to realize how heavy I was.

"What are you doing?" he asked.

I froze. "I, um...you said to...am I doing it wrong?"

He gripped my thighs and pulled me right down. He took the full brunt of my weight across his strong thighs so my core, wet behind my panties, was lined up and pressed against his jean-covered erection. "There," he said, staring into my eyes with a fierce determination. "From now on, if you're in this club, this is where I want you. Right up on my cock like you own it."

He was so hard beneath me. The instinct to grind on him was there, but I didn't dare. I must have looked like a baby deer caught in headlights, all shocked eyes and too afraid to move, but I didn't complain. The urge to shout 'sandwiches' had long passed.

He reached around me, grabbing a saltshaker and a tequila shot. He passed them both to me, and I shook the salt over the spot I'd licked on his neck, letting the little crystals stick to him.

"You're gonna have this all down your shirt," I laughed, watching some of it roll beneath his collar.

He grinned. "Good. You can lick it off me there too."

Oh, sweet baby Jesus. I wanted to do that. His white T-shirt was so tight beneath his open cut, and the man's stomach was as solid as marble.

I was definitely up for licking it if that's what he wanted.

But there was a salt trail on his neck, and I was pleased for the excuse to put my tongue back on his skin. I dragged it up his neck again, and the salt exploded on my tongue. Reluctantly, I pulled back and downed the shot. The fiery liquid didn't scald so much anymore, now that we'd had a couple, but I still looked around for something to chase it with. "Lime?"

War stared at me, eyes full of heat. He reached up, gripping the back of my neck. "No lime. I wanna taste that tequila on you."

Before I could even comprehend what he was doing, he leaned forward and drew my head down at the same time. Our lips collided, his tongue instantly pushing inside my mouth.

I didn't fight. I sank down into the kiss like I'd kissed the man a million times before.

His grip on my neck was punishing, but it only added to my arousal. I'd never had someone hold me so possessively, like if I even thought of trying to pull away, he'd drag me right back. Our lips moved together, fast and hard, and he kissed me like he'd been waiting a lifetime to do it and not just the hour I'd been here at the party.

He groaned into my mouth, never letting up the grip on my neck, but his other hand slid over my thigh to grab a handful of hip. At the same time, he thrust up, rubbing his erection against my core. "Fuck, baby girl. I've been wanting to kiss you since the moment I saw you in that dress at the club the other night. Why the fuck aren't you wearing that dress now?"

I didn't know if it was the alcohol or just the fact I was the center of his universe in that very moment, but it made me bold. "Because I'm clearly very stupid."

He kissed me again, his fingers digging in and rocking me over his erection. "You know what I'd do to you right now if you were wearing that dress instead of jeans?"

Oh God. I wasn't sure I wanted to know. I was already really regretting how thick the denim was between us. But I found myself whispering, "Yes," into his ear.

It came out something like a breathy moan, and he shivered in response.

"I'd have had you on my lap, right like you are now. Except I would have hiked your skirt up around your waist so everybody could see your delicious, completely fuckable ass."

His hand slid around to squeeze me there, holding me even tighter against him, encouraging me to rock on him and take what I needed.

"Then I would have slipped my hand inside your panties to find out if you were wet for me."

Too turned on to stop, I ground over his dick, rocking my hips back and forth, increasing the friction. A gasp slipped from my lips at the building sensation inside me.

"Are you wet for me, baby girl?"

I couldn't answer that. I was drowning for him, but I couldn't say it.

"Say it. I know your cunt is fucking dripping for me right now."

I couldn't. It was too forward. And so dirty. I didn't even know what the hell I was doing. I barely knew this man and yet I was dry humping him in the middle of a party like I was a teenager.

But I didn't want to stop.

With a growl that was practically feral, War took my mouth again. The kiss a punishment for not giving him what he wanted. He drove his tongue into me, tasting and taking, dominating, and controlling. I moaned, pleasure coursing through me.

In the next instant, he was on his feet, me in his arms.

"War!" I yelped, struggling to get down. I'd break the man's back. "Put me down, I'm too heavy."

"That's real fucking insulting, baby girl." He strode through the party with me in his arms, while some of the guys clapped for us. "You think I can't carry your sweet ass to my bed?"

My cheeks went hot as I was carried toward the hallway where Rebel and Fang had disappeared earlier.

But I didn't stop him. Because making out with him on the couch wasn't enough. I wanted more. I wanted him alone.

To War's credit, he wasn't struggling with my weight. He carried me like I was as tiny as Siren and Kiki. He was so big and solid, he made me feel small in a way I never had with any other man. The sounds of the party filtered away the farther we went down the darkened hall. We passed several other rooms, their doors closed, but the sounds coming from within made it clear what was going on behind them. I had no idea how long War and I had been making out, but we clearly weren't the only ones.

It only added to the heat building at my core. "Are these all bedrooms down here?"

"Yeah. We all have one. Some of the guys live here full time. Some of us just use it as a crash pad when we've had too much to drink and can't drive home." He chuckled in my ear. "Some of us just use it as a place to get a beautiful woman naked and lick her pussy until she screams."

Oh my God.

There was a promise in that last statement that had me trembling.

At the very end of the hall, War opened a door, stepped past it, then kicked it shut behind him. He finally let me go, and my feet slid to the floor.

We were suddenly very alone.

"Just you and me now, huh? Seemed to me like you were kind of into being out there with everyone." I gazed around his room. It was sparsely furnished but clean. There was a bar fridge in one corner and a writing desk beside it. As well as a door that presumably led to a bathroom, but the main feature was definitely the bed. It was made up with dark-colored sheets, and a comforter was folded neatly at the end.

War leaned on the writing desk, crossing his arms over his chest, and watched me wander around his room, trailing my fingertips over his things. His grin was full of wry amusement. "Oh, I am. If I'd thought you'd be down for it, I probably would have laid you out on that couch and ate your pussy for everyone to watch. Fuck, Bliss. I'd love to do that; you have no fucking idea how bad I want your thighs around my head while every other man in the room watches and creams himself with jealousy because it ain't him."

I laughed. "That wouldn't happen."

He raised one eyebrow. "Why not?"

Ugh. I knew it would only be a matter of time before I made things awkward with my hang-ups. "Maybe if you did it with Siren."

He frowned. "Why?"

I raised one shoulder. "She's gorgeous."

"And you're not?"

"I've had a lifetime of people telling me how pretty I'd be if I just lost some weight. And they're right."

His eyes darkened. "Take your jeans off."

I glanced sharply at him. "Sorry?"

"Take your jeans off, Bliss. Now."

A shiver ran through me at the demand in his voice. The only light in the room came from a small lamp in the corner he'd flicked on. I wanted to do what he'd said. I'd willingly come down here, knowing, or at least hoping it was going to turn into sex. I knew this was my only chance to have him. He'd have lost interest by the next day, but I didn't care. I had so much pent-up frustration inside me, I desperately needed to give it an outlet.

But I never had sex with the light on. And I sure as hell wasn't about to start now, with him, the man who probably had models in his bed every other night. "Turn the light off."

He stared at me, mulling something over in his head. Eventually, he nodded and pushed off the table to go to the lamp. "One time, Bliss. You get tonight in the dark, because I can see I've probably already pushed you out of your comfort zone. After tonight, every time I fuck you, it's gonna be with the lights on. Don't deprive me of watching you."

I sucked in a breath at the promise. At the idea he'd even want to see me.

Caleb had never come right out and said it, but I'd always suspected he'd never wanted the lights on because he was too busy picturing someone else beneath him.

War bent over and flicked the switch on the lamp, plunging the room into darkness once more. "Take your jeans off, Bliss," he said again.

My heart pounded, but God, I wanted to. Even if this was just a quick screw with the rest of our clothes still on, I wanted to feel him inside me. My core begged to be filled.

The darkness was familiar and comforting. It wasn't absolute, but it was enough to feel sexy. He would only see my outline, a dark figure moving in the shadows, not all the little lumps and bumps and rolls I hated.

He sat on the side of the bed, the springs squeaking slightly beneath his weight.

I stepped out of my heels, my bare feet finding the

scuffed wood floorboards. I undid the button on my jeans and then the zipper on my fly before pushing them down my legs and toeing them off.

"Panties too."

I couldn't breathe. Caleb had never made me feel like this. There'd never been any sort of foreplay or buildup with him. It was just him rolling on top of me and pushing his dick between my legs, whether I was ready or not. I'd gotten used to it, but it was never particularly fun for me. I'd always had to go to the bathroom later and handle it myself if I wanted to come. Most of the time I didn't bother.

I tucked my fingers into the sides of my panties and lowered them to the floor, barely daring to breathe.

War stood so we were face-to-face. His fingers found my chin, and he tilted my face up. "You like it when I tell you what to do."

It was more of a statement than a question.

I nodded. All I'd ever done in the past was lie quietly beneath men while they grunted and sweated over me. I didn't know anything else. Caleb never even kissed me in public, let alone pulled me onto his lap and told me to grind on him. I needed War's guidance.

"Good girl." He kissed me deeply, his tongue plunging into mine. It was so sexy I almost forgot I was half naked.

His fingers found the hem of my top, and he lifted it over my head. The shirt joined the rest of my clothes on the floor, and a moment later, my bra was beside them too.

"Just how I like my women," War purred in my ear. "Fully naked before I've even taken my cut off. If we're in here, baby girl, I don't ever want you in clothes."

I wasn't experienced enough for this man and his mouth. He was the starring character in every sex dream I'd ever had. In those dreams, I was just as confident as he was.

The reality was very different.

"Hold on to the bed frame."

I had no idea what he was doing. But I did as he said, crawling across the bed to kneel at the top. I placed both hands on the wrought iron that decorated the headboard.

I didn't dare look over my shoulder at him when the bed dipped and squeaked behind me. He moved in close, still fully clothed, so he was kneeling right behind me.

His hand landed on the back of my neck, squeezing tightly. His palm was warm, and the tight grip turned into a kneading massage, his fingers digging into the tense muscles there before slowly moving lower. His massage became a featherlight touch, dancing down my spine and fluttering over my lower back. There, it smoothed out into a flat palm against my skin, sliding down until he cupped a handful of my ass. "Gonna spank you now, baby girl."

Without waiting for me to say yes or no, his palm connected sharp and fierce with my naked behind.

I yelped, not at the pain, but at the pleasure it sent spinning straight into my core. A gush of arousal bloomed there.

War's palm smoothed over the sting, massaging it away. "I don't ever want to hear you talk about yourself like you did just before. It's insulting. To you, and to me for wanting your body the way it is."

I nodded quickly. Though I knew it wouldn't be that simple. I couldn't simply turn off years of hating the way I looked just because he told me to. But for tonight, I could pretend I could.

"Spread your legs. I'm gonna kneel there."

I widened my knees, and War moved between them, his hands roaming all over my ass. Every now and then, his erection, still locked behind his jeans, brushed against me, but he never let me feel it properly.

"You wet for me, Bliss?"

I nodded.

"I want to feel it."

I let out a tiny moan of approval. He moved in closer, one hand circling around to the front to stroke my pussy.

His finger found my clit, and at the same time, his palm smacked my ass again.

The feeling was electric. I slumped forward onto the headboard, while War made encouraging little noises in the back of his throat. "I've got you."

He picked up the pace on my clit, rubbing two fingers in circles over it while he spanked me again. Every time his hand landed on my ass, it was with a practiced speed and strength that left me tingling and wanting more, rather than actually in pain. My ass would be pink, no doubt, but not bruised.

All the while, he never let up on my clit. The pleasure vibrated through me until I had my head resting on the headboard, along with my arms, my ass jutted back while he drove me toward orgasm.

"Look at you, fucking presenting yourself to me like that," he murmured. "How could you ever think you aren't beautiful, Bliss? I'm so fucking hard right now that if I didn't have to taste you, I'd be slamming myself inside you."

His big hand moved to between my shoulder blades, and he pushed me down so my face was buried in his pillows, my ass in the air. I panted into them, feeling incredibly exposed, and yet all I wanted to do was exactly what he told me. I was on display, but it was the dirtiest, most erotic thing I'd ever done, and I wanted more.

His hands slid up the backs of my thighs, spreading them as wide as I could go before coming to rest on my ass. He spread me there too, and I gasped.

"Shh, baby girl. Ain't nobody ever touch you there?"

"No," I murmured.

"Good."

Oh God, why was the possessiveness in his voice so damn hot?

I didn't get time to think that through because then his mouth was covering my pussy.

He kissed me there like he kissed my mouth. Long, open-mouthed sucking with slow and intruding strokes of his tongue. It flickered over my clit, sending the little bud wild, then switched to licking up my arousal. He plunged in and out of me like his tongue was his cock, fucking me. He speared me deep, then drew back to my ass, tonguing there as well.

"Oh my God," I yelled into the pillow, grateful they muffled my surprised shout.

War chuckled. "Yell it louder, baby girl. Until you're comfortable with me fucking you in front of other people, I want everyone out there to at least hear what I'm doing to you."

I was so out of my depth with him. There was no way this was ever going to happen again. I couldn't be that girl he wanted me to be, having public sex and God knows what else because I was sure that was just the very tip of the iceberg with him.

But this would be enough. This would be enough to fulfill every sexual wish I'd ever had. In reality, I hadn't even been able to dream up something like this. My fantasies had never even come close, and they were all with nameless, faceless men.

From now on, they'd all have War's grin and green eyes.

I never knew having someone lick you so thoroughly, in such a private way, could feel like this. War's tongue was demonic, eliciting pleasure everywhere it touched. His fingers joined the action, one plunging into my core before a second joined a moment later.

"Fuck, baby girl. You are so wet. You're dripping down my hand."

I froze, embarrassed at how into it I was.

His palm smacked my flesh once more, my ass jiggling. "Wherever you just went in your head, stop it. Your entire body just locked right up. You don't even know how much I love this."

I relaxed again, and to prove his statement, he added a third finger, angling them perfectly so they hit that spot deep inside me. He thrust them into me at the ideal speed, better than I could have even instructed him to do it.

"I'm gonna come," I moan-shouted. "Oh God, War! I can't!" I rocked my hips faster, chasing down what I needed.

"Yeah, you can, baby girl. You're gonna cream all over my hand and my face."

He dove into my pussy, licking and sucking me until a

scream built in the back of my throat. His fingers drove into me, and on instinct, I slammed my hips in time with the rhythm he set, meeting each punishing thrust with a grind of my own. My inner thighs were coated, and my legs shook with the force of the orgasm barreling down on me.

One finger pressed to my ass, three deep inside my pussy, and his tongue on my clit, I came with a scream. I yelled his name at the top of my lungs, so loud I was sure it echoed before moans overtook any ability to form words. I ground against him while he plowed into me, never letting up on my clit. We bounced and squeaked on the bed, pleasure surging through me in a light so blinding it could have lit the room if it hadn't been inside me. I moaned and tried to breathe, but the waves of pleasure kept coming and coming, and War rode out every one, eventually moving his lips to my inner thigh and pressing sweet kisses there, in between luxurious licks.

I couldn't move. I was locked in place by sheer bliss, even after the orgasm subsided.

War laughed and smacked my ass playfully. "You still breathing, baby girl?"

I flopped onto his bed on my stomach, eventually turning my head to one side. "You made me forget how."

"Mission accomplished then."

He lay down on the bed beside me, on his side, his head propped up on his arm while he watched me.

"Are you...?"

He was still fully dressed. He hadn't even attempted to remove his clothes.

"Am I what?" The fake innocence in his voice was ridiculous.

"You haven't..."

"Come? Nope."

I twisted onto my side, mirroring his position. "Is that another of your kinks? Delayed gratification or something?"

He leaned in, brushing his lips over mine. "Nah. I was fully satisfied tasting your cum on my lips, hearing you scream the fucking building down, and feeling your sweet pussy clamp down on my fingers like a vise."

"No sex then?"

He chuckled. "I'm a gentleman, Bliss. I don't fuck on the first date."

I raised one eyebrow. "Never?" I found that hard to believe.

"Can't fuck on a first date if you don't date."

"Oh." That made more sense. Why date someone when you had a clubhouse full of women throwing themselves at you every night? "This technically isn't a date though. I came with Rebel."

"You came on my tongue. This totally counts as a date. 'Cause, baby girl? Next time we go out it'll be our second date. If I had you screaming like I did just now, and that's date one behavior, wait until you see what date two will get you."

24

BLISS

*R*ebel's hand hitting me square in the boob woke me from my hangover-induced slumber.

"Your fucking phone, Dis. I swear, you are not sleeping at my place ever again if you're gonna get calls at this time of morning."

She was curled up in her bed next to me, a pink silk eye mask crooked on her face, her short hair sticking up in every possible direction.

I squinted in the bright sunlight and then rolled over, groping blindly around the floor for my phone. When I found it, my eyes widened at the time. "It's midday. Shit. We wasted a whole morning."

"Sleeping is never wasted time. But you're gonna find yourself permanently sleeping if you do not answer that phone. What the hell is that ringtone? It sounds like something out of *Hannah Montana*."

I shoved her, and she buried her head beneath the covers while I hit the answer button.

"Morning, Sandra."

"Bethany-Melissa! You're alive! I've been worried sick."

I rubbed at my sleep-dry eyes. "Uh, why?"

"Caleb said you were too sick to attend last night, so I've been calling to check on you, but when you didn't answer, I imagined all sorts of horrid things. I was about to start calling the hospitals."

I ground my teeth. Caleb still hadn't told everyone we were broken up, even after everything Nash had said? I was so done with this. "Are you free for lunch?"

Sandra hesitated. "Well, yes... But no offense. I don't want to bring you chicken soup. I love you and all, but I don't do illness. Not even for you."

That was hardly surprising. I might have known Sandra for years, and I knew she cared about me in her own way, but making someone soup or holding their hair back while they puked or anything else that could be deemed gross or domestic was out of her skill set.

"I'm not sick. I'll explain, but can you meet me somewhere for lunch? I need to talk."

"Sure, the club?"

I grinned, an idea forming. Might as well throw her in the deep end. "A club. Yes. But not the country club. I'll send you a drop pin and meet you out the front. See you in an hour?"

"I'll be there."

I hung up and opened my map app, ready to drop directions to Sandra's phone.

"Did you just invite your country club buddies to Psychos?" Rebel mumbled from beneath the blankets.

"Just one of them."

"Guess I'm getting outta bed then, because I ain't missing the look on her face for nothing."

$\mathcal{I}$ met Sandra out in front of Psychos, and as Rebel had predicted, the look on her face was hilarious. I waved when she pulled up, but her hand didn't lift from the steering wheel. Fighting back laughter, I walked over and tapped on the window.

She lowered it a crack. "What in the name of all things holy are we doing here? Have you been abducted and need help? Are your kidnappers just on a smoke break or something?"

I snorted. "What? Of course not. Get out and come in."

She shook her head furiously. "Oh no. No-no-no. Are you doing porn in there? Is it a porn studio? You aren't going to ask me to be an extra, are you? I heard the rumors about your dad's company, but I didn't believe it was true. Honey! I can spot you some cash if you need it, you don't have to turn to selling yourself like this."

"Sandra!" I didn't know whether to laugh or roll my eyes. From anyone else I would have assumed they were joking, but I had a feeling Sandra was dead serious. "It's not a porn studio. It's a bar."

"With a deranged clown on the door." She rolled the window a little lower and glanced around like someone might mug her at any moment. "Why on earth would you bring me some place like this? In Saint View, of all places. I saw a homeless person on the way in!"

"Oh, the horror," I said dryly.

This was probably what I'd been like the first time I'd come here too. At least internally, if not verbally. It was a wonder Nash and Rebel had been as kind to me as they had, because if I was half as obnoxious as Sandra was being right now, then they really should have just booted me out the door on my ass.

Slowly, like she was being held at gunpoint, she climbed out of the car. I winced at her smart pantsuit and jacket. It looked completely out of place next to the jeans and tee I'd worn to the party last night. I'd showered at Rebel's apartment, but I hadn't had time to go home and change.

She took in my outfit at the same time and cringed. I couldn't blame her though, when I'd just done the same thing to her. I pushed it aside, because she was the best friend I had and because she was the biggest gossip I knew. I'd learned early never to tell her my secrets. Not after I'd told her about my crush on Bobby Ornith in seventh grade. The entire school had known before lunch, and Bobby had rather publicly announced that he didn't date fat chicks.

He'd been the boy who didn't want to hold my hand.

So in the end, she had done me a favor, showing me that my affections were misplaced on a someone who could be that awful. But I'd never told her anything super personal since.

It worked in my favor now though. I dragged her inside the bar, ignoring her shocked gasp.

This was only the bar side. Imagine if I'd drawn back the curtain and revealed the door to where the parties were held. She would have immediately got to ordering a billboard to make sure everyone knew.

"Bethany-Melissa," she whispered loudly. "This place is terrifying. That man is staring at us."

I glanced over and grinned at Vincent, standing silently at one side of the room. He'd started the day before, but I hadn't been working. "That's just Vincent. He wouldn't hurt a fly."

"He looks like he pulls the wings off flies for fun!" she hissed.

I totally didn't agree. But maybe it was because I'd first met him as a childcare worker, and I'd seen how gentle and intelligent he was. But today, Vincent was dressed all in black, right down to his shitkicker boots. He didn't smile. He had his arms crossed over his chest, his biceps popping, and his gaze a little too focused on me. He probably did look intimidating, but I knew he was the man who'd sat in my bathroom and never once sneaked a peek. He was the man who played Spider-Man with four-year-olds for hours, because he secretly kinda liked Spider-Man too.

And he was the man I'd kissed so softly a couple of nights ago. The one who'd kissed me back so gently and tentatively it had curled my toes.

I smiled, just thinking about his kiss. I knew better than to think that whatever I'd done with War last night was something that could turn into a relationship. I was too newly out of one to even consider it anyway. But my date with Vincent had me looking forward to when I was ready. I wouldn't ask him to wait for me, of course, but maybe if he were still single in a couple of months...

I dragged my attention away from Psychos' new body-guard and forced it to stay on my friend. She still stared at Vincent with a mixture of terror and awe, and I had to snap my fingers in front of her face to get her attention. "Sandra! Focus."

"Right." She squinted at me. "What on?"

"I wasn't sick last night. Caleb and I broke up."

Her mouth dropped open. "Is your fever so high you lost your mind?"

"Like I said, not sick."

Her blue eyes were round, and her perfect eyebrows had inched up on her forehead. "Caleb didn't say a word!"

"He's...not taking it well."

Her eyes widened. "Wait, are you saying you dumped him?"

I nodded.

"Why on earth would you do something like that? He's handsome. Wealthy. Influential. He's the perfect man."

Caleb was about the furthest thing from the perfect man. But it was degrading to think about all the abuse I'd put up with from him. And not just the big stuff, like when he hit me and raped me. It was all the little things. The never saying thank you when I made him a meal. The complete disinterest in my pleasure in the bedroom. The way he never introduced me by name to his colleagues. I was always just expected to be there in the background, smiling and waiting patiently on him to throw me a scrap of attention.

I'd thought that was the way relationships were. It was how Sandra and her husband were.

I'd thought the money was important enough that I could overlook all his flaws. I certainly had enough flaws that I could be tolerant of other people's.

But I'd never hit someone.

I'd never forced myself on them just to hurt them.

I'd never cheated.

"Nobody is perfect," I murmured. I wasn't going to rehash it all for Sandra. It was embarrassing to admit I'd put up with it for as long as I had and painful to constantly go over it. "But we're done. I gave back his ring."

Her mouth formed an O. "I can't believe this. I thought you two were next on the wedding train. Poor Caleb. He must be devastated. What other secrets have you been keeping all this time?"

I tried to keep my features schooled into something that didn't give away how I really felt about 'poor' Caleb. Caleb would act the victim anyway. I might as well get used to it.

"Actually, there is more. I've left the daycare center—"

"Oh good, you working there was really so unnecessary. I never understood why you bothered." She clapped her hands together. "Ooh! We can play tennis during the day now!"

I shook my head. "Actually, no. I have another job."

"Already? Boo. That's no fun. Where?"

"Here."

"In...Saint View? Is it a children's charity or something?" Her face wrinkled like the very mention of Saint View was dirty.

"No, I mean here, in this club."

"You're waitressing?"

I shrugged. "I own the place. So yeah, waitressing. Pouring drinks. Cleaning. Doing admin. Whatever needs doing."

She stared at me. "Why would you buy a bar in Saint View?"

"I inherited it when my brother died."

She held a hand up, her expression flickering through so many different emotions I couldn't keep up. "Okay, start talking. What brother? Clearly not Everett."

I launched into the tale, telling her everything in detail, about how Axel and I shared a mother but had different fathers. I told her how he and Nash had always looked out for me, and how after he died, I inherited the bar.

Sandra quit interrupting me every five seconds and listened to the entire story with huge eyes, like she was watching a movie with a killer plot twist that had her glued to her seat.

I sipped at my drink, needing it after talking for so long.

Sandra used the opportunity to get a question in. "So it had to be the best friend, right? Wow. This is better than the true crime shows on Netflix."

I frowned. "What do you mean?"

"We're playing 'Whodunit', right? I've watched enough of this stuff to know the murderer is always known to the victim. There's no way this was a random gang thing, just for shits and giggles." She sat back, crossing her arms beneath her breasts. "I've got my money on the best friend. What did you say his name was? Nate?"

"Nash."

"Him for sure. You mark my words."

Irritation prickled at the back of my neck. I clenched my fingers around the tabletop and squeezed hard so it had somewhere to go. Sandra was so off base it wasn't funny. "No way. Nash loved Axel."

"Murderers usually do."

"Nash is not a murderer, Sandra!"

I hadn't meant to yell it. But it echoed around the quiet bar. Rebel and Vincent both looked in my direction. Vincent's gaze burned me, unspoken questions in his eyes, but I quietly shook my head, trying to let him know that it was all fine.

"Sorry," I muttered to Sandra. "I didn't mean to yell."

"It's fine. It's hard to hear the truth. But think about it. You need means, motive, and opportunity, right? Means —the man lives in Saint View. Guns are a dime a dozen. No problem there. Opportunity—"

"He was here the night Axel died. Working."

"He was at Psychos when *you* got here that night. He was also very conveniently around to take you right to the murder scene and act the devastated best friend for the cops. How far is Axel's place from here?"

"Five minutes."

"So it's pretty feasible that Nash could have disappeared from a crowded bar for ten minutes on the guise of a smoke break. Nobody would have noticed. Are there cameras in here?"

"No."

"Then he has no real proof he was here all night, does he?"

This was ridiculous. "Nash didn't do this. You don't know him. He wouldn't."

She pointed a finger at me. "And your feelings for him make you too close to him to have an objective eye."

I didn't comment on her observation of how I felt about Nash. "What's his motivation then?"

She shrugged. "Could be anything. Jealousy over the bar. You said they ran this place together, like co-owners. Maybe Nash was pissed that Axel hadn't signed over half of it. Maybe Axel slept with his girlfriend. Or ran over his puppy. I don't know, people kill for all sorts of stupid reasons as well as big ones. But don't you think you should find out?"

I shook my head. "Axel was involved in more than Nash or I knew. It had to have been a deal gone bad."

Sandra lifted a shoulder. "Maybe. But are you really comfortable working here with Nash when he might have been the one to put a bullet in your brother's head?"

25

BLISS

*N*ash and I moved around each other for the next few days without talking much. I busied myself with creating a new lunch menu with one of the Psychos bartenders, who also had some experience working in a kitchen. But George had picked out some problems with my plans for a full lunch service, a proper coffee machine, and loyalty cards.

"This ain't Starbucks, Bliss. You think War and his guys are gonna come in here, handing over their little pink cards to get a hole punched?"

He had a point. "Okay, fine. The loyalty cards might be a bit much, but nothing wrong with offering something other than stale peanuts to eat, right? We want to encourage people to stay here longer. They currently can't do that because they have to go elsewhere to get a proper meal. War and the guys already have a bar at their compound. We have to offer more than what they can get there."

George nodded his bald head. "I like it. I'll go shopping if you can get the menus printed?"

I was so excited that he liked my ideas that I swept the poor, startled man into my arms and hugged him. "Yes! Nash will hate it, I'm sure. But if you're on board, I'll get the menus printed this week, and we can launch the new menu on Monday."

George untangled himself from my embrace and got busy with a pen and paper, scribbling down meal ideas and the ingredients he'd need for them. He had a little smile on his lips, and I liked that. I had a feeling he was pleased about his role at Psychos expanding. I wanted that for all the staff. I wanted them to feel like this place was their home and be proud and excited to come to work. Which meant treating them well and paying more than I had to.

I wanted all those things, but they all took money.

With that taken care of, I turned my attention to the party I'd decided we were having on Friday night. My breath got quick whenever I thought about it. I wasn't sure if it was because of the things I'd see once it got rolling or because I knew it would bring in the last of the money I needed. This party would mean I could pay Axel's drug supplier as well as start putting some more of my new plans into place. They were plans I hadn't confessed to Nash or to anyone really. But I was itching for the meeting with our drug supplier to take place at the end of the month, despite the terror I still felt when I remembered the man's finger crawling over my skin.

I was going to ask him to double our quantity. We needed more. I wanted a party every weekend. If not twice a weekend. Once or twice a month with no consistency wasn't enough. I'd already organized the performers, and they were all in, grateful for the regular work. But a huge side of the business was the drugs. People needed a little extra something to get them going, and a couple of tabs of E or a little bag of coke wouldn't kill anyone. There would be nothing more than that done on my premises, but I wanted people to let loose and have a good time.

And spend big.

Nash wouldn't like it, but he could lump it. He'd barely spoken to me since he'd snatched the phone from my hand and told Caleb where to go. Caleb hadn't called since, so I was grateful, but Nash was making the entire thing awkward.

Or maybe we both were.

Sandra's warning that murders were normally carried out by someone close to the victim kept ringing in my head.

Nash was the closest person to Axel.

I just couldn't picture it. I couldn't come up with a reason for something to come between them enough that Nash would do that.

I wandered back out to the bar area, instantly feeling Vincent's gaze on me from where he stood in the doorway. I'd offered him a stool a hundred times since he'd started working here, but he'd refused every time, preferring to stand, his dark-eyed gaze constantly moving around the room but always returning to me.

I liked it. I liked having him here. He was infinitely better at his job than Solomon had been, though the party on Friday night would be a true test of Vincent's newfound bodyguarding skills.

Dragging my gaze off the man who looked entirely too good in all black, I found Rebel restocking beer bottles into a refrigerator. "Is it just you out here? Where's Nash?"

She shrugged. "Boss Man said he had to run out for a bit. It's quiet so we don't need him 'til later. If you're searching for something to do, he put some boxes on his desk for the party on Friday night that he said you need to go through."

"What are they?"

She shrugged, not really paying attention to me. "No idea. Something he found out back, I think."

Curious, I left her to her restocking. In Nash's office, I found the boxes she was talking about. The label on the front simply said, Quantity: 500. "Well, there's a lot of something in here," I mumbled.

The boxes were unsealed, but the flaps were tucked into each other, closing their contents off to dust. I opened the first one, pushing back the thick cardboard to reveal the contents.

Inside was a sea of black silk. I reached in, unsure of what I was looking at, and then pulled one out.

A mask. They were blindfold-shaped, long rectangular pieces of material, but with holes cut for they eyes. A Psychos logo was embroidered into the end.

"Haven't seen those for a while," Rebel commented from the doorway, paused there with a box of drinks in her arms. She shifted the weight to her side, jutting out her hip like she was holding a baby.

"What are they? I mean, I can see they're masks. But what are they for and why do we have so many of them?"

Rebel grinned. "We haven't done it for a couple of

months, but we used to give them out at parties. Everybody wore one. Then took it home as a little souvenir."

"Did people like that?

She shrugged. "Axel thought they would. It's sexy. It adds to the mystery. I mean, it's not like they really conceal anyone's identity, but you can kind of pretend for a minute, can't you? It gives people a sense of bravery they might not otherwise have when they don't have anything to hide behind. And the whole aim of our game is to get people dropping those inhibitions so they spend more money, have more sex, and keep coming back, right?"

I understood completely. I already wanted to be wearing one at the next party. Even though I'd be working, not participating, there was a safety in being a little anonymous. "There's so many here. We should definitely start using them again."

"Agreed." Then a smile spread across her face. "Axel fucked up the initial order. He meant to order a thousand. But then ten thousand arrived. The company wouldn't take them back because they were personalized. He was so cranky. I'd bet there's tons more boxes of them out back somewhere."

I smiled at the imagined image of my brother standing helplessly by as box after box of sex club masks were unloaded off a truck.

I turned back to the box. "How many do you think we'll need for Friday?"

She shrugged. "Anywhere from three to six hundred? It depends on the night really."

I eyed the box critically. "I'm going to count how many is in this open box so we can be prepared. And think up some sort of display for them so everyone can take one as they enter."

"Have fun. I've got more drinks to deal with, so I'll leave you to it."

"Thanks."

When she left, I squinted at the box critically. Design and aesthetics were not really my thing, but I wanted it to look nice. And handing them out of a brown cardboard box was not going to fly. I dumped them out onto Nash's desk, thinking again how much I needed an office of my own. Nash was going to kill me when he saw the mess I was making.

The masks tumbled out, a piece of paper fluttering after them. I picked it up, turning it over to see the writing, and then laughed. It was the invoice from the company who'd made the masks. "That definitely says ten thousand in the quantity section, Axel. Not 1000. You really should have checked your order before you hit send."

My heart gave a little squeeze, realizing this was as close as I'd ever get to talking to my brother again. I was about to put the paper back into the box when Axel's email address caught my eye.

The police had seized all of Axel's possessions from the club in the days after his death. His house was still locked up as a murder scene under investigation, until whenever the gang task force got around to Axel's case, so I hadn't been able to get in there yet to search through any of his things.

But this email address was web based. I hadn't thought much about it until now, because it's not like he would have just been sending emails back and forth with drug dealers.

But he clearly did have an email he used.

I glanced out of the doorway, but Nash was still nowhere to be seen. Shoving aside the masks, I uncovered Nash's laptop but was halted at the sign-in page. I didn't know his password.

I pulled out my phone instead, bringing up the email website's login page. I hesitated for a second, because trying to break into someone's email didn't sit well with me. But neither did the notion that Nash might not be what he seemed. And maybe Axel's emails would hold some sort of clue as to what had been going on in his life.

I desperately wanted to know.

So I pushed aside the part of me screaming that this wasn't morally right.

Neither was selling drugs or running a sex club, but those lines had already been crossed. Might as well jump a few more.

"Okay, username or email. That one is easy." I copied out the email address from the top of the invoice and then sat back, staring at the password field.

The cursor blinked at me accusingly.

"If I were Axel, what password would I choose? Maybe something to do with football." I knew he'd played in school for Saint View High, so I plugged in their team name, plus a couple of variations. They all came back with a red "Incorrect password or username" message.

"Okay, fine. Not football. What about Psychos..."

That was a no-go too.

"What's the password, Axel?" I drummed my fingers on the desktop.

It jogged a memory loose in my head.

"You need to say the magic password to get those candies."

"Sandwiches!"

With trembling fingers, I typed it in.

Axel's email opened in front of me. "Oh my God. I can't believe that worked." I glanced up at the ceiling, like Axel might be lurking up there somewhere. "I really hope your bank account passwords were harder to crack than that one."

Though I knew that not just anyone would have guessed it. Only me, him, and Nash had been there that night in the tent where I'd forgotten my manners because I was desperately hungry.

Axel's inbox had a red circle around the number 1587, and I cringed at the number of unread emails. "I don't think even death excuses an inbox this out of control."

I scrolled through the main inbox page, reading the titles of emails and not finding anything all that interesting.

It wasn't until I was four pages of unread emails in, that I found one that caught my eye.

I clicked on it to open it.

———

Dear Mr. Fuller.

Thank you for meeting with us earlier today. We appreciate the opportunity to assist you with the sale of your business. Please find attached our rates and charges. If you have any questions, please forward them at your earliest convenience. We'd be happy to assist.

Regards,
High Street Real Estate.

—

I checked the date on the email.

Two days before his death.

A sinking feeling washed over me.

With a nauseating gut instinct, I searched Nash's name in Axel's emails. It brought up a whole list of results. Some just silly things, like memes and YouTube videos they'd passed back and forth between them. But there were a ton of automatic bank receipts too. They were all addressed to Axel's email, but Nash's name was listed as the owner of the receiving bank account, which was why they'd shown up in the search.

There was one for every month, going back as far as I could find.

I sucked in a breath when I saw how much each transaction was for. It was far more money than his salary.

If Axel sold Psychos, he wouldn't have had the money to keep paying Nash, surely. I knew how much the business was worth, and it wasn't much. What if Nash had found out? What if they'd argued, and it had escalated into something more? I had no idea why Axel would even want to sell the business or why he'd be paying Nash so much money, but the proof of it was right there in front of me.

A more sinister thought crept into my mind.

What if the man who'd come to my room wearing a mask in the middle of the night and demanding his monthly payment had actually been Nash? These payments were regular as clockwork, one a month, just like he'd demanded when he'd told me he didn't run credit.

I shivered, remembering the man's threats to take his payment out on my body if I didn't produce the money.

"Jesus, Bliss. Could you have made any more of a mess in here?"

I snapped my head up, frantically jabbing at the buttons on my phone, trying to get Axel's bank account receipts off it. "What? Sorry! I'll clean it up." I shot to my feet, shoving my phone quickly into my pocket.

Nash leaned on the doorway, a grin on his face. "You were watching porn, huh?"

"No!"

"Mmm-hmm. Sure. It's okay, Bliss. Nothing wrong with a little porn to get you through the working day."

My heart pounded. But standing in front of me, Nash was as charming and handsome and harmless-looking as always.

I was letting my head get away from me. So I glared at him, just like I would have if I hadn't seen those things on Axel's email.

He chuckled. "Sorry. I forgot you rich uptight people think it's dirty and forbidden."

"We don't think that. We just—I just—don't watch it personally."

His teeth dug into his bottom lip. "Never?"

"No!"

"You realize how ridiculous that sounds, right? You own a sex club."

"I own a dive bar."

"That throws sex parties after hours. You own a sex club, Bliss."

"Fine. That doesn't mean I have to watch porn." I was more flustered from getting caught than from admitting I didn't watch guys ramming their massive dicks down some poor woman's throat. But I didn't want him questioning me any further.

Nash sniggered. "Why bother when you can watch it live, right?"

I rolled my eyes, picked up my box of masks, and tried to get past him. "I'll take these out to the tables then. I don't want to be in your way."

Nash lifted the box from my hands and set it down at his feet. "I've got a better idea." He held out his hand to me. "Come."

I bristled at the demand. "Do you talk to all the ladies like they're dogs?"

He took a step closer, staring down at me, his gorgeous blue eyes pinning me to the spot. "Normally when I tell women to come, they're naked in my bed and begging me to let them."

A wildfire erupted around us. Or maybe it was just inside me, but it consumed my body in a second.

Nash chuckled and put his hand beneath my chin. "You ain't ever heard of delayed gratification, Bliss?"

I had. I'd accused War of being into it. I just hadn't ever thought about it in conjunction with Nash.

Though it would now be all I thought about from

today until the end of eternity. I was sure my face was burning.

Nash took pity on me and picked up my hand, pulling me out of the office. "Come on. I really do want to show you something."

I followed him dumbly to the secret door. Vincent's gaze dropped to Nash's hand around mine. He took a step to follow, but Nash called back over his shoulder, "No dangers back here, bud. Watch the bar."

Vincent didn't seem at all happy about that, but his gaze focused on me. "Bliss?"

I bit my lip. It was so hard to look at Nash and suspect anything bad when he still had the face of my childhood hero. But the building was huge. And this door was soundproof. If I went down there with Nash and something did happen, nobody would hear me yell for help.

The things I'd found on Axel's computer could paint a nasty picture if I let them.

I hated that Sandra had me thinking all these things.

But I didn't want to be that woman in the horror movie who followed a guy into the dark.

My gravestone would not read "Too Stupid to Live."

"Wait a sec," I said to Nash, disentangling my hand from his. I went to Vincent and pulled his head down, putting mine on the opposite side so Nash wouldn't see my lips moving. "Keep the door open," I whispered in his ear.

I let him go, and he straightened, his dark gaze boring through mine. His eyes were full of questions, his entire body tense, but he stood rooted to the spot while I followed Nash through the secret door. I glanced back over my shoulder at him, and he nodded ever so slightly.

"Something going on with you two?" Nash asked, fumbling around on the wall of the main room for the light switch. He found it, and yellow light flooded the windowless room.

It was completely innocent-looking right now, in the middle of the day, the last party long cleaned up and done. The couches were all in their rightful places, the cages dismantled and stowed away. The bar was clean, and Rebel had refilled all the drinks in the glass-fronted refrigerators, ready for Friday night.

"Me and Vincent?" I raised a shoulder. "That's not really any of your business."

"It is if you're both working here." His voice was strained.

"Is there a workplace rule about colleagues dating?" I knew full well that there was no such thing. And even if there were, I could have terminated it in a second.

He glowered at me.

"Didn't think so. Careful, Nash. You sound jealous."

He dragged his gaze away. "You're too young for me, Bliss. You don't want to go there."

The words slipped out of my mouth before I could even stop them. "Says who?"

He spun around so quick I had no time to react. In a second, he had my back to the wall, caged between his arms. His nose ran up the side of my neck while he inhaled. "You have no idea of the things I'm into."

"Try me," I whispered back, instantly forgetting everything Sandra had been filling my head with.

His gaze dropped to my lips, and he let out a groan, pressing his body against mine.

He was hard. So very hard it took my breath away.

The door slammed open, and Vincent rushed through.

"What the fuck?" Nash jolted back.

I held a hand up to Vincent in a stop motion. "I'm okay."

He stopped instantly, halting in his tracks. His gaze flickered between the two of us. "He's not hurting you?"

The growl that started up in Nash's chest was feral and angry. "What the fuck do you mean? Of course I'm not hurting her!" His gaze tore to mine. "What is this? You're scared of being alone with me?"

I shook my head, instantly knowing how stupid I'd been to let my imagination get away from me. "No, no. I'm not."

Nash's hurt expression gutted me. "Yeah, you clearly were. Enough that you had your guard dog follow us in. What the fuck did I do, Bliss?"

I couldn't bear the expression on his face. I felt awful. I knew in that moment that no matter what Sandra thought, and no matter what Axel's emails had said, Nash wasn't the one who'd killed Axel. "Nothing! Nothing! I just let someone get in my head, and it all got confused, and then I found some emails about the money Axel was paying you..."

Nash staggered back, running a hand through his hair. "This is about that stupid money? Why didn't you just ask me?"

"I was going to!"

He narrowed his eyes. "Sure you were. Right after you took out a restraining order? Not that it's any of your business, but I never even wanted that money. A while back, I did a stint in jail. Axel started paying me when I got out to make up for the money I didn't earn while I was inside. Plus some."

I blinked. "Why would he do that?"

"To ease his guilt. It was his fault I went away. Or so he believed anyway. I tried telling him a hundred times to get over it, and that he would have done it for me too. But he needed the money to make it right in his own head."

"He let you take the fall?"

"More like Nash fell on a sword for him," Rebel said from the doorway.

I hadn't even heard her come in. She didn't seem too pleased with me, and I couldn't blame her.

Nash shook his head. "I wasn't innocent. We were young and stupid. We were both in the wrong, but there wasn't any point to both of us doing time for it."

I had to try to explain myself. I hated the disappointed expression on his face. "Axel was going to sell Psychos. I found an email from a broker. He would have stopped paying you. That gives you..."

It all sounded so stupid now when I wasn't all wrapped up in my own fears.

Nash's eyes flashed. "Motive? Is that where you're going with this, Bliss?" He leaned hard on the door behind him. "Jesus fuck. Anything else you want to accuse me of? Rape? Torture? How about global fucking warming?"

He was so angry. And it was mixed with a healthy dose of hurt and betrayal.

Tears pricked the backs of my eyes. "I'm sorry."

"Yeah, me too." He twisted the doorknob behind him and let it swing open. "Here. This is what I brought you back here for." He turned and glared at Vincent. "Not to fucking attack her."

He stormed from the room, back into the bar. Rebel gave me a sad look but followed after him, which told me she was upset with me too.

That left me with Vincent. "I'm sorry. I owe you an apology, too. I really messed that all up. I'll talk to Nash and explain. He won't make things hard for you here."

Vincent shook his head. "I don't care about that. As long as you aren't hurt."

I put my hand on his chest. "I'm not. I swear."

Vincent hovered, but I just wanted to be alone.

"Can I have a minute, please?" I asked.

"I'll wait by the main door."

I thanked him and watched him walk away. Embarrassment and guilt washed over me. I couldn't stop seeing the hurt on Nash's face.

I'd make it up to him. I'd grovel and beg forgiveness.

I didn't want things to be weird between us. Not when we were running this business together.

I stepped into the little room Nash had opened up and gasped. The walls had been freshly painted a soft pink, the chemical scent from the paint still lingering. A stained wooden desk sat in the very center of the room with a small love seat pressed to one side. The room was full of natural light courtesy of a skylight, which made up for the fact there was no window, and it fell over a couple of indoor plants in rose-gold-colored pots. A little pink name plate sat on the desk, and when I picked it up, I almost burst into tears.

Boss Girl was printed in gold lettering.

He'd made me an office.

A beautiful one that was me through and through. It was perfect. It was right by where all the main action happened on the party side, just like his office was right where all the action happened on the bar side.

I wanted to cry looking at it.

I'd been working so hard to change. I didn't want to be a sheltered, naïve, stuck-up woman from Providence who let her fiancé hurt her and her best friend fill her head with elitist rubbish. I didn't want to be the sort of person who jumped to conclusions about a man who'd done nothing but help and watch out for me.

Nash had seen what I needed and given it to me without even asking.

All I'd given him were unfounded accusations and a blatant lack of trust and respect.

"I'll earn it back," I promised the silent room. "I swear, I'll earn it back."

26

BLISS

I was going to throw up.

That was the overwhelming gut reaction I'd had all evening while I counted the clock down to midnight, when the party would begin. One minute I was hot and sweaty, the next I was cold and clammy. I couldn't settle down. I gravitated between the bar and the hidden back rooms, checking and checking again that everything was in place and ready.

"You're making me dizzy with your pacing," Vincent commented from his spot by the door.

I grimaced at him. "Sorry. I'm getting in the way, aren't I?"

He shook his head. "No, but why are you so worried? Nash and Rebel have done this many times before. So have all the other staff."

"But I haven't," I wailed, sidling up next to him. "The outfit I'm wearing is very skimpy."

His dark-eyed gaze rolled over my jeans and Psychos

T-shirt. "Your arms are bare, I suppose. But it's hardly revealing."

I laughed. "I'm not wearing this once the party starts." I wondered whether to tell him about the outfit I had planned but then decided I'd just surprise him.

Nothing had happened between us since our first date and kiss. But Vincent followed me around everywhere, glaring at anyone who so much as dared to glance in my direction.

Nash had continued to call him my guard dog, but as far as I was concerned, Vincent was doing exactly what I paid him to do. It wasn't just me he looked out for. He watched Rebel cautiously when patrons got too rowdy. He'd only had to step in once, and Rebel had kissed his cheek and told him he was the sweetest.

Vincent's cheeks had stayed red for an hour after that.

He was protective of all my employees. Even Nash. Not that Nash would let himself notice.

He was still hurt over Wednesday night.

I couldn't blame him. I knew I had to give him time.

At eleven thirty, I did two shots of tequila, knocking them back hard and fast because I needed the Dutch courage. Then I went into my beautiful new office and sat at my desk. With my palms flat on the desktop and the door locked, I took three deep breaths.

I didn't have to do this.

But a part of me wanted to. I'd felt sexy and wanted in my black ripped-up dress last time. I'd liked the way people—especially War and Nash—had looked at me in it.

War was going to be here again tonight, and I wanted to look good. For him, but also for me. Rebel was planning on nude waitressing again, but I couldn't do that. I didn't have her confidence. But I pulled out the bottom drawer of my desk and lifted out the Victoria's Secret bag with trembling fingers.

Inside was the most beautiful piece of lingerie I'd ever seen. I lifted it from the tissue paper it was wrapped in and took a deep breath. "Are you seriously going to wear that, in public?" I murmured.

But it was either that or jeans. I hadn't brought any other options because I knew I'd wimp out and take them.

"Just do it. You'll fit right in. You know this. Nobody is going to stop and stare and be like, 'OMG! Bliss is in her underwear!' when they're all in theirs, or less, too."

I was glad I was alone for the pep talk. Because it was embarrassingly lame. I was a twenty-five-year-old woman. I could own this. If Rebel could get her gear off entirely, I could strut my stuff out there in a sexy outfit that was no more revealing than a bathing suit.

Determined, I toed my shoes and socks off, placing them neatly in the bottom drawer. My jeans went next and then my shirt.

I was down to my underwear and suddenly paralyzed.

"Bliss?" Vincent's voice came through the door with an accompanying knock.

I yelped, covering myself with my hands. Then realized that was stupid, because the door was locked. "Yes?" I called back.

"Whatever you're wearing, you'll look beautiful."

I slumped, my hands falling away from my body.

I was tempted to throw the door open and kiss him. It

had been exactly what I needed to hear. Just one person to say I looked great.

Vincent didn't lie. He didn't tell people what they wanted to hear.

When he gave a compliment, he truly meant it.

"Thank you," I said quietly through the closed door.

"You're welcome."

I shed my boring, cotton, everyday underwear and slipped on the midnight-blue panties. They cut halfway across my ass, full enough to provide some coverage and not ride up, but cute and cheeky at the same time. There was no bra. It was more of a lace tank top that plunged deep between my breasts. In the light of my office, it was sheer enough to show a hint of nipple, though once the lights were off in the club, I knew that wouldn't be noticeable.

But the parts I found sexiest were the thigh-high stockings and the little belts and clips that held the entire outfit together. They were tight across my thighs and held the top from moving out of place.

I blew out a shaking breath and then put the lingerie out of my mind. It was done, and I needed to move on to hair and makeup. The last two things I added were my favorite pair of heels, ones I knew I'd be able to work in for hours without getting a blister, and my mask.

I slid it over my eyes, fastening it in place behind my head. My hair fell in soft waves over my shoulders.

I was done. Ready to begin the party.

There was the urge to vomit again.

I opened the door anyway.

Vincent was still standing on the other side, guarding

it like there were thousands of screaming fans trying to break it down.

He turned around. "Are you ready..."

His eyes flared, and unashamedly, his gaze rolled down my body. The lights weren't out yet, so I knew he was getting a little more than everybody else would, but that felt okay, because he already owned a little part of me. After what he'd done for me with Caleb, and then our kiss...

I wanted him to think I was beautiful.

I was desperately terrified he wouldn't.

"What do you think?" I whispered.

"What are you wearing?"

Every time someone had said that to me in the past, it had been with scorn. *"What are you wearing, Bethany-Melissa? Your arms are really too fat for that. Go put something with sleeves on."*

When Vincent said it, it was with awe.

"Do you like it?" I asked.

"Very much."

I beamed at him, confidence filling me up and over-flowing. I handed him a mask. "Come on, let's get this show on the road.

---

*T*he wall sconces glowed yellow around the room so there was enough light to see by, but not so much people couldn't hide in the shadows. Heavy bass thumped through the club, the DJ we'd hired playing pump-up music in the hopes of getting people geared up and excited to party.

It was early, so the performers in their cages were still in the tame beginnings of their acts. They danced seductively, running their hands over their bodies while the room filled.

I hid away behind the bar with Rebel and the other staff, my heart in my mouth.

Rebel, in her panties and nipple covers, leaned on the counter, watching the crowd of people stream in. "Turnout looks good, Dis. We're filling up fast. You ready to make some money?"

I was so ready to make some money. With days until my end-of-month meeting, tonight had to go well. I needed the cold hard cash in my hand.

I picked up my tray of champagne flutes and balanced them carefully on my arm. The shining gold bubbles glimmered in the lights, and Rebel and I took to the room, going in opposite directions, offering every person a complimentary glass to get the party started.

Everyone wore the Psychos masks they'd been handed at the door, and I loved the added element of mystery it brought the room. People mingled in small groups, talking and chatting like they would have at any normal club, some taking to the floor to dance while they sipped their drinks. Others headed straight for the cages, staking out positions in the front row, knowing what would soon be coming once the crowd was warmed up.

One couple made a beeline for the corridor where my office was, disappearing into the darkness with a key dangling from a gold chain. Nash passed me by, and I nodded in their direction.

"What's with the keys?" I asked.

"They're for the private rooms. People book them on

entry, and they get a key to use whenever they want throughout the night."

"Oh, right." I knew there were rooms back there, of course. I'd seen them when I'd wandered around. "I just assumed they were for private lap dances. Or for when people got so turned on they couldn't wait to get home. I didn't think people would be practically running down there the minute they got here. Seems to kind of defeat the purpose of a sex party. Like, isn't the point to have sex where people can watch you?"

Nash raised an eyebrow. "Fuck. I forget how innocent you are or I would have deliberately shown you before this. I just assumed you knew. Come here."

My tray was empty anyway, and I needed a refill, so it wouldn't matter if I disappeared from the main floor for a moment. I followed him down the corridor, and he paused at the room the couple had disappeared into. The door was painted black, like the rest of the corridor.

"Notice anything about the door?"

I shrugged. "It's black?"

He put a hand to the little metal peephole covering. "It has a peephole. Except instead of people seeing out, people can see—"

I blushed. "In. Okay, right. Gotcha."

I hovered for a second. Nash's gaze flickered over me. His tongue pressed to the side of his cheek while he studied me. "You want to look, don't you?"

I couldn't help the giggle that escaped me. "Do you?"

He grinned. "Would be insulting not to since they're putting on a show. I mean, they get off on people watching. I'd hate for them to walk away disappointed in their evening."

"You go first."

He slid aside the covering, ducked his head, and peered through.

"Well?"

He turned to me with fake shock on his face. "There's people having sex in there!"

I sniggered and elbowed him out of the way. "Show me."

He stepped to the side, and I took his spot, squinting through the peephole.

There were indeed people having sex in there. I watched for a moment and then crinkled my nose at what I'd seen.

Nash was laughing. "It's not always that sexy, is it?"

I made a face. "It really wasn't! Poor woman. She looked like she was making out her shopping list in her head while he jack-rabbited her."

That was nothing like what I'd witnessed in the main room last time I'd been at one of these parties. "I think I'll stick to the pros."

"Probably a good idea. There's other little delights for you to find in the other rooms, but we should probably check on the party. It'll be filling up quick."

He went to walk away, but I grabbed his arm. "Wait, Nash. Are we okay? After the other day..."

He shrugged. "I'm over it. I was hurt, but I get it. Everyone feels like a suspect. I'd be lying if I said I wasn't looking at people in a different light as well."

His gaze flickered to my breasts for half a second before dragging back up to my face. He grimaced when he realized I'd caught him staring. "Shit, sorry. I swear, I wasn't..."

Except we both knew he was.

"You can look," I whispered.

He groaned and ran his hand through his hair. "Fuck, Bliss. Don't say things like that. Not here."

"Why not here?"

"Because everything is different at these parties. There's no inhibitions. There's no outside world. I could forget you're Axel's little sister and young enough to be my daughter."

"So don't look at me then."

His eyes burned through me. "I fucking want to look at you, Bliss."

His gaze rolled over me, slow and sexy, lingering on my breasts, my hips, my belly, and then the junction of my thighs.

I didn't dare breathe. People milled around us, moving toward rooms with their keys clutched in their hands or sidling up to peepholes to watch what other people did behind them.

But all I cared about was Nash and the way he made me feel. I didn't care that he was older. He was gorgeous and rock-hard beneath his tight T-shirt. His biceps popped. I wanted to stare at him as much as he wanted to stare at me.

He put one hand at the back of my neck and drew me in.

My breath hitched.

His gaze dropped to my lips, and unconsciously, I ran my tongue over them.

His mouth hovered over mine but then changed course, brushing against my ear. "Have sex with someone tonight, Bliss. Because you look way too fucking good in that not to."

I blew out a breath as he pulled back and disappeared into the crowd, leaving me weak and turned on.

Have sex with someone.

Just not him.

It didn't matter that he was attracted to me. I still wasn't enough.

Straightening my shoulders and lifting my chin, I strode back out into the main room. I refilled my tray with drinks, and I did what I'd come here to do.

Work.

Sex was not on the table.

Well, it was. There was a couple going at it right on the table to my left.

But not for me.

27

WAR

"So, we've got everything set for Tuesday. All the clubs have been notified, and everyone is coming."

I glanced over at Hawk while we stood in the line outside of Psychos, waiting to get in. "All of them?"

He cringed and nodded. "Yeah, man. All of them. They should start arriving Sunday."

"Where the hell are we going to put them all?"

Hawk shrugged. "We've got plenty of room for camping. I ordered a couple of those portable toilets with the showers too, 'cause fuck, having everyone trying to use the one bathroom in the clubhouse. That thing would get clogged in about ten minutes flat."

"Food?"

"They'll sort themselves out except for the night of the funeral. I figured we better handle that."

I sucked on my cigarette and let the nicotine smoke fill my lungs. I blew it out so slowly it burned. But it helped relieve the pressure ticking away inside me like a fucking time bomb. "Get Aloha to smoke some meat. Heaps of it. Queenie will get the girls making some sides, but as long as there's meat and beer, that'll keep most people happy." The line inched forward, and I went with it. "I can't believe they're all coming."

"Your old man was well-loved. Everyone wants to pay their respects." Hawk glanced at me. "And..."

"And they want to gawk at how I'm handling being prez."

"Yeah. That."

"Assholes." We were all Slayers. Different chapters of the same club. We were supposed to be one big happy extended family.

We weren't.

Half the men who arrived at our complex this week would shake your hand in one second, then stab you in the back in the next. Literally. Then they'd pull the knife out of your bleeding body, wipe it on their T-shirt, and use it to cut their dinner.

Some would have been genuinely upset to find out about my old man's passing. They'd be here to pay their respects and mourn. But there'd be just as many looking for a weakness.

Because knowing other people's soft spots was the best way to manipulate them into doing what you wanted.

I didn't trust anyone as far as I could throw them. Especially not the men outside my own chapter.

I stubbed my smoke out beneath my boot as we reached the door. "No more club shit tonight, yeah? Let's just have a good time. The rest can wait."

"I'm all for that." Hawk eyed Rebel, standing at the

door with her tits out and her toned, flat belly on display beneath them.

She grinned up at him, holding out two black strips of cloth. "Evening, boys. Ready to have some dirty fun?"

Hawk eyed her little tits with only the nipples covered by stick-on tassels. "Always."

"Mask up then. Keep 'em on all night, or you're out the door."

"You're all of five feet. Good luck throwing anyone out."

I chuckled, nudging Hawk. "You clearly haven't seen Rebel when she's pissed. People run out, just to avoid her wrath."

Rebel beamed like I'd given her a compliment. "I'm so glad you noticed!" Then she scowled at Hawk. "And for the record, if you aren't scared by my wrath, which you really should be, I got my new buddy, Vincent, over there. He's more than willing to throw down."

Hawk and I both glanced over at the new bouncer. He was a lot smaller than the last one, though not a small man by any means. He was over six foot, but he was slimly built, though muscled for sure. He didn't look particularly threatening. He didn't acknowledge our presence with anything other than a steady stare.

"Hey, you got any private room keys left?" I asked Rebel.

She raised an eyebrow but picked up a key from a hook on the wall behind her. It was on a thick gold chain with a little tag that had the number thirteen on it. She dangled it in front of me. "You and Hawk wanna get freaky in private?"

I grinned. "Hey, Hawk. Wanna blow me in private or

out in the middle of the floor where Rebel can watch and get jealous?"

"It'd be like blowing my brother. Hard pass on both the private and public oral sex offer." He rolled his eyes at me. "Thanks so much for thinking of me though."

I shrugged. "Guess I'll have to save it for someone else." I plucked the key from Rebel's fingers and handed over a none-too-small wad of cash for the privilege.

She tucked it away and gave me a wink. "Lucky lady."

"Lucky man." Because if the woman I wanted in that room tonight was up for it, I really was going to be the luckiest son of a bitch in the room.

I hadn't stopped thinking about Bliss all week. My palm tingled with the urge to spank her luscious ass again. I wanted her coming on my tongue and bellowing my name. I couldn't wait to have her riding my dick, but that would come in good time.

I moved into the party, bobbing my head a little with the beats that filled the room. Hawk and I were late, and everything was already in full swing. I shook my head, passing a woman on her knees sucking off two guys. She had her hands wrapped around both their dicks and used her mouth to alternate between them. Farther in, a group of men surrounded a woman they'd stripped naked on a couch. They were pleasuring her in every way possible. Their hands and fingers worked her intimate areas, while she watched on like a queen, not reciprocating in any way. "Good for you, sister," I murmured as I walked by.

"You wanna join in, honey?" She trailed her fingers in my direction.

Any other time I would have. I got off on watching women get off. I fucking loved how their faces changed when they were mid orgasm, blissing out, and there was no better feeling than them dragging their nails down your back and shouting your name when they exploded. "Got other plans, sweetheart. Enjoy though."

She went back to paying attention to her men, and I spotted Bliss at the bar. "Jesus fucking Christ," I muttered, stopping dead in my tracks. My dick instantly went hard, begging to be closer to her.

She was busy at work, taking drink orders, smiling and chatting with people. She'd painted her lips a deep red that I desperately wanted wrapped around my cock. But then she stepped out from behind the bar with her tray of drinks, and I nearly came in my jeans like a fifteen-year-old.

She caught sight of me on her way to a table and detoured in my direction. "You made it."

I almost couldn't speak. Bliss in lingerie, for the entire room to see but not touch? Yes fucking please. I couldn't even pretend to make polite conversation with her. "Your ass is on display."

She gave me an overly innocent grin and then peeked over her shoulder at her behind. "Is it?"

My fingers twitched, but I held them at my sides, knowing the rules. Nobody touched the staff here. That Vincent guy might not be as big as Solomon, but there was something about him that made me not want to cross him. "You asking me to spank you, baby girl? That why you got your ass all out on display for me?"

Her eyes flared, and I would have bet anything she was reliving the other night at the clubhouse, when I'd spanked her ass until it was pink and then made her come on my tongue. I leaned down so my two-day stubble scratched over the side of her face. "I think you chose those panties while thinking about what I did to you, didn't you? Were you wet in the store, picking them out for me? Did your clit throb, wishing it was on my tongue again?"

She let out a shuddering breath, which gave me all the answers I needed to know.

"If I put my fingers into those little panties right now, I'd bet they'd come out gleaming."

She pressed white teeth into her bottom lip.

I freed it with my thumb, running my finger over her lip and tilting her head up so she had to look me in the eye. "Put the tray down and meet me in room thirteen." I pressed the key into her hand. "I want you naked and fingering your pretty pussy when I get there."

She sucked in a shocked breath, and for a second, I worried I'd gone too far. Except then she put the tray down. "Those rooms have peepholes."

"I know. Don't worry. I'll be the only one watching you."

She swallowed so hard that for a moment, I didn't think she'd do it. I was so freaking hard for her that I'd have to go jack off in a bathroom if she said no. That would be bitterly disappointing.

But she nodded, taking the key from my hand, and with a final glance from me, disappeared into the crowd in the direction of the private rooms.

I could have cheered out loud and punched the air. But I didn't. I gave her a three-second head start and then I followed, stalking her like she was prey.

My gaze flickered along the corridor of rooms, knowing that behind each of them would be some new kink to get off on. But the only one I wanted to watch was Bliss.

Finally, I found number thirteen, and my fingers clenched into fists at the guy already at the peephole. I shoulder barged him out of the way with a feral snarl. "Get the fuck away from there."

He stumbled to the side, giving me a dirty look. "What the fuck, man? You don't own the peephole."

I got up in his face. "I do right now. You wanna watch her?"

He nodded.

"Then come back when I'm in there with her, blowing her goddamn mind. But you don't fucking watch her when she's alone."

Watching her when she was alone was for me only.

28

BLISS

I slipped the key into number thirteen as quickly and quietly as I could, twisting the lock and then pushing open the door only enough that I could fit through it before closing it again. I fumbled for the lock on the inside, flicking it with one hand while I leaned against the door, my breathing out of control.

I had to be having some sort of midlife crisis. At twenty-five. A quarter-life crisis? Either way, this was not what I did. I did not go pleasure myself in the middle of a sex club, in lingerie, while anybody could watch me through the door.

And yet, when War told me to, I knew I would.

"I want you naked and fingering your pretty pussy when I get there."

I moaned at the memory of him murmuring that in my ear with a club full of people around us.

I wanted to do it. I was so turned on by the thought of him standing outside, watching me, that all other doubts disappeared.

The room had matte black walls with gold accents, like the rest of the club. There was no bed in this room, though I knew others had them. This one had a long, wide, three-section leather couch that faced the door. It was a tiny room, so there wasn't much else. Just a little side table, presumably for people to stow a handbag or wallet on.

I unclipped the straps holding my stockings to the rest of the outfit and perched on the couch to roll them down my legs. There was muffled conversation from outside the door, and I froze at the knowledge somebody was out there, right now, watching as I took my clothes off.

I had no idea if that was hot or creepy.

But then War's grumbly baritone cut through the door, and everything inside me turned to molten lava.

War was every ounce the bad boy.

It didn't matter that we barely knew each other. The connection between us was purely physical. I'd never had that with anyone, but I craved it now like I craved air.

I wanted him to want me.

I lifted my lacy top over my head, facing the door, staring right into the little peephole because I knew he was out there. I could feel his gaze on my breasts even through the door, and my nipples beaded at the thought of him watching me like this.

It was dirty, and wrong, and yet my whole body felt alive.

Caleb liked to hide me away until I was needed to be his dutiful girlfriend at an event. There was no hiding here. War never made me feel like I had to.

I tucked my fingers into my panties and pulled them

down. I leaned back on the couch, closed my eyes, and imagined War watching me.

An instant tingle started between my legs in anticipation. I took one handful of my breast, tweaking and teasing the nipple in the way I knew I liked from so long of taking care of myself because Caleb never bothered.

Fuck Caleb.

Fuck his judgmental bullshit. I knew exactly what names he'd call me if he could see me right now. None of them were pretty. They were hateful, and awful, but they were more about him than me.

That was what being around these people had taught me. I didn't have to conform. I could be free. Sexy and sweet and a good person all at the same time.

I could make myself come for a man I barely knew, just because it turned me on to do so.

So I pictured War watching me and pressed two fingers up inside my slick center.

I moaned a little at the intrusion, grateful for something to fill the ache even though I needed more. My other hand lowered to my clit and rubbed little circles on it while I rode my fingers, hooking them to hit my G-spot, and getting wetter and wetter the longer I went on until my fingers were coated.

The door flew open, and I jerked upright with a squeal.

War slammed his way into the room, kicking the door shut behind him. He didn't bother locking it. "How did you get in here?" I yelped. "That was locked!"

He didn't answer. He just dropped to his knees in front of me and spread my legs wide. "Look at you, fucking glimmering."

"War, the door…"

He shook his head, leaning over me to sweep his tongue into my mouth. He kissed me so hungrily, and it was so wet and dirty that I pulled him down on top of me, desperate for the contact.

"I want them seeing how wet you are for me, baby girl. I want people knowing how turned on you are, just because I was watching you. I want them watching you coming while you scream my name and hold my face to your cunt."

He dove between my legs, his mouth fitting to my clit and tonguing it wildly. His fingers speared up inside me, and I instantly rocked on them, encouraging him to go faster, harder, deeper.

"God, you taste good. Like spun fucking sugar," he groaned into my thigh. He sat back and ran a finger through my juices. "You're so wet you're dripping on the couch, baby girl, and it's the sweetest sight I've ever seen. Every man outside that door right now is so hard looking at your sweet slit."

War was the king of perverted dirty talk and exhibitionism. But I was beginning to think I got off on it too, because the more he talked, the more he put me on display for whoever was outside, the more I wanted it. I could feel how wet and needy I was, and my mewling noises of need begged for him to just give it to me.

His fingers still fucking me, he kissed his way up my stomach to my breasts. One nipple disappeared into his mouth, the other tweaked and teased by his fingers. "First it was closed doors. Now a peephole. What next, baby girl? You gonna let me pound you out in the main room with everyone watching? I'm not gonna lie. I can't wait for that."

I had a feeling I would let War do whatever the hell he wanted. "You gotta let me come here first," I pleaded.

"Then come."

He added a third finger, and I completely unraveled. The thickness stretched me so good, it rolled through my body like a wave, taking out everything else in its path. Nothing existed except me and the orgasm and the man who'd given it to me. I screamed and writhed, until War backed off and gave me something else to do with my mouth.

He undid his fly, lowering his pants just enough to free his erection. His dick was thick and hard and huge, just like I knew it would be. His fingers speared into my hair, pulling it tight, my scalp prickling deliciously.

"Open your mouth, baby girl. Wanna feel your moans on my cock."

I did so eagerly, taking him inside me and sucking on the head of him. He was soft velvet skin over steel, and his precum tang hit the back of my tongue, only encouraging me further because I wanted to take it all. As much as he'd given me and more.

I gripped his hips, letting him thrust into my mouth, more and more turned on by the control he had over me. I was so wet and slippery on the couch beneath me. I stared up at him, my legs still spread wide so he could stand between them. His gaze met mine while he thrust in and then pulled out of my mouth, his hand on my head exerting just enough pressure to let me know what he wanted.

I wanted to show him that I could do a good job of this, even without his guidance.

I took him deeper and deeper into my throat, delighting in the way he cussed out my name.

"Fuck, Bliss. Stop before I come down your throat."

I wouldn't have minded. But then he was pushing me onto my back and settling between my thighs, and I wanted his cock there even more.

He rubbed his dick along my slit, teasing and torturing me with every swipe, so close to where I really needed him. I squirmed and shifted beneath him, trying to line us up, desperate for him to fill me. When he finally did, it was with an effortless slide. I cried out once more, still sensitive from my earlier orgasm. I clutched him to me, feeling how thick and hard he was and thrusting up to meet him because I needed to. It was a primal, basic urge, a desperation to come that drove me on, grinding against him until I was panting, groaning, and then screaming.

I screamed so loud as the orgasm hit me that there was no doubt the people outside would hear. I couldn't help it. I came harder than I ever had before, everything inside me swirling and exploding and ripping noises from me I couldn't possibly contain.

The door slammed open again.

War looked up, but in the next minute he was gone, thrown into the floor.

"What the hell?" he stuttered, grabbing at the man looming over him with murder in his eyes.

I squealed and on instinct scuttled away from the two men grappling with each other, trying to cover my nakedness with my hands and arms.

Vincent's fist slammed into War's cheek with a sickening thud of flesh against flesh.

I screamed. "Vincent! No! What are you doing? Stop!"

But it was like he didn't hear me. His fist pounded into War again, and though War tried to give it back, Vincent had had the element of surprise and definitely had the upper hand.

The shock subsided, and common sense found its way in. I wasn't going to just sit here and scream while the two of them tried to kill each other. I threw myself between them, getting in Vincent's face, shoving at his shoulders, trying to get him to focus on me, not War.

He pulled back to swing again but stopped when I screamed, "We were having sex! He wasn't hurting me!"

He stopped. Blinked. And then pushed back to his feet, backing off to the corner.

Relief crashed through me. I turned to War. "Are you okay?"

He spat blood out on the floor, prodding at his bleeding lip and then wincing. "Fine. Not like I've never been punched before, but I'm gonna fucking kill—"

No he wasn't. Nobody was going to hurt Vincent if I had any say in it. "No. You're not. Wait here. I'll be back."

Without waiting for War to reply, I grabbed Vincent's arm and shoved him down the corridor toward my office.

Nash stormed into the action, but he stopped dead in his tracks when he saw me. His eyes widened, darting between me and Vincent and the crowded hallway full of people all staring at us.

"Bliss, what the fuck?" Nash gaped at me.

I was still fully naked. I could feel both mine and War's arousal on my inner thighs, and yet it didn't seem the worst thing in the world. Separating the two men—two men I cared about—and keeping them from killing each other seemed more important.

"Can you go help War? He's in room thirteen and he's hurt."

I didn't wait for Nash to agree. I knew he would. I punched in the code for my office door and glared at Vincent. "In."

"Bliss, I—"

"No, I don't want to hear it, Vincent! At least not until I have some fucking clothes on!"

29

VINCENT

*T*he darkness flickered at the edges of my vision, seeking to find a way in, inching forward with long, slender fingers that threatened to drag me down and pull me under. I sucked in deep breaths, filling my sight with her. If I could see her, if I knew she was okay, then maybe I could keep him away.

Scythe laughed somewhere in the back of my mind, the sound sending chills down my spine.

Bliss shut her office door behind us and stormed to her desk. She yanked out the bottom drawer and took out the jeans and T-shirt she'd been wearing earlier in the day, throwing them on top of the desk top with jerky movements.

She was angry.

I wasn't sure why.

She was also naked.

That wasn't something I'd ever really noticed about people before. My father had dumped a bunch of old, crude magazines on my bed when I'd been fourteen.

He'd told me to go through them and do what felt natural.

I'd looked. And then I'd put them away in a drawer and gone about my day. The naked women inside them hadn't been of any interest.

But Bliss was different. I couldn't drag my gaze away from the soft creaminess of her skin. It looked so smooth, I wanted to reach out and touch her just to find out if it was as silk-like as it seemed.

She scowled at me. "No turning around to face the wall this time?"

She yanked up her panties, covering her mound and the swollen slit between her legs. Her inner thighs glistened, and my fingers clenched at what that man had been doing to her. I dragged my gaze away, but the moment I did, *his* voice was in my ear.

"I'm coming for her."

It took everything I had to push it out. I groaned at the effort and turned back to watching her.

Her eyes widened at my clear disregard for her request for privacy. "Vincent!" she snapped.

"I need to see you. I need to know you're okay."

Her gaze burned through me, full of a fire and defiance I'd never seen on her before. But then it softened, and she sighed, taking her bra from the table. "I suppose it doesn't really matter now. The entire club has seen everything I have going on. I don't know what I was thinking. This whole thing is mortifying."

Her breasts were large and full, her nipples a light brown.

The urge to suck them and run my tongue around the ridges and little bumps rushed me hard and strong.

The urge to take her like War had been, followed straight after.

My dick went hard behind my black uniform pants, and I gripped the wall at my back to anchor me so I didn't move.

She pulled her bra on, fastening it at the back, and then all her gorgeous skin disappeared beneath denim and cotton.

The entire time she eyed me, her perfectly shaped eyebrows drawn together in a frown. When she was dressed, she pointed at the chair on the opposite side of her desk. "Sit."

I sat without question.

She lowered herself in the chair on her side of the desk and blew out a long breath that lifted the loose tendrils of hair from around her face. "Vincent... What the hell?"

"He was hurting you. I heard your screams."

She scrubbed her hands over her face and groaned. "He wasn't hurting me. I was...enjoying it."

I stared at her. "You were screaming."

"Because it was good! Jesus, Vincent. You know how it is when you're on the verge of an orgasm."

I didn't. *He* did. But I didn't. He taunted me with those memories, of women writhing beneath me, but none of them were mine. They belonged to Scythe.

And so will she.

"No!" I ground out.

Bliss jumped. "You don't?"

My head swam in dizzying circles, the blackness always trying to creep in. It hurt to keep it out. I squeezed my eyes shut and pressed my hands to my ears, trying to force his voice away. I didn't want to hear his thinly veiled threats. His promises that he'd take the one thing I really wanted.

Soft fingers wrapped around my wrists, drawing my hands away.

I opened my eyes.

Bliss was on her knees at my side, staring at me with huge, worried eyes. All the fire and anger had disappeared. "What's going on? Talk to me."

Her voice was like honey. It soothed through everything inside me that felt frazzled and raw. "I told you I had a medical condition. It's called Dissociative Identity Disorder."

She stared at me blankly. "Okay. What's that?"

"Most people know it as a split personality. Or multiple personalities."

Her eyes widened. "Well, that was not what I was expecting you to say. And this conversation clearly requires me sitting down." She stood and grabbed the chair from her side of the desk, dragging it around to mine. When she was sitting, her hands in her lap, she tilted her head to once side. "Okay. Tell me."

I'd never explained this to anyone. Not in all the years since I'd turned eighteen and taken myself to a doctor, where they'd run every test under the sun, eventually confirming the diagnosis I'd always known. "Do you remember how I said I didn't date in high school?"

She nodded. "Sure."

"I did... Apparently. I just don't remember most of it because I wasn't the personality in control for all of those years. *He* was."

She bit her lip. "Who's he?"

"Scythe."

Her gaze fell to my hand. "Like your birthmark?"

I nodded.

There was no judgment in her tone. No fear, but that was only because she didn't know him. I didn't want her knowing him.

"How does it work?"

I wanted to say it right. I wanted her to understand and not be scared. All I could do was tell her everything.

"Me...Vincent... I'm the dominant personality. Mostly."

She nodded. "But sometimes you aren't?"

"Sometimes I can't keep him out. I try, but sometimes there's no stopping him."

"Have I...met him?"

I shook my head quickly. "No. You'd know if you had. He's nothing like me."

"The breathing...and the covering your ears. That helps you keep him at bay?"

"Tonight it did. It doesn't always. Sometimes he comes on too strong and too fast. I have no hope of winning when he's like that."

Her hand landed on my leg, just above my knee, her thumb smoothing over the fabric of my pants. "Why do you fight so hard to keep him in? It looked painful."

"It is. But bad things happen when I let him out."

She froze. "Like what just happened with War?"

If getting into a fight was the worst thing that Scythe had ever done, I would have let him out as often as he liked. It would have been a lot easier. A lot less painful. His demands grew by the day, silently eating away at me.

"Worse," I murmured. "That was nothing compared to what he's capable of."

Her voice shook, the fear I didn't want her feeling creeping in. "Tell me. I need to know."

I didn't want to say it, but I wouldn't lie to her. Not ever. "Murder. Mayhem. Violence. Sometimes I can regain control in minutes. But sometimes it takes me years. Like when I was in high school. I barely remember anything from that time. He keeps his memories locked away where I can't reach them."

She rubbed the back of her neck, kneading the muscles there. "I really needed a drink for this conversation."

I stood and grabbed a bottle of vodka from the shelf behind her desk, cracking the top open. I glanced around, but there were no glasses in her office.

She held a hand out. "After everything that just went down? I'll chug it straight from the bottle. Hand it over."

I did as I was told.

She took a long swig, wincing as she swallowed, then held it out to me.

I shook my head. "I can't. Alcohol makes me weak. It's harder to fight him off."

"So did he take over tonight? Is that why you attacked War? What about the other night at the ice-cream parlor?"

"That was still me, but his voice was loud in my ear, urging me on. When I do things like that, it's because he's trying to take over. If I'm quick enough, I can fight him off."

"And if you aren't?"

I shrugged. "Then he wins."

She bit her lip. "That doesn't sound like a good thing."

"It's not."

She took another swig from the bottle. "Was it my fault?"

I frowned. "That I have DID?"

"That Scythe pushed through tonight?"

I didn't say anything.

"Shit, it was, wasn't it?"

"The doctors say his appearances are triggered by trauma. When something comes up that I can't deal with, Scythe takes over. Seeing you like that with War...I thought he was hurting you. That hurt me. So Scythe intervened." I met her gaze. "I clearly owe you an apology."

She shook her head. "I think I owe you one. I should have told you about War. We're..."

"In a sexual relationship."

She blinked. "I...I don't know. I guess so. I mean, yes, we were having sex tonight, but I don't know if that's an ongoing arrangement..." Her cheeks went the prettiest shade of pink when she was embarrassed. "I should have told you."

"It's not my business who you sleep with. But perhaps if I'm working, you could just let me know in advance, so I don't ruin things for you."

Her mouth pulled into a line. "It is your business. We had a date. And a kiss..."

That kiss had been like nothing I'd ever experienced before. I could still taste her on my lips if I thought hard enough about it. But that didn't give me the right to dictate who she was intimate with.

Mine.

She grabbed my hand, and Scythe's voice faded away. "I like you. I want another date. Another kiss. I want more everything. But I just got out of a long-term, very horrible relationship. I just want to live for a little bit. Without restraints."

My life was all about restraints. The hold I constantly had to put on Scythe was only part of it. My family's business and demands and threats made up the other half.

I would have loved to live without any of that. To know what it truly felt like to be free. That would never happen for me, but I would never stand in her way.

Maybe I could live it vicariously through her. "I won't barge in next time you're having sex with someone."

She raised an eyebrow, then stifled a giggle. "Okay. That's a good start. And you'll take me out on a second date?"

She could have asked me to fly her to the moon. I would have said yes.

She could have asked me to kill for her. Fuck, I would have killed that Caleb asshole in the middle of the daycare parking lot, but what did you do? Nothing. Pussy. Who do you think she'd prefer? Your little boy romantic notions? Or me?

He'd be in my head for days now. He always was after I slipped and let him out for a moment. The urge to go find a knife to run my fingers over was there, and that was a very Scythe thing to do.

I should have said no. I was a danger to everyone around me.

Especially her.

But when I opened my mouth, all that came out was, "Yes."

30

WAR

*T*he roar of motorcycle engines had droned on, nearly constantly, for the past two days while steady streams of riders arrived for my old man's funeral. Hundreds of them turned up at the gate, got checked over by Fang, and then were let in. They were everywhere I looked from the little porch of my property, deep in the woods within the compound's fences.

I hated it. I had a room at the clubhouse when I wanted to be around people, but the rest of the time, I spent in my cabin. It was far enough away that I didn't hear the noise of the other guys in the club, but with hundreds of extras, there was no hiding from people.

I stifled a groan as another figure strode through the trees surrounding me.

"Hey, Prez."

At least it was just Hawk.

"I wish you wouldn't call me that."

Hawk rolled his eyes. "I'll go back to 'hey, fuckhead'

after everybody has left, but until then, you're the prez, so quit being a whiny bitch and get used to it."

I sniggered. "Fine. What do you want? Or you just out here, lurking around like a Peeping Tom, hoping to get a glimpse of my dick when I get changed?"

Hawk didn't even bother responding to that. We were so used to each other's ribbing. "We got a problem."

I groaned. "Twelve hours 'til the funeral, so of course something has to go wrong. What now?"

"One of the Saint View Sinners is at the gate. Wants to talk to you."

I blinked at him. "Does he have a death wish? Does he not know we have three hundred members here right now?"

Hawk lifted a shoulder. "I think he knows. It'd be near impossible not to with all the fucking racket they're making. You can probably hear us from the main road."

"You think he's a spy?" I wouldn't put anything past the rival club, though I used the term 'club' loosely. They were wannabe gangbangers for the most part. Mostly, they stuck to their side of town, and we stuck to ours.

Hawk shrugged. "Not a very good one since he walked right up to the gate and asked for you."

I groaned. "Fine. I'm coming."

I pulled my boots back on, not bothering to do up the laces, and trudged along the path that led to the front of the compound with Hawk by my side.

"How's your shiner?"

I shot him a dirty look. "Do you want me to give you one of your own?"

His laughter mingled with the noises coming from ahead of us. "I'm never gonna forget walking into that room and seeing you laid out flat on the floor with your dick still hard and your pants around your ankles. Of all the places to get jumped, the great War Maynard goes down when he's dick-deep in some ho."

I shoved him so hard he stumbled the right. "It was Bliss. And she's not a fucking ho. Don't ever call her that."

Hawk raised an eyebrow. "Touchy, touchy. I hope her pussy was worth it."

We kept walking, and I started planning how I'd kill my best friend because the asshole kept fucking laughing.

She'd been worth it. The single punch to the face hadn't been my favorite way to end an evening, and Hawk and Nash had hustled me out of there without even saying goodbye to Bliss. I hadn't seen her since, but I'd been reliving the feel of her wrapped around my cock. If I didn't have three hundred unwanted visitors, I would be camped out on her doorstep, begging her for another round.

People called out to me as we passed the clubhouse. I waved or nodded at them in acknowledgement but ignored their offers of drinks, smokes, food, and pussy.

Drinks, smokes, and food would be plenty tomorrow after the funeral. I'd socialize then.

As for pussy, unless it was Bliss's, I wasn't interested.

Fang grunted in our direction when we arrived at the gate and pointed at the short, weedy-looking guy on the other side. "I gave him the option to leave. Multiple times. He's still here."

"You check him for weapons?"

"Yeah, he's clean."

I nodded, letting myself out of the gate, my boots

crunching on the gravel. "You're either a very brave man or a very stupid one. What's your name?"

The guy hurried forward. "Winger."

He was at least five inches shorter than me and thin as a reed. The track marks up his arms were a dead give-away for the reason he was so twitchy and agitated.

"If you're hoping to score, we ain't selling nothing," Hawk spat out from behind me.

He always had my back, and I knew Fang did too. Not that I would need backup if this guy was dumb enough to try something. I was itching to punch someone after Vincent had got his lucky hit in on me. If it wasn't going to be him, this guy would do if he gave me a good enough reason.

But Winger shook his head. "I got information."

I glanced at Hawk and then back at the Sinner. "Go on then."

He shook his head, his greasy hair hanging limply around his ears. "It'll cost you. Money up front. Two K."

I raised an eyebrow. "Or I could just beat it outta you for free."

The man stopped his twitching. "Come on, War. I need the fucking money."

"To inject into your arm?"

"What's it to you?"

I shook my head and turned around, striding back toward the gate. "Not interested."

Fang and Hawk followed close behind me, and the gate was almost shut when Winger yelled out.

"It's about who killed your dad."

I froze. "What did you say?"

"Your dad. I know who killed him."

I was on the runt of a man before he could blink, lifting him by his shirt and dragging him up against the fence.

He yelped like a little bitch. "Two K and I'll tell you everything!"

"You tell me everything and I won't leave your body cold and dead on your mama's lawn."

He blanched. "I need the money."

My fingers crept around his throat. "Your mama need a new lawn ornament? Start talking."

The fight went out of him. "Fine. I don't know who set it up. But I know who carried it out."

"I'm waiting, and my fingers are getting the urge to snap something. Considering the nearest something is your neck, you're gonna want to give me a name."

I let my fingers flex tighter around his neck, eyeing the bluing color of his lips as his oxygen supply was cut off.

Fuck, that was satisfying.

Winger scratched and grappled at my fingers, and eventually, that was annoying enough for me to drop him back onto his feet. He coughed and wheezed, staring at me with big bloodshot eyes.

Hawk blew out a plume of smoke from his cigarette. "A name, asshole. Or start digging your own grave, 'cause you ain't walking out of here alive."

Winger's big eyes darted between us while he rubbed his rapidly bruising neck. "The hitman the club uses when they want someone gone." His voice was raspy and weak.

I could barely hear him. But when he uttered out the name of the man who'd taken my father and left my mother in a coma, I committed it to memory, carving it into my heart until I could carve their names into his.

"Scythe."

---

*I*t rained the morning of my father's funeral. Which was fitting, 'cause the old bastard had actually liked it. Nobody else did though, and the service we held at the cemetery was full of black leather jackets, umbrellas, and somber faces.

I let the rain drip down the back of my neck, staring blankly at the minister in front of me who'd fucking promised not to drone on with religious bullshit and yet didn't seem to be able to help himself.

"Allister 'Army' Maynard, was a friend and brother to his club members. A doting father to Warrick—"

Somebody behind me let out a guffaw of amusement at the use of my full name, and I cracked my knuckles.

"And a devoted husband to Alegra."

"Who the fuck is Alegra?" someone commented none too softly.

"He means Fancy, you moron," someone hissed back.

The minister tried to get control back of the large crowd, but something off to the left caught my eye.

Bliss.

She stood at the very edge of the graveyard, a black dress skimming her knees, a black umbrella clutched in her hand. Her auburn hair was pulled back in a low ponytail, which hung over one shoulder.

I waved her over.

She shook her head.

I frowned and waved her over again.

She bit her lip uncertainly.

"Fuck this," I muttered. "Can we get on with it. We've got a party to have."

A cheer went up around me.

It wasn't that I didn't love and respect my father. But this wasn't him. He would have been chomping at the bit to get back to the compound and a bottle of scotch too.

The minister fumbled around and huffed a bit, but there wasn't much he could do when I stepped forward and took a clump of dirt from the pile next to the open grave. I threw it in, watching it spread over the shining mahogany of my old man's coffin. "See you in Hell, old boy. I hope they have air-conditioning."

After the life he'd led, there was no way he was getting through Heaven's pearly gates.

None of us were.

Except maybe Bliss, because even dressed in all black, she was so fucking beautiful she had to be heaven sent. "See you all back at the clubhouse." I strode away through the rain, my steps quickening the closer I got to Bliss.

"Hey," she said when I approached. "I'm sorry. I know I wasn't invited, but I just wanted to come pay my respects—"

I grabbed her hand as I passed but didn't slow down. She hurried in little heels that sank into the soggy ground while trying to keep up with me.

"War, wait. I'm really sorry about the other night. By the time I got out, you were gone. I knew everything was happening with the funeral, so I didn't want to intrude."

My bike was too fucking far away. I could feel the

stares of the rest of the club on my back while Bliss babbled. I increased the pace, forcing Bliss to practically run after me, but I couldn't stop it. I needed to get out of here. At my motorcycle, I spun on her and yanked the umbrella out of her hand, tossing it on the side of the road. "You ever ridden one of these before?"

She was still staring at her discarded umbrella. "A bike? No."

"You're about to learn." I swung a leg over and then motioned for her to get on the back behind me.

"I've got heels on."

"Then lose 'em. I don't fucking care. I just need to get out of here. Now get the fuck on."

She did it instantly, kicking off her heels and discarding them on the side of the road along with her umbrella and car. She held me tentatively, her hands limp at my sides.

I grabbed them, wrapping them around my middle, pressing her palms to my abs. "I ate you out until your pussy wept, Bliss. You had my cock in your mouth. You can fucking touch me."

She settled in behind me, holding me tighter and turning her face to one side to rest her head against my back. I stomped viciously on the kick start, and the engine roared to life with a satisfying bellow I never got sick of.

"Where are we going?" she yelled over the noise.

"No fucking idea." As long as it was anywhere but here.

I peeled out of the graveyard parking lot and just let myself get lost in the feel of a woman on the back of my bike.

I'd never had one there.

Not once in the sixteen years I'd had a license, nor all the years before that when I was riding beat-up old junkers around the compound.

You didn't take just anyone on your bike. That seat was sacred ground in my world.

And I'd just put Bliss on the back for the entire fucking club to see.

I drove aimlessly, loving the way she was so soft but held on so tightly. Her hand snuck inside my open jacket to press against my stomach. My dick kicked to attention, which wasn't ideal, but there was no controlling it when she was up against me.

I soon found I did have a destination in mind and took the winding road along the coast, gunning the bike harder, pushing it up to the cliffs.

I steered off the main road and down a short bumping path that led to the Saint View Lookout.

There was still police tape everywhere, but not a soul around, so I drove straight through it. It tore easily and flapped in the strong breeze that buffeted us. I drove us right up to the edge of the cliffs, as far as I could possibly go while still keeping her safe.

Then I killed the engine and let the roar of the ocean below us become the new noise that filled my ears.

That, and Bliss's breaths, warm against my neck.

She didn't let me go. She just sat there on the back of my bike, holding me.

A wave of emotion clogged my throat.

My parents' car had hit the rocky walls right around here somewhere. I couldn't tell where, the rain was too thick, the weather too gray and dull to see, and yet the two of us sat here in the middle of the storm, getting drenched. Neither of us seemed to notice.

I reached a hand back and gripped her thigh, holding on to her as tightly as she held me, because somehow, she felt like the only thing keeping me together.

"I'm so sorry," she murmured. "So sorry you lost him."

I couldn't stand it. The sensation of loss was suddenly so deeply raw that it felt like it was shredding me from the inside out.

I hated the way it felt.

It was foreign and painful, and I just wanted it to stop. I yanked open my fly, pulling out my dick. With my other hand, I tugged on her thigh, dragging her legs up and around me while I hoisted her to straddle my lap. She gasped when she felt my erection, prodding at her inner thighs, but she instantly reached between us to stroke me, her other hand on my shoulder while my feet planted flat on the rocky ground balanced us.

My lips went for her neck, kissing and licking away the trickle of rainwater and sucking on her sweet skin that smelled faintly of honeysuckle, even though she was soaked.

She gripped my cock, jerking me up and down, getting me harder and harder until my balls were clenching, and I was desperate to take her. "Ride me, Bliss," I murmured in her ear, moving her panties aside. "I need to be inside your sweet pussy."

Her panties were soaked through, and I held them to her thigh as she lifted and then sank down onto me.

She was warm where everything else was cold and miserable. And for a moment, we just sat like that, staring at each other, my cock buried in her core.

Abandoning her panties, I put my hands to her back and pulled her flush against my chest. She rocked, grinding over my lap. I guided her movement with my hands and rolled my hips in time with hers, thrusting up when she impaled herself on my cock.

"I want you naked," I murmured into her neck. "I want your tits in my face when I finally get to come inside you."

She moaned when I bit her neck, but she didn't say no, so damned if I wasn't going to take that as permission. There was no one around. Nobody would be out here at the bluffs in such shitty weather, but the idea that someone could be had me so excited I could barely hold my shit together.

Roughly, I found the zipper on the back of her dress and yanked it down, undoing her bra strap since I was there. The dress fell easily off her shoulder, pooling around her middle and between us, but she never stopped her rhythm.

I groaned at the sight of her full breasts, the rain hitting her skin and sliding down her tits like a fucking waterfall. If it was cold, neither of us paid any attention. The heat radiating between us was so great there should have been steam. I took her tits in my hands, squeezing her, loving how they bounced while she rode me, chasing down her pleasure. I buried my face between them, kissing and licking every inch until she writhed on top of me.

"I want you to come," I groaned amongst sucks of her nipples. "Fuck, Bliss. I want you to come with me."

"I'm close," she said around sharp little "Ohs" that punctuated every drop of her hips down onto mine, her cunt taking everything I had to give like she was built for me. "Oh. Oh. Oh."

I put a hand straight to her clit. The thing was swollen and soaking, and I pinched it between two fingers, eliciting a cry from her that had my balls drawing up.

Her inner walls clenched on my cock in response.

"I'm coming," she screamed into the wind. She was wild, all inhibitions abandoned and lost to me inside her and the orgasm we'd created together. "War!"

Her pussy went so tight it was like being punched in the gut. And yet then there was the sweet release of unloading inside her and filling her with my cum.

I groaned, driving my fingers into her hair and pulling her head down to claim her lips, giving her everything I had. "Fuck, baby girl. I want you on my bike every night, taking my dick just like this."

She shuddered, wrapping her arms around my neck as the orgasm slowly subsided.

I claimed her lips again because she was so fucking kissable. I'd never really cared much for kissing, but Bliss's lips were addictive.

She kissed me back, our movements becoming slower and sloppy, out of rhythm now that we were both completely spent.

I held her for as long as she wanted, needing the contact more than she did.

It had been a lifetime since someone had hugged me.

"This isn't what I came here for," she whispered. "But I'm glad it happened."

"Come back to the clubhouse with me. We're having a big party, though it's the last thing I want to do. I'd rather take you somewhere and do this all over again, but I have to make an appearance."

She nodded. "Okay. Whatever you want. I'm yours for the rest of the day. I need to go have a shower first though." Her cheeks went pink. "I'm kinda sticky."

I shook my head, lifting her off my dying erection and putting her panties back in place. "No. No showers. I want to know my cum is inside you, coating your panties and your inner thighs. I want any asshole who tries to get you naked tonight to know that I was there first."

Her breath hitched. "Nobody else is getting me naked but you."

I gazed into her eyes. "What about Vincent? You're fucking him, right?"

"What? No, we're not..."

That surprised me after the way he'd acted at the club the other night. That had been the markings of a jealous boyfriend. "But you want to?"

Something hardened in her eyes. "You aren't exactly offering me monogamy, War. This isn't a relationship. You don't even know my surname."

My dick hardened instantly, because Bliss with a backbone was fucking hot.

I pulled her in and kissed the angry look off her face. "I don't do relationships. But I do want to know your last name."

She drew back. "Arthur."

I nodded.

"I want to keep doing this, Bliss Arthur. I haven't wanted anyone like I want you in a very long time."

"I want to keep doing this, too. What I do with Vincent, or any other guy, doesn't concern you."

I chuckled into her mouth. "Who knew you were all fire and ice beneath that sweetheart exterior? I never would have guessed it." I grinned. "But here you are, setting your boundaries, letting me get your tits out while you ride my dick on my bike. You're a fucking wet dream, baby girl. I hope you know that."

The little smile on her face said that maybe she was beginning to.

31

BLISS

*E*verett and Verity ran around the kitchen chasing each other in their pajamas, their little giggles like sunshine on a cloudy day. I loved when they were home, filling this big house with laughter. It was a stark difference to the worries that plagued the adults who lived here.

Nichelle rummaged through the pantry, dropping packets of snack food at her feet. "Everett, here. Take this and put it in your school bag for tomorrow. We were so late this morning; we need to be more organized."

Everett groaned. "A packed lunch again? When do we get to eat at the cafeteria with everyone else?"

I hadn't realized they'd cut the kids' cafeteria allowance. I wouldn't embarrass Nichelle in front of them, but I made a mental note to contact the school tomorrow and at least pay for that. The party last week had been successful, and I had a fat stack of cash in the safe at Psychos to prove it. I'd have some left over after I paid Axel's supplier.

Not enough to do much more than that though. I'd severely underestimated how much these parties actually cost to run, but it was the beginning of getting myself and my family back on track.

It was rapidly approaching the end of the month, and I was on pins and needles, waiting for some sort of sign from the dealer. The fear had mostly disappeared, leaving behind only a low thrumming excitement about the potential these parties had. But I needed more product.

Guilt nibbled at me for supplying an illegal substance. What I was doing was dangerous and reckless, but what choice did I have? I was already locked into Axel's contract. Making it bigger only made it more beneficial for me. And everyone was over twenty-one. All consenting adults.

I patted Everett's little blond head. "I happen to know that your mom makes the best packed lunches in the world. So much healthier than the cafeteria stuff."

Nichelle raised a questioning eyebrow to me. We both knew she was hardly Martha Stewart in the kitchen.

I shrugged, and she went on with her organizing of the kids.

I slid off my stool, grabbing my car keys from the countertop. "See you little monkeys later. I gotta get to work."

Everett and Verity threw themselves at my legs, wrapping them tight with their sweet cuddles, and I hugged them back. I missed working with children every day. "Go brush your teeth, okay?"

Nichelle poked her head out of the pantry again as my little siblings ran up the stairs. "Is that where you've been going at night? To the daycare? What kind of daycare runs a night shift?"

I paused. I still hadn't told her or my father about Axel and Psychos. Every time I thought about it, I just imagined the disappointment on my father's face. It had just been easier not to. "I'm actually working at a bar."

She wrinkled her cute nose. "Gross."

I laughed because her assessment actually wasn't all that wrong. "It is a bit actually. Sometimes anyway. Spilled beer gets sticky really fast."

"Your father won't be happy. He'll say that sort of work is beneath you."

It would be even worse if he knew which bar it was and where it was located. "I know. That's why I haven't told him. I don't really need the lecture."

She nodded thoughtfully. "I won't say anything either. It's your life. If you want to work in a stinky bar and put up with men swearing at sports games and dropping food on the floor like toddlers, then that's your prerogative."

I was almost a little disappointed that she agreed with my assessment to not tell my father. The truth was, he'd be embarrassed. He'd maybe even try to force me into quitting to save face if any of his friends found out what I was doing. Working at the childcare center had been bad enough. A bar was just the height of slumming it.

Nichelle's manicured fingernails tapped against the pantry door. "You had some mail today, by the way. I left it on the entrance table for you if you want to grab it on your way out."

"Okay, thanks. See you tomorrow."

I left Nichelle to her attempts at organization and walked to the door, grabbing the small bundle of envelopes on the table as I passed, as well as my bag from the coatrack. When I tugged the door open, cool night air smacked me in the face, and I shrugged my jacket on, relishing the fluffy interior on my goosebump-covered skin.

I was seated behind the steering wheel before I got a chance to look at my mail.

Bill. Bill.

The third envelope had me frozen.

It was gold, where the others were business white. The other thing distinguishing it as different was the fact my name was typed on the outside, but not the address. There was no postmark.

Someone had hand delivered it.

I tore the back open and pulled out a single gold card, the edges beveled and embossed with an intricate black design. It was so pretty it could have been a wedding invitation.

Except that all it had was a date and time and place.

8:00 p.m. Saint View Bluffs.

The date was today.

My stomach clenched. "Fuck," I whispered. I glanced at the clock on the dashboard. It was already seven-thirty.

With my heart hammering, I started the car and put my foot down so hard on the accelerator that the wheels screeched a little.

I navigated the now familiar route from my house in Providence, through the streets toward Saint View, the houses outside getting smaller and more run-down with every mile I covered. "Hey, Siri? Call Nash."

The ringtone sounded through my car speakers as I pushed the car as fast as I could. It was a fifteen-minute drive to the bar. And then another five or so minutes from the bar to the bluffs. I was going to be cutting it super fine to get there on time, and I didn't want to know what would happen if I was late with the money. "Come on, Nash," I muttered. "Answer the phone."

It went to his voicemail. I changed tack and called Rebel. Voicemail again. "Goddammit!"

There was no point trying any of the other staff because I was only around the corner. I parked my car right by the doors, not bothering to turn the car off before I dived out of it and ran for the bar entrance. I yanked open the heavy doors, and a wall of sound hit me. I balked at Vincent who was standing guard in the doorway, the bar packed behind him. "Jesus Christ. Where the hell did all these people come from?" I hadn't even noticed vehicles in the parking lot, but I hadn't exactly been doing a head count. I was more worried about getting in, getting the money from the safe, and then getting back out to the bluffs in time to meet the dealer.

"There's some sort of gathering at the Slayers compound, it seems. They all descended here when the alcohol there ran out."

"Shit. Nash and the others must be run off their feet."

I squeezed through the people, pressing up on my toes, trying to find Nash among the crowd. His trademark flannel shirt open over a white tee jumped out at me from within the sea of black leather, and I pushed my way over to where he was frantically clearing glasses from a table.

"Nash!"

He glanced up. "Thank fuck you're here. There's way more people here than we have the staff for. Can you—"

"I can't stay. I'll be back as soon as I can. But I can't stay now."

"What! Bliss! For fuck's sake. We've never been this busy in the history of the damn bar, and you're skipping out on work? We need you."

I silently held up the gold card with the date and place engraved.

Nash snatched it from my hand. "What the hell is this?"

But then he stared up at me as realization dawned. A fierce determination morphed his features. "I'm coming with you."

I shook my head. "I only came to get the cash. I'll be fine alone."

Even as I said it, I wasn't sure I was.

His blue-eyed gaze went dark. "Like hell you will be. This might be the guy who killed Axel for all we know. I'm getting my keys."

I gripped his arm. "You can't leave Rebel here to run the place alone. We don't know half these men. That's not safe."

Nash looked torn. "She can call someone in."

"I've got to be there in ten minutes! I don't have time to wait for you."

"I'll go with her."

I spun around at the voice behind me. I hadn't even realized Vincent had followed me.

I opened my mouth to protest, because Vincent was clearly needed here just as much as Nash was, but Nash cut me off with a glare. "He goes with you, or you aren't going at all."

I ground my teeth. "The guy said not to bring anyone."

"I'm really very good at being quiet and staying hidden. We'll take two cars. I'll follow you at a distance. I swear, he won't know I'm there."

I knew they were right. As much as I wanted to think I could do this alone, I'd be stupid to when I had Vincent offering his protection. The rapid thumping of my heart slowed to a steadier beat, and I nodded. "Fine. I'm getting the money, and then we'll go. See you in the parking lot."

I hurried back toward the entrance and the secret door into the sex club section. It was dark inside, but the open door left just enough light to see. I punched the code into the safe and grabbed the money I'd already carefully counted out and put in a bag.

Vincent was in my doorway waiting for me.

By this point, I wasn't even surprised that he'd disobeyed my orders to wait in the parking lot. I didn't have time to argue. My watch said I had three minutes to get somewhere that needed at least five, so we'd have to argue about his stalkerish tendencies later.

We stormed back out into the night, Vincent slamming shut the door behind him.

My breaths came a little too fast, and a sudden rush of nerves engulfed me. "You'll be close, right? You promise?"

His fingers came to the side of my face, and his deep-brown gaze captured mine. "You won't see me, but I'll be there. He so much as touches you, and he's dead."

There was that Vincent intenseness again. Right now, it was the thing I liked most about him. His complete and utter faith in his ability to protect me was reassuring.

I pressed up onto my toes and brushed my lips over his. It was a peck of a kiss, nothing more, and yet my lips sparked to life like they'd been electrocuted. Everything inside me screamed and shouted demands for me to wrap my arms around his neck and deepen the kiss, even though kissing was the absolute last thing we had time for.

I slid behind the wheel of my car, putting the money in its little bag on the passenger seat. By the time I looked up again, Vincent had disappeared into the darkness.

32

BLISS

*T*he light rain that had been falling ever since War's dad's funeral turned into gusty blasts that hammered against the windshield as I took the winding road along the coast and up to the cliffs. I'd been here just yesterday, on the back of War's bike, and yet tonight, the vibe felt entirely different. Tonight there was no warm body to wrap my arms around. Just a stormy darkness, well fitting for the meeting that was about to take place.

I peered into the rearview mirror, but I didn't see anything.

The nerves that Vincent wasn't there crept up my throat, threatening to turn into panic. But he'd said I wouldn't see him, so I drove on, using my focus to stay on the slippery road instead of worrying about everything else.

My headlights flashed over the small signpost that indicated the lookout, and I put my blinker on, taking the turn slowly and carefully. The road beneath me turned bumpy, the asphalt giving way to gravel and dirt that led to the cliff edge that jutted out over Saint View Beach.

Well away from the ledge, I stopped the car.

I glanced around, feeling sick in the darkness. "What the hell are you doing, Bliss?" I murmured. "This is such a bad idea. You are one hundred percent the basic white bitch who's about to get murdered or bitten by a vampire."

I waited, but there was nothing. No headlights. No masked figure stepping from the shadows. Even the rain let up and the moon peeked through the cloud cover. It was still eerie as hell, but at least I could see a little better.

I was late. Only two minutes, but maybe that was enough for him to have left.

No. He'd want his money. He wouldn't have given up that easily.

But maybe I was in the wrong spot. The bluff was long, and there was a walking trail that I couldn't access by car.

That had to be it.

"I don't even have an umbrella, thanks to War making me ditch it." I grabbed the bag of money from the passenger seat, clutching it between my fingers, and opened the door. The dirt lot had turned to mud, and I grimaced when I put my foot down into it with an unappetizing squelch.

On instinct, I locked my car and cautiously moved for the walking trail, fighting the slippery mud with every step. The rain started up again, because that was just my luck, and I trudged along, my sneakers gathering more and more muck with every step.

I was soaking and annoyed enough that I almost missed the figure step out of the shadows.

I froze, but then a boom of thunder cracked, and I jumped a mile.

He didn't say anything. His black hood covered his hair and shaded his face from the one tiny strip of moonlight.

I forced myself to breathe and act cool, like I did this every day. I tossed the money through the darkness, letting it arc up, and then land at the man's feet. "It's all there," I called. "Every dollar. You can check it if you want."

He didn't say a word.

He didn't make a move to pick up the bag.

I swallowed thickly. "I want to make a change in our agreement. Three times the product. So we can do a weekly party..."

I could feel his gaze on me. It crept over me like dirty, dark spiders, crawling and creeping, inching their way across my skin, searching for a way inside me.

I didn't want to look intimidated. But my body took an involuntary step back before my brain could issue a command not to.

The man took a step forward.

"I'm good for the money," I tried again, fighting to keep a tremble out of my voice. "I can pay more often than once a month if you want."

He took another step forward, stepping over the bag I'd tossed to his feet.

My heart seized.

He wasn't picking it up.

I stumbled backward, fumbling in my pocket for my

car key. I clamped my fingers around it, pointing it in the man's direction and praying that in the darkness it would look like a knife. "I'm armed!"

The man's laughter cackled across the space between us. "You stupid bitch. Do you really think I'm that dumb?"

Lightning flashed, lighting up Caleb's face.

My gasp was lost to the wind, but it brought with it a rush of fear. I spun and fled, running back to the car. My thighs burned with the effort of propelling my body, and my feet slid out from beneath me, sending my hands down into the mud. Pain jarred through them, but I pushed myself upright and kept going.

I couldn't hear if Caleb was behind me. The roar of my blood in my ears and the rain coming down around me drowned everything else out. I was sure I was screaming, but I couldn't hear it.

The car loomed in front of me, like a flashing safety beacon. If I could just get to it, I could lock myself inside.

I ran for the driver's side door and yanked up the handle.

It didn't work.

I jerked it again and again, screaming out my frustration, all while knowing that Caleb was right behind me.

A sob burst free.

"Searching for this?"

I spun around.

He had my key clutched in his fingers. I didn't even know when I'd dropped it.

I lunged for it, but he was taller and quicker. With a glint of pure malice in his eye, he threw the key over the cliff face.

I watched it sail over the edge and disappear into the blackness of the night.

Caleb stalked me, advancing on me like a demon in the night. "I was going to make you my wife, Bethany-Melissa!" his shout pierced through the buffeting wind. "I gave you a ring. A house. Everything you wanted. All you had to do was be good."

"Vincent!" I screamed. "Vincent!"

Caleb's fingers were around my neck in a second, the force pushing me up against the side of my car. My spine thudded on the cold, slick metal with a bone-jarring thud that rattled my teeth. "Vincent!" My screams turned to sobs.

"Who the fuck is that?" Caleb snarled.

I tried to recoil from the stench of alcohol on his breath. Up close, he didn't look well. His normally clean-shaven jaw was dark with several days' worth of stubble, and even in the dim light, his eyes were clearly bloodshot.

"Is he your lover, Bethany-Melissa? Is that who he is? Do you scream his name like that when he's fucking you?" He laughed. "I know all about the men you've been fucking behind my back. Sandra told me everything. How many men have you let into your pussy? More than just one. Three? Five? You filthy slut."

He let go of my throat and grabbed my breast roughly, squeezing it so hard I yelped.

"You like that? You like it rough? Is that how they give it to you?"

I shook my head. "Caleb, please. You're hurting me!"

"I thought you liked it like that?" He slammed his lips down on mine, hateful and hard.

I tried to scream again, but that was a mistake. Caleb

took the opportunity to plunge his tongue into my mouth, disgusting and thick and slimy with the taste of scotch.

I scratched and tore and slapped at his face, but the man was stronger and bigger than me and wouldn't be swayed. He attacked my mouth before dragging his lips across my cheek, his sharp stubble scraping along my skin. "Scream my name like you scream his, whore."

"Vincent!"

His hand cracked across my cheek. "Say my name!"

"Vincent!"

He shoved his hand down the front of my pants, savagely prodding and grabbing between my legs. "Say it! Say it! Say it, bitch, or I will shove my dick so far up your cunt you'll fucking taste it."

Tears streamed down my face. But I couldn't let Caleb rape me. Not again. The first time had made me want to die.

I needed help. Vincent had said he'd be here, but there was no one. My sobs got lost into the dark night, each of them sounding like Vincent's name and the heartbroken realization he wasn't coming.

33

VINCENT

*S*itting low behind the wheel of my car, my black ball cap pulled down on my forehead, I watched Bliss toss the money onto the passenger seat of her car and drive out of the Psychos parking lot.

Like a shadow, I followed smoothly behind her, keeping an eye on her taillights as I trailed her through Saint View.

Every muscle in my body hurt. From my toes to my fingers. Every muscle in my back and in my gut.

I'd been fighting an internal battle all week. Ever since I'd dragged War off Bliss at the club, *he'd* been in my ear. While I was at work, surrounded by noise, it was easier to drown him out. But now, in the silence of the car, his taunts started again.

You let another man touch her?

"She said she wanted him to," I muttered.

Jealous?

I refused to listen. Bliss and I had talked. She liked War. He was allowed to touch her like that. Her screams hadn't meant he was hurting her. But seeing them like that. Thinking she was being hurt, had opened up something inside me. It had given Scythe room to move around, and I'd been paying for it ever since.

War wasn't going to hurt her. And neither was Nash. Neither of them were threats to her.

Scythe was.

His laughter mocked me.

I focused on the road ahead. The rain was worsening, bucketing down now in heavy sheets that seemed to only get worse the higher up the cliff face we went. I could barely see Bliss's taillights through the onslaught.

I needed to be closer.

I accelerated, ignoring the slippery roads and lack of visibility. I couldn't lose her.

She flashed through a green light, but by the time I got there, it had turned red.

You know you're going to lose her, Vinnie boy.

I wasn't. And I fucking hated when he called me that. I put my foot down harder.

The truck hit the back end of my car with a sickening screech of metal against metal.

It spun me around the slippery road in dizzying circles. My head bounced off the window, a sharp pain splintering through my brain while black flickered at the edges of my vision. Around and around the car spun, sliding through the intersection, finally coming to a stop on the other side, facing in the wrong direction.

Things moved slowly. Outside, the dark was pierced with lights and horns.

None of them were Bliss's.

The pain in my head only added to the rest of the pain in my body.

"Bro! Are you okay?"

The rapping of knuckles across the glass window to my left jolted me, and I twisted my neck to see who it was. An unfamiliar face peered through, his eyes big with worry.

"Can you move? You need to get out of the car! There's gas leaking everywhere!"

Well, that wasn't ideal. The moment he mentioned it, the toxic tang seared my nostrils.

I pushed on the door, and it gave way.

The man's hand gripped my arm as he helped support me, half dragging me away from my car and over to the side of the road. "Fucking hell, bro. That was the most intense thing I've ever seen. Look at your car!"

But my car was the last thing on my mind. My gaze landed on the black motorbike behind the man.

The keys still dangled from the ignition; a black helmet abandoned to the side of the road. I staggered toward it.

"That truck just cleaned you right up! I can't believe you walked away from that. Are you sure you're okay— Hey!"

I slammed my foot down on the kick start and shot off into the night, the wail of police sirens and ambulances forgotten in the need to get to Bliss.

Well, you fucked that up, didn't you? One simple task, Vinnie. All you had to do was follow her.

I pushed the bike as hard as I could, a rising sense of danger growing with every mile I passed. The road curved, and I leaned with it, back and forth, winding my way up the mountain while a clock ticked in my head, each movement of the second hand whispering, *Bliss, Bliss, Bliss.*

The rain started up again, soaking through my clothes and jeans, the wind whipping at my bare skin like ice.

The lookout loomed ahead, and I took the turnoff too fast, the tires skidding out on the dirt and gravel.

Thunder cracked above me, sending arcs of pain through my head once more, but the lightning that followed lit up the scene.

Bliss's car.

Her pushed over the hood.

A man fumbling with his pants behind her, while he pinned her down with his free hand.

Her screams cut through the night, piercing right through my heart.

Time to let me out, Vinnie boy. You know this ain't your forte.

I pushed back on his demands, running to get to Bliss.

You sure she ain't enjoying that? You know you already fucked this up once. You go in there and rip that guy off her and slit his throat like I know you want to, and she'll never forgive you.

I stopped dead. She'd been so mad at me when I'd interrupted her and War. She'd forgiven me, but I didn't know that she'd give me a second chance if I screwed up again.

I hated when she was mad at me. "Bliss?""

Caleb looked up from behind her.

Confusion swirled around me, pulsing through my

brain, mixing with Scythe's laughter. "What is this? You said you were meeting Axel's supplier..."

"Vincent!"

Caleb's lips twisted in an ugly snarl. "This guy? For fuck's sake. I told you he was a faggot. Is he retarded too? Just standing there, watching like a pervert? You want to watch while I pound her, buddy? Go right fucking ahead."

Caleb yanked at her pants. Her gaze met mine, and she screamed my name again.

Let me out. Let me out. Let me motherfucking out, Vincent!

I pressed my hands over my ears, everything going blurry.

Voices swirled around me in a void I couldn't make sense of.

"Gonna take what I want from your used-up cunt, and then I'm gonna leave you out here to die, like the stupid bitch that you are. Everyone will be better off when you're dead at the bottom of those cliffs. They'll rule it a suicide, and I'll tell everyone you did it because I wouldn't take you back."

"Vincent!"

I couldn't fight the storm. I couldn't break through the swirling pressure that built inside my head until I was sure it was going to explode.

"Scythe," she begged between sobs, so softly I barely heard her.

But I did.

Everything vanished. The confusion. The fight. The pain.

My gaze slammed into hers, and I saw it all. The

terror in her eyes. The desperation in her voice. The fact that motherfucking asshole had his hands on my girl. My lip curled back in a snarl.

Our girl, Vincent pleaded.

"Scythe!" she screamed this time.

A grin slowly spread across my face.

I was back.

THE END...for now.

The story continues in Half the Battle, Saint View
Psychos #2
http://mybook.to/HalfTheBattle

Want signed paperbacks, special edition covers, or Saint View merch? Check out Elle's new website store at
https://www.ellethorpe.com/store

ALSO BY ELLE THORPE

Saint View High series (Reverse Harem, Bully Romance. Complete)

*Devious Little Liars (Saint View High, #1)

*Dangerous Little Secrets (Saint View High, #2)

*Twisted Little Truths (Saint View High, #3)

Saint View Prison series (Reverse harem, romantic suspense. Complete.)

*Locked Up Liars (Saint View Prison, #1)

*Solitary Sinners (Saint View Prison, #2)

*Fatal Felons (Saint View Prison, #3)

Dirty Cowboy series (complete)

*Talk Dirty, Cowboy (Dirty Cowboy, #1)

*Ride Dirty, Cowboy (Dirty Cowboy, #2)

*Sexy Dirty Cowboy (Dirty Cowboy, #3)

*25 Reasons to Hate Christmas and Cowboys (a Dirty Cowboy bonus novella, set before Talk Dirty, Cowboy but can be read as a standalone, holiday romance)

Buck Cowboys series (Spin off from the Dirty Cowboy series)

*Buck Cowboys (Buck Cowboys, #1)

*Buck You! (Buck Cowboys, #2)

*Can't Bucking Wait (Buck Cowboys, #3)

The Only You series (complete)

*Only the Positive (Only You, #1) - Reese and Low.

*Only the Perfect (Only You, #2) - Jamison.

*Only the Truth - (Only You, bonus novella) - Bree.

*Only the Negatives (Only You, #3) - Gemma.

*Only the Beginning (Only You, #4) - Bianca and Riley.

*Only You boxset

Add your email address here to be the first to know when new books are available!

www.ellethorpe.com/newsletter

Join Elle Thorpe's readers group on Facebook!

www.facebook.com/groups/ellethorpesdramallamas

ACKNOWLEDGMENTS

Ah Vincent. My sweet little psychopath. I had more messages and emails about him when he showed up in Saint View Prison than I have ever had about any other character. I never had any intention of writing him a book of his own, let alone a trilogy.

But here we are, at the end of book 1. You guys wanted it, so I wrote it. And we've really only just begun with the Vincent/Scythe drama. There's so much more to come. Scythe is...not like Vincent, let's just say that lol. I can't wait for you guys to read book 2.

Thank you to Jolie Vines, Emmy Ellis, and Karen Hrdlicka who make up my stellar editing team. Thank you to Jo Vines, Zoe Ashwood, Sara Massery, DL Gallie, Lissanne Jones, and Kat T Masen for all the chats and support. Book writing is hard and can be lonely, but you guys make long days fun. Thank you to Shellie, Dana, Louise, and Sam for your early feedback. A massive thank you to my promo and review team for always being there for me. Thank you to the Drama Llamas for being my honorary extended family.

And as always, a huge thank you to my family. To Jira, Thomas, Flick, and Heidi. You four are the loves of my life and I couldn't do any of this without you.

Love, Elle x

ABOUT THE AUTHOR

Elle Thorpe lives in a small regional town of NSW, Australia. When she's not writing stories full of kissing, she's wife to Mr Thorpe who unexpectedly turned out to be a great plotting partner, and mummy to three tiny humans. She's also official ball thrower to one slobbery dog named Rollo. Yes, she named a female dog after a dirty hot character on Vikings. Don't judge her. Elle is a complete and utter fangirl at heart, obsessing over The Walking Dead and Outlander to an unhealthy degree. But she wouldn't change a thing.

You can find her on Facebook or Instagram(@ellethorpebooks or hit the links below!) or at her website www.ellethorpe.com. If you love Elle's work, please consider joining her Facebook fan group, Elle Thorpe's Drama Llamas or joining her newsletter here. www.ellethorpe.com/newsletter

facebook.com/ellethorpebooks

instagram.com/ellethorpebooks

goodreads.com/ellethorpe

pinterest.com/ellethorpebooks